LEGENDS

Stories in Honour of David Gemmell

To MIKE -

LEGENDS

Stories in Honour of
David Gemmell

Edited by Ian Whates

ENJOY!

ALL BEST!

NEWCON
PRESS

NewCon Press
England

WFC 2013

First edition, published in the UK November 2013
by NewCon Press
in association with The David Gemmell Legend Awards for Fantasy

NCP 063 (hardback)
NCP 064 (softback)

10 9 8 7 6 5 4 3 2 1

ISBN: 978-1-907069-56-7 (hardback)
978-1-907069-57-4 (softback)

Cover art © 2013 by Dominic Harman
Cover layout by Andy Bigwood
David Gemmell silhouette courtesy of the David Gemmell Legend
Awards

Text layout by Storm Constantine

CONTENTS

1. Introduction – Stan Nicholls   7
2. Or So Legend has It – James Barclay   13
3. A Blade to the Heart – Gaie Sebold   33
4. Return to Arden Falls – Ian Whates   51
5. The Drake Lords of Kyla – Storm Constantine   75
6. A Tower of Arkrondurl – Tanith Lee   101
7. Who Walks With Death – Jonathan Green   119
8. Skipping Town – Joe Abercrombie   135
9. The Land of the Eagle – Juliet E McKenna   147
10. All Hail to the Oak – Anne Nicholls   167
11. Swords and Circle – Adrian Tchaikovsky   199
12. Fairyland – Jan Siegel   219
13. Mountain Tea – Sandra Unerman   231
14. The League of Resolve – Stan Nicholls   237
    About the Authors   261

Honouring Fantasy

An Introduction by Stan Nicholls

In a speech at our awards ceremony a couple of years ago, Alain Nevant of French publisher Bragelonne, our principal sponsor, referred to the international fantasy and science fiction community as a family. One that could sometimes be likened to both the Walton and Addams families, but a family nonetheless.

The generosity of the family members who have provided stories for *Legends* made this anthology possible.

When David Gemmell died on 28th July 2006, aged 57, friends and colleagues wanted to find a way to honour his life and work. The consensus was to create an award in Gemmell's name.

Apart from commemorating a widely admired author, we felt there was a need for a proper award for fantasy. By which I mean what might be called 'pure' fantasy – the kind Gemmell wrote – that, at least here in the UK, seemed unregarded. Science fiction, horror, crime and other genres have their prizes, we reasoned, so why not fantasy?

We made a false start. Perhaps we were too many cooks, with too many diverse ideas about what we wanted to do and how to do it. In any event the project went into abeyance for a while.

The impasse was broken by the writer and Gemmell protégé Deborah Miller. Rather than endless discussion and urging other people to do something, she argued, we had to roll up our sleeves and get on with it. More than anything else, Deborah's drive and determination was what made the dream a reality.

A core committee was formed, with Deborah as Award Administrator. Gareth Wilson, who has a good claim on being David Gemmell's Number One Fan, came aboard as our

Webmaster. Mike "Sparks" Rennie, who has provided the Tech and Logistics for numerous conventions, agreed to do the same for us; and Christine Harrison brought her fiscal expertise to the role of Treasurer. My wife, Anne Nicholls, took on editorship of the award ceremony programme book, and I had the honour of being offered the position of Chair, which, after a brief period of trepidation and false modesty, I accepted.

We wanted to create an award recognising the best fantasy novel of any given year. What else could we call it but the Legend Award, after Gemmell's first, most celebrated novel?

There were three options: 1) have a jury decide; 2) have the public determine a shortlist and a jury settle the final outcome; 3) have a completely open vote with no jury.

Every juried award, particularly in a specialist area like fantasy, has the perennial problem of finding suitable judges. We considered a number of ways to resolve this problem, including the possibility of having a judging panel drawn from a pool of fantasy readers. But the massive amount of reading involved – our first longlist ran to over ninety titles – and the fact that we couldn't reimburse people for their time and effort, made that a big ask.

Adopting the second option – part public vote, part jury – would boil the longlist down to a manageable number, but didn't solve the practical difficulty of finding suitable judges.

In arriving at the decision to adopt a totally open vote we weren't being critical of awards that choose the juried route. We've no doubt that their verdicts are reached honourably. But apart from the practicable considerations involved in mustering juries we have what might be called a philosophical objection to that way of doing things. Frankly, the idea of a small group handing down pronouncements about what deserves an award and what doesn't strikes us as almost elitist, and against the spirit of our times. In an age when masses of ordinary people use technology to topple despotic regimes and change government policies, surely they can be trusted to vote for a book award.

When our committee has to confront difficult decisions we have a simple rule of thumb – 'What would Dave have wanted?' Knowing the importance he placed on readers, we're sure Gemmell would have favoured as democratic a system as possible when it came to an award bearing his name. So we put our faith in the wisdom of crowds.

We attracted some criticism for having a public vote. In the same way that we would have been criticised if we'd gone with a jury. One objection was that readers would band together to vote for their favourite author. But unless people are being strong-armed into voting in some unimaginable way, then presumably they really do favour the writer they're voting for, whether in unison with others or not. If some kind of partiality should creep in – although it's difficult to think how it might – our contention is that a sufficiently large pool of voters dilutes it to the point of insignificance.

This is how the process works. A longlist is compiled from titles submitted by publishers, and the public are welcome to suggest additional titles they think worthy and eligible. The longlist is voted on and the five titles with the most votes form the shortlist. A second round of votes determines the winner. We have robust systems in place to prevent multiple voting.

We didn't know what to expect in our first year. In the event, the Legend Award garnered almost 11,000 votes from 75 countries.

Simultaneous with working out *how*, we were looking for *where*. After investigating numerous venues, we decided on The Magic Circle headquarters in London's Euston. To say the place has character would be an understatement, and we loved its eccentricity and intimacy from the minute we stepped over the threshold. Securing The Magic Circle as the annual location for our ceremony is thanks to our aforementioned sponsor Bragelonne, France's leading publisher of fantasy and sf. Bragelonne's Alain Nevant and Stephane Marsan were also friends of Gemmell, and his French publishers,

With the *how* and *where* sorted, we turned our minds to *what*. We wanted something special as a trophy. Simon Fearnhamm of the Raven Armoury volunteered the perfect solution – a half-sized replica of Snaga, the awesome axe wielded by Gemmell's illustrious hero Druss. Simon's Snaga is a truly beautiful hand-crafted artefact. With a price tag of approximately £2,500 when made to commission, we believe it to be the most valuable trophy on offer in the fantasy/sf fields.

With the permission and support of Dave's widow Stella and the Gemmell family, and the backing of the publishing and speculative fiction communities, our first presentation took place at The Magic Circle on 19th June 2009. We were particularly pleased that Dave's daughter Kate and son Luke were able to join us for the ceremony. We began with a spirited reading from *Legend* by James Barclay, yet another of Dave's friends. James' opening recitations from Gemmell's works, and his conduct of an auction of fantasy memorabilia that precedes the presentation, have become invaluable staples of our ceremonies.

Other 'Friends of the Awards' as we like to think of them – people not actually on the committee but who have proved unstinting in helping the process run smoothly – include, among others, Deborah Miller's daughter Tiffany Lau, Mark Yon, Nick Summit, Elaine Clarke, Anna Kennedy, Rachel Oakes and, again keeping it in the family, our daughter Marianne Fifer.

The first winner of the Legend Award defied expectations – Andrzej Sapkowski's *Blood of Elves*, a novel translated from Polish. The four runners-up each received a 'mini Snaga' by way of compensation, a practice we've continued.

Buoyed by the success of our initial ceremony, we decided to add two new categories in 2010. The Morningstar Award honours the best debut novel, something we thought especially important as David Gemmell was noted for the help and encouragement he gave to many aspiring writers. The Ravenheart Award was designed to recognise the best fantasy cover art, an aspect of the genre we felt deserved acknowledgement. We were now officially

The David Gemmell *Awards* For Fantasy.

That year the Morningstar went to Pierre Pevel for *The Cardinal's Blades* and the Ravenheart to Didier Graffet for the cover of Joe Abercrombie's *Best Served Cold*. The Legend was again a surprise but richly deserved. It went to Graham McNeill for *Empire*. 15.500 votes were cast overall.

2010 was also notable in that we welcomed *SFX*, the UK's number one sf and fantasy magazine, as our media partner.

2011 saw the Morningstar awarded to Darius Hinks for *Warrior Priest*, the Ravenheart to Olof Erla Einarsdottir for the cover of *Power and Majesty* by Tansy Rayner Roberts, and the Legend to Brandon Sanderson for *The Way of Kings*.

Patrick Rothfuss' *The Wise Man's Fear* took the Legend Award in 2012; Helen Lowe's *The Heir of Night* the Morningstar, and Raymond Swanland the Ravenheart for his cover for William King's *Blood of Aenarion*.

One of the things that has delighted us about the awards is their international flavour, with prizes going to authors and artists from France, Iceland, Poland and the US as well as the UK. Proof, if it was needed, that the literary expression of the fantastic knows no borders.

This year has seen a tragedy, and great sadness for everyone involved with the awards. On 6th May Deborah Miller passed away. She was 50 years old.

Deborah had first been diagnosed with breast cancer in 2001, and went into remission several times. The condition surfaced again early in 2013, and she fought it with her usual resolve, but treatment proved ineffective. She passed peacefully, with her husband, Bill, at her side.

Deborah faced her illness with courage and good humour. It's a testament to her tenacity that, despite her illness, she found the strength to do so much for the Gemmell Awards. This book is dedicated to her, with love and fond remembrance.

The proceeds from *Legends* will help perpetuate the Gemmell Awards, and for that we have Ian Whates and Newcon Press to thank. We're also indebted to all the writers who have selflessly contributed their time and talent.

But that's what families do.

Stan Nicholls
Chair, David Gemmell Awards For Fantasy
August 2013

www.gemmellaward.com

Or So Legend has It

James Barclay

"Get back in line! You're opening up my right flank."

Hirad ignored the shout from his left, blocked a sword thrust, ducked beneath a wild swing and buried his blade in the chest of his enemy. The man fell, blood surging from the wound and spurting from his mouth.

The smell of blood was in Hirad's nose and fear was in the eyes of those he faced. Here he was just twenty years old, or something like that, and fighting for Lord Arlen against Baron Pontois. This was what he had been born to do. It would make him rich. It might even make him famous.

Hirad made to move further up into the thick of the enemy. He was hauled backwards, a hand clamping on to the collar of his leather jerkin, almost pulling him on to his back and two paces from his next target. Fighting elsewhere was fierce. Spells crashed to the ground, keeping reserve forces back. Spell shields glowed bright under impact.

"Stand in line!" barked the voice.

"Who put you in charge?"

"I'm not in charge, just keen on living through the morning. Focus."

The enemy came again. Hirad was desperate to look at the warrior to his left. More, he was desperate to punch his fat mouth but that would have to wait. Here on the mud and blood of the battlefield, Arlen's forces faced perhaps three hundred men and mages who were seeking to annexe the key routes to Gyernath harbour. Hirad stood with around half that number but with their flanks well-defended by mages and around fifty horsemen; they had successfully narrowed the skirmish line and the odds were beginning to even out.

Hirad's face burned with humiliation but he waited. Their section of the line closed. To his left, Hirad could hear the sound of a sword tip beating time on the ground. The tapping ceased. Hirad sensed the tension in the warriors flanking him. He attacked.

The man in front of him was wiry and tall, holding a dagger and long sword. Hirad feinted to strike to his left. The man moved his dagger to counter. Hirad switched his sword to his right hand and sliced it into the man's side. The man rocked back. Hirad took a pace forward.

"No!" roared the voice from his left, joined this time by another voice to his right.

The tip of a double-handed blade missed Hirad's left arm by a hair before chopping into an enemy midriff. The unfortunate was slammed sideways into another Pontois fighter, his guts spilling onto the mud.

Hirad stabbed his blade through the heart of his opponent and spared the warrior a glance. He was massive, a bit older than Hirad, with a shaven head and a very broad chest. In other words, a typical slow-moving, muscle-stuffed, walking corpse like so many he'd seen already. Mostly face down in the dirt.

"Next time you walk in front of his arc, he'll take your kidneys out too," came the voice from the right.

The fighters in front of them were hesitating. Hirad turned back and growled, beckoning them on. If anything, they backed off further. Orders rolled across the battlefield.

"Back. In. Line," said the lumbering one.

Unbelievably, a third voice chimed in. Hirad felt his blood bubbling.

"They're breaking off across the front. Perhaps we could all step back and cool down."

Hirad stared at the man who would have been his next

victim, seeing the relief in his face and the shake in his arm. The Pontois lackey nodded in what was presumably supposed to be respect. Hirad spat on the ground. Orders rang across the lines once more. The two sides parted and the stretcher and healer parties raced in.

Hirad, his sword still dripping blood, turned to the loud mouth. There he was, cleaning gore from his two-handed blade with an already filthy rag. A mage, presumably the one who'd piped up just now, landed nearby, dismissing the ShadowWings spell. He was an elf; probably thought himself more important, like most of his kind. Hirad walked up close to the muscled one, aware the blood of his sword was dripping on the other's boot. He had to tip his head back a little to glare into the smug face.

"Risk my life again and I will dance in your guts once I've opened your fat stomach."

The big man continued cleaning his sword, not looking at Hirad while he replied.

"You misunderstand what was happening," he said. "Despite my advice to stay in line, you chose to move up. You also moved slightly left, placing you in the arc of my blade. You risked your own life. You risked mine twice and the man on your right flank too. Don't let it happen again."

"Think you can teach me how to fight, smart mouth?" said Hirad, his head hot and his grip tightening on his blade. "Want to try right now?"

Hirad bounced back a couple of paces and brought his blade to the ready. The sword cleaning continued, though at least the eyes looked towards him now.

"If you're looking for someone to vent your anger on, our opposition will be back once the battlefield is cleared. Your energies are best directed that way."

Every word he said stoked Hirad's anger. "Is that so? And yours are in assuming command to cover up your lack of ability as a fighter, right?"

That got his attention. The eyes in that bull head narrowed

and colour appeared in his cheeks. He dropped the rag on the ground. His sword tip traced a line in the mud as it moved in Hirad's direction.

"Now, gentlemen, let's not fight," said the other warrior.

"You keep out of this, dandy man, or you'll be next," growled Hirad over his shoulder.

"My concern is that I live," said the big man. "And if I have to dump you on your arse to make sure that happens that is exactly what I'll do."

"You aren't quick enough to beat me," said Hirad.

He switched his blade between his hands three times then snapped it forwards. The big man batted it aside with his sword, stepped in and slammed the heel of his palm into Hirad's chest. Hirad fell flat on his back. A heartbeat later, the rock-steady tip of that two-handed blade was at his throat.

"You were saying?"

"Fine, you're quick; but do you have the balls to push your blade home?"

The big man shook his head. "I have no desire to kill you or harm you in any way. We're here to do a job and unless I miss my mark, we all want to live to collect our wages."

His voice was completely calm. Hirad wanted to down him so badly it hurt but he was not in the best of positions. He dropped his blade to the mud and held up his hands. The big man nodded.

"Good. So let's get ourselves ready and try and help each other get through the day. All right?"

Hirad shrugged. The sword tip moved from his neck and the big man turned his back and began to walk away in the direction of a water butt. Hirad surged to his feet, leaving his blade and meaning to finish what he started with his fists. He felt arms about him from the back, strong arms.

'Whoa there, my friend,' said a voice by his left ear. 'Best leave it at that unless you want another lesson.'

Hirad froze. 'Let me go or I'll break both your arms.'

'Good with threats, aren't we?' said the elf, sauntering up.

Hirad spat towards him. The arms hugged tighter, pinning Hirad's to his sides. He kicked backwards, hearing the man grunt as his shin was barked.

"He wants to humiliate me. He has no respect for my talent. I will not let that lie. Get off me!"

Hirad tried to break the warrior's grip. He kicked back again, flung his head backwards too, hoping to smash the bastard's nose, but all he found was his shoulder.

"Enough!" The big man dashed water into Hirad's face and closed in until their noses were practically touching. The smells of blood and sweat mingled unpleasantly. "You're doing the job of humiliation all by yourself. Time to calm down and while you're doing so, let me tell you something: if I had no respect for your talent, I would not have pulled my blade past you earlier.

"How old are you?"

Hirad shrugged, his ire subsiding ever so slightly. "Twenty-ish, maybe twenty-one. I'm not one for counting, really."

"And how long have you been fighting?"

"I don't know... five years probably."

The big man moved back a little. "I'm amazed you're still alive."

Hirad puffed himself up as much as he good with the other one still holding him.

"I'm not. It's because I'm quicker than them, better than them."

"But mainly luckier," said the big man. "I think you can let him go now... what's your name?"

"Sirendor Larn," said the dandy man.

Hirad was released. He rolled his shoulders a few times and glanced back. Sirendor looked as if he'd just got dressed. His clothes and light leather armour were almost spotless and if Hirad hadn't known he'd been fighting all morning, he wouldn't have believed it.

"Thank you, Sirendor," said the big man. "And we'll have

your name too."

"Hirad Coldheart. Remember it. Everyone else will."

"I have no doubt about that," said the elf. "Though the reasons might not be those you would wish. I am Ilkar."

"Then we are introduced."

"All except you, clever mouth," said Hirad. "What's your name?"

"It's of no consequence," said the big man.

"God's drowning but you're a prat," said Hirad.

"But a fast one. Faster than you. And a couple of years older and still alive and do you want to know why?"

Hirad didn't. "You're going to tell me anyway."

"Yes, because you need to hear it or your unforgettable name will soon be followed by R.I.P."

"I seriously doubt that."

The big man held a finger to his lips. "Humour me, at least... After five years, you really should have noticed that the ones who tend to live long are those who work with the fighters either side of them and with a nearby mage if they have any sense."

"I've noticed I'm still alive."

The big man blew out his cheeks. "Give me strength to survive the tests before me."

"Don't bother. I don't need your lecture. I can look after myself."

"I know!" the big man's shout ruffled the braids in Hirad's hair. "I saw you this morning before I joined the line. I saw you fighting with Blackthorne's men last year and I saw you during that debacle up by Rache not thirty days ago. What you did there was... impressive. You're good. You're really, really good. But every time you go into combat you leave yourself, and those you stand between, exposed by your reckless moves. It will cost you your life. It has already cost others theirs."

"That's their problem," said Hirad.

"No you moron it's yours," snarled the big man. Hirad was

startled in spite of himself. "Dear Gods drowning why are you so stubborn? Born in the north, were you?"

"And proud of it."

"It figures. Right, I'm going to try one more time. Do your best to follow what I'm saying, all right?"

"I'm not stupid," snapped Hirad.

"We've not seen a great deal of evidence to support that statement thus far," said Ilkar.

"And you can shut your mouth too, sharp ears."

"A three thousand year old insult too. Such an intellect," said Ilkar. "Why are you wasting your time with him?"

"Why are you standing here if not to see what happens next?" asked Sirendor. "I know I am."

Hirad felt his cheeks burning again. He wished his sword was in his hand, not lying on the ground with blood drying on the blade.

"Listen to me," said the big man, waiting until Hirad looked back at him. "You're here because you're talented. Arlen knows who he's hiring. Pontois' militia are tough and loyal and they work together. Tell me, Hirad, what pay do you get if we lose this fight?"

"Nothing, of course."

"Right. And do you get extra shares if fewer of us survive to collect our pay if we win?"

"No, but it's a good idea."

"It'll never happen, believe me," said the big man. "And do you think your chances of survival are better if more of us fight for longer?"

Hirad cast his eyes skywards. "Obviously."

"Good. So you see what I'm getting at."

Hirad stared at him while the sounds of warriors and mages beginning to ready themselves for another fight began to gain in volume.

"Are you trying to say I need you alive to improve my chances of getting paid?" he said eventually.

The big man cracked a smile. "Absolutely. So I'm suggesting that we work together. I've seen you fight, Sirendor, you've very fast hands and nimble feet. And you, Ilkar, a high quality mage. Care to work with me... us?"

The two of them nodded their heads.

"Hirad?"

"The better I look alone, the more I get paid next time."

The big man sighed. "And the sooner you die. So just this once, do it my way?"

Hirad looked at his accidental companions. This wasn't at all how he'd seen this or any other fight. But something about this great pile of muscle was utterly compelling. He shrugged.

"Good. We're going to take a flank, the left, I think."

"What, to get as far from the action as possible?" asked Hirad.

"No," the big man's voice held a note of exasperation. "Because Pontois hasn't set his best on us yet. That'll happen now and they'll try and break us on the flanks and the left looks weaker to me as it will do to them. We'll be waiting. I want this over in a couple of hours and you can help that happen."

"You don't want us in line?"

"No, we'll do better stepping into the inevitable breach," he said. "I'll inform the field commander. See you over there."

"Why are you doing this?" asked Hirad.

"Let's just get through the day first."

Hirad smiled, intrigued. "Some sort of test, is it?"

"I've just had an idea. Old theme, new angle."

The big man trotted off. Hirad looked at Sirendor.

"You're stronger than you look."

"And you're smellier."

Hirad saw the sparkle in his eyes and the warmth in his smile. "At least you'll know where I am without looking."

Sirendor laughed, stooped and picked up Hirad's sword and handed it over hilt first. "Painted with Pontois blood though I note a couple of bare patches."

"I'll see what I can do," said Hirad.

They started walking across the back of the line reforming in response to a gathering of Pontois militia. It didn't look weighted any differently to Hirad. Still, so long as there were enemies to fight… Ilkar fell into step beside them. Hirad glanced at him, feeling a little abashed.

"Sorry about the sharp-ears thing," said Hirad.

Ilkar raised an eyebrow. "Don't worry about it."

"I mean your ears aren't even sharp, are they? 'Leaf-ear' would have been more accurate."

"There really is no answer to that," said Ilkar.

"Was that supposed to be a compliment?" asked Sirendor.

"Dunno really." Hirad shrugged. "So are you old old or, y'know, young old?"

"Me?" said Ilkar.

"Well I can see how old Sirendor is."

"Got a lot of friends, have you?" asked Sirendor.

"Not really," admitted Hirad.

"Who'd have thought it?"

"In answer to your rather clumsy question, no I'm not old. Not for elves and not for humans either." Hirad stared at him. "I'm thirty seven, all right?"

"Just about old enough to be my father," said Hirad.

"That is a truly appalling thought."

"Can I ask you something else?"

"Do I have a choice?"

Hirad grinned. "Not really. Thing is, won't you get bored of being alive?"

"What? No, of course not. Why, will you?"

"I won't live to be as old as you," said Hirad. "Reckon by the time I'm sixty or so, that'll be about enough. But you'll go on to four or five hundred, won't you?"

"Something like that."

"I've always wondered what it would be like to know you had that long to go."

21

Ilkar stared at him for a moment. "You know that's actually a really good question. From your point of view, I mean. I guess we just view time in a very different way. From my perspective, you humans hardly get going before you die. I'm amazed you aren't depressed by the paucity of time you have."

"Who says we aren't?" said Sirendor.

Ahead of them, cavalry were assembling. Hirad took a quick glance about him. Behind them, the town of Gyernath went about its usual business untroubled by the conflict outside its borders.

It was daft, really. They were fighting over a road that was impassable half the year anyway. Arlen owned it, Pontois wanted it whoever controlled it set the tariffs to and from the docks. Big money.

Hirad knew he shouldn't care but Arlen's way had always seemed right and proper whereas Pontois was just a cock. That meant everyone who fought for him was a cock and those who opposed him had something about them, mercenary or not.

"...anyway," Sirendor was saying. "Our anonymous friend seems to have a plan."

"What *is* his plan? I mean for after today," said Hirad.

"Well, mercenary teams are all the fashion," said Ilkar. "I hope that's what he's thinking."

"Oh really? Is that it?" Hirad curled his lip. "And why wouldn't he tell us his name?"

"So he can disappear if it doesn't work out, I suppose," said Sirendor.

"Him? Six foot lots, shiny head and built like my father's prize bull? He'll be a spirit in the wind."

As if summoned by being discussed, the big man trotted over to join them.

"All friends now, are we?" he asked.

"Well, I don't want to kill them anymore, if that's what you mean," said Hirad.

"It'll do. Right, it's all arranged. Section commanders are

passing on Pontois' likely attack, we've another reserve group on the right flank and we've strengthened the centre to make sure we hold firm. I need you all to follow my lead. Ilkar, that goes for you too."

"Er, all right," said Ilkar.

"You'll have doubts but watch it unfold and if you trust my calls go with them."

"I can do that."

"Good. And you two?" He stared at Hirad after Sirendor had nodded. "Think you can curb your inclination for suicidal moves?"

"I've no idea."

"All right, then, how about you agree to step back when I yell at you?"

"I'll give it a go."

"And duck when I tell you."

"That I can do."

"Good enough. Hirad, take centre; I'll take left; Sirendor on the right. Ilkar, a Hard Shield to begin, please. I foresee projectiles."

They weren't kept waiting long. Pontois' forces were heading in at a run. Across Arlen's lines, orders were barked and the energy of magical shields snapping into place warmed the air. Horsemen to their left, maybe twenty five of them, gathered in loose formation, their eyes on the approaching enemy cavalry cantering easily over open ground. Wan sunlight flashed against armour.

Thirty yards distant, the sword lines split, first ranks heading on, second rank stopping.

"Incoming!" called the big man.

Arrows surged across the open space. Arlen's archers returned fire. Shafts flared against shields, seeking weakness, seeking gaps. Volleys continued to fall. Hirad was yet to hear a cry of pain. It would have to be a loud one over the roars of the advancing militia and the taunts of Arlen's defenders, mind you.

The arrow barrage ended. The lines clashed. Enemy cavalry moved to the gallop, Arlen's responding, moving to meet them. Hirad saw the pressure that was hitting their flank. He itched at his sword grip.

"You'll get your chance soon enough," said the big man. "Ilkar, SpellShield."

"I hear you."

Knots of enemy mages were moving behind the enemy lines. While their brothers and sisters defended the militia, they had specific targets in mind. Hirad watched them come when the press of bodies in front of him allowed it.

"Arrows on the incoming mages!" called the big man. "Get pressure on them."

Blood fountained into the air in front of Hirad. One of Arlen's men fell back, his throat ripped apart. Another moved to fill the breach, straddling the dying mercenary. Hirad recognised both of them. Arrows fell on and around the advancing mage teams; shields flared.

"We could take 'em," said Hirad.

"That's why I'm calling it," said the big man. "Wait on."

The opposing horsemen clashed on open ground about twenty yards from the skirmish line. The noise of fighting, already extreme, became deafening, drowning out the shouts of orders and the cries of the wounded and dying. The knots of mages stopped. They cast almost immediately.

"Bloody hell," muttered the big man. "SpellShields. Now!"

His call was taken up but not quickly enough. FlameOrbs seared across the sky, dropping on to the flanks of the fight. Pontois' men were well-prepared and stepped back on command, their defending mages already with shields in place. Heat and flame poured from above. Orbs detonated on unprotected men, reducing them to ashes and steam. Vibrations rocked the ground.

The enemy cavalry broke and wheeled to charge in. Pontois' elite ran into the holes in the line.

"Ilkar, hail or ice, your choice. Do it now. Hirad, Sirendor, stand by me."

There were enough of Arlen's men to fill the breach but the shock of the attack was in too many faces and some were walking corpses to Hirad's eyes. To his left, Arlen's cavalry were galloping to intercept Pontois'. Some had broken away to scatter the mage groups. The big man moved forwards, tapping his blade on the smouldering ground. The stench of burning was everywhere, smoke irritated their eyes. The trio closed up quickly to the end of the new left flank.

"Ready," said Ilkar from behind them.

"Perfect," said the big man. "Ilkar, I trust you. Hirad, Sirendor... down."

Hirad dropped prone, almost at the feet of the burly warrior in front of him. He heard a cry of warning. Intense cold swept over his body, blown on a howling gale. He could hear flesh and cloth creaking as it froze and the half-called cries strangled in petrified throats. IceWind; most effective.

"Up and in," said the big man. "Ilkar, perhaps a ForceCone ready, I'll leave it to you."

"About time."

Hirad came to his feet. Ilkar's spell had been horribly effective. Blackened corpses were scattered across the ground in front of him. The edges of the wind had caught the enemy cavalry and their order was shattered. Three horses were down, two were staggering, mortally wounded by the freezing gale. Hirad could see a wounded man staring at where his right arm once was, screaming over and over. The limb itself lay black and ruined on the ground next to him.

Hirad kept pace with the big man and Sirendor. The atmosphere of the battle had changed. Two blows had been struck, one by either side, and the momentum was back with the defenders. Hirad raised his blade. The three of them struck forwards in concert. Hirad's blow was partially blocked but it left his enemy open. Hirad made a return blow and carved deep into the warrior's neck. Next to him, Sirendor had confused his enemy and buried the point of his sword in the unfortunate's chest. The big man hadn't bothered with subtlety, taking his victim's blade with his on the way to smashing his skull.

"Hold!" he shouted. "Ilkar what do you have?"

Hirad stilled his impulse and, instead, watched those in the next rank glance down at their dead comrades before moving up to close their line. He could hear cavalry clashing once more. A horse screamed. Hirad heard a horn sound a break. Hooves thundered on the mud.

"ForceCone," said Ilkar.

"On my go." The big man's sword tapped on the ground. "We'll take these. Move up."

Hirad paced forwards, switched his blade between his hands and hammered it into his opponent's flank. Sirendor fenced briefly before delivering the killing blow and the big man kicked his enemy in the gut after his strike was blocked high and away.

"Hold!" he shouted, chopping his blade into the fallen man's gut. "Ilkar, break their horsemen."

"Oh, right. Good plan."

Ilkar moved his focus. Hirad felt the sting of magic across his shoulders. He glanced left. Pontois' cavalry were reforming, still lacking cohesion when Ilkar's ForceCone struck them, an expanding circle of magic, hard as stone, emanating from his palms. Undefended while their mages gathered themselves after the last skirmish, horses and riders were driven across the ground. Legs buckled, horses collapsed and riders were crushed beneath their rides.

"Step up."

Next to Sirendor, the Arlen mercenaries were gaining courage and this time they moved up simultaneously. Hirad found a firm footing, fielded a heavy overhead blow, swayed inside and dragged his sword across the chest of his enemy. The big man deflected an axe strike to his side, butted the axeman on the bridge of the nose and carved his blade up, splitting his enemy's body from groin to ribcage.

"Hold."

Arlen's cavalry drove into the flank of Pontois' militia. Spells fizzed from shields covering them from desperate attack. Horns sounded along Arlen's lines and everywhere, men pushed forward and the roar of battle intensified.

"It's as good as over," said Hirad.

"So it is," said the big man. "Two hours, no more. Better my way, don't you think?"

Hirad shrugged. "This time," he said.

"Every time. Come on, let's point them back home."

"I did not."

"You bloody did. In fact, you said about halfway here that it was the *only* reason you were coming."

Hirad took another long swallow of very good Blackthorne red wine and held out his goblet for a refill. The big man obliged.

"It was not the only reason," said Hirad, a smile cracking his face. "I also mentioned the free lodgings as critical."

"Told you he was just a free-loader," said Ilkar.

"And I told all of you I knew what I was doing," said the big man.

"I think the serious stuff might be coming," said Ilkar.

"Then I need a lot more to drink," said Hirad.

So here they were and Hirad couldn't quite believe it, free food, drink and lodging or not. He'd been riding the road to Korina with Sirendor and Ilkar the morning after the victory party at Gyernath and the big man had trotted up, invited them all back to this inn and said he had something to discuss. Hirad still couldn't really work out why he'd agreed to hear what the man had to say. Probably because, and he'd never admit this to anyone, he rather liked all three of them and he'd sworn he'd make no friends on the skirmish line. It was too fleeting a life.

But he hadn't turned his back and he hadn't ridden off towards Rache or up to Orytte where he had heard there was work. He was here in *The Rookery* with two men and an elf he'd wanted to kill a couple of days ago, sitting in a back room full of comfortable chairs set around a log fire.

Hirad shook his head and chuckled while the big man refilled his goblet again.

"What is it?" he asked.

"Nothing. Just the turns of life I suppose. So what is it you want to talk about?"

The big man placed the wine jug on the mantel and stood to one side of the fire where he could see them all.

"I'm not about to patronise you, you know I want to put a team together but it can't be like anyone else's team."

Hirad scratched his head. Ilkar put his confusion into words.

"In what ways not the same? I presume you're not talking about composition."

"No, I'm not. Clearly warriors backed by a mage is the only sensible option for a fighting team. Although I can see a place for groups of mages hiring themselves out, I'm not one; so I want the more traditional make-up. No, I'm talking about attitude and approach and that's why I'm talking to you three and I have another trio already working together that I think will fit us."

Ilkar spread his hands. "And which attitudes and approaches do you think we all meet? I don't wish to insult anyone but Hirad but we don't exactly conform to a type, do we?"

"Not in hygiene terms anyway," said Sirendor.

"I have a bath every year even if I don't need it," said Hirad, punching Sirendor on the shoulder. "Play your cards right and I'll even share my bath water with you."

"I wouldn't fit, what with all the other creatures trying to swim away from your filthy hide."

The big man cleared his throat. "And that's an example of why I've picked correctly. You're not just outstanding at what you do, you're also more comfortable together after two days than most teams are after two years.

"What I see on the battlefields of Balaia are teams only together because they earn more that way. They still fight as individuals, they squabble about leadership, shares and inevitably end up either breaking up, killing each other or getting killed by their opposition. I don't want a short mercenary life. I want to earn my money, retire and run *The Rookery* with Tomas while I grow old.

"I can only do that if I fight alongside those I trust. We can build that trust between us, fight as one. And the more successful we get, the more we can command. But I don't want our reputation simply to be that of effective fighters. I've watched you, more particularly, I've watched the contracts you've taken and the way you conduct yourselves so I know you believe how I believe. And I want to set down what that means."

"I'm not going to fight by rules, muscle-head," said Hirad, not liking where this seemed to be going.

"If I tried to impose that, I'd make you a lesser warrior," he said. "What I want is for us to swear to a simple moral code. It will set us apart. Make us the first to be signed up by the barons and lords we want to fight for. Few teams fight exclusively for those on the right side of disputes. We can break that and make ourselves the key stone of future fights for people like Blackthorne, Gresse and Arlen."

"You'll make us targets," said Ilkar.

"I'll make us rich," said the big man. "Look at this."

He picked up a sheet of parchment from a table next to the mantel. He laid it on the table in front of them. Hirad stared at it, seeing there were words on it and nodding in what he was confident was a sage fashion.

"Absolutely. It's very, y'know, perceptive and interesting." They were all looking at him. "What? Just giving my opinion."

"You have no idea what it says, have you?" said Sirendor.

Hirad felt himself blushing. "Well, some of the words I had to guess at a bit."

"Which ones?" asked Ilkar.

Hirad gestured vaguely at the parchment. "The last four."

"So you're completely comfortable with 'to'," said Sirendor.

"Well it's a start."

"Bloody barbarian," said Ilkar.

"I am not."

"By my definition, you are. Or did you actually get an education?"

"Farming," replied Hirad.

"Fabulous. Reading and writing?"

"I can sign my name," said Hirad.

"That's all we need," said the big man. "It reads: 'To kill but never murder'. It's the code I want us to live by as a team. It will set us apart from every other team in Balaia. I don't just want us to be the best, I want us to be the best by doing our jobs right every time."

Hirad shrugged. Ilkar and Sirendor were both looking at the big man as if they'd received some sort of major revelation.

"This might actually work," said Sirendor.

"We have to believe it," said the big man. "Or this is just a piece of parchment."

He held out a quill and placed a pot of ink on the table. Ilkar took the quill and signed his name with a flourish. He handed it on to Sirendor who scratched his name below Ilkar's. He held the quill out to Hirad.

"I've left room for your 'X' or hand print or whatever it is."

Hirad smiled. He dipped the quill in the ink, bent to the parchment and wrote his name carefully next to Ilkar's.

"There," he said. "Neater than yours, dandy boy."

Ilkar roared with laughter. "Bugger me but he's right!"

Sirendor sniffed. "Fucker."

Hirad pointed the quill to the big man. "Your turn. Get to find out your name now, don't we?"

The big man smiled. "I don't need to sign, it's not important. I wrote the code and that is enough."

Hirad snorted. "We don't want any mystery man on the team so either sign up or bugger off."

"Yeah, what are you, some kind of mystical *unknown warrior* or something?" said Ilkar.

The big man shook his head. He took the quill, dipped it and signed.

"Excellent," said Hirad. "What does it say?"

"It says 'Unknown Warrior'," said Sirendor.

"Unknown... I like that," said Hirad. "Good to meet you, Unknown."

"Thank you," said the Unknown. "We're now a team. I've already thought of a name."

"Oh, yeah? Pray tell," said Ilkar. "Coldheart's Killers?"

"Larn's Lacerators?" said Sirendor.

"Ilkar's..." began Hirad. "Um, incinerators?"

"Those are all utterly terrible," said The Unknown, smiling. "I was looking for something less flashy, more, I dunno, worthy...something that says we're serious and exceptional in our field."

"Oh dear," said Ilkar. "So more along the lines of 'the Moral Marauders' then?"

"None of the rhyming crap," said the Unknown. "We formalised our arrangement here in *The Rookery*. 'The Rook' is rubbish but I thought something in the same family of birds would work."

"Yes?" said Hirad. 'Which one do you want to name us after? Jackdaws? Magpies? Not going to earn us respect, I'd say."

The Unknown let the silence settle like an actor might for dramatic effect.

"We should call ourselves, 'The Raven'."

Hirad thought for a moment. "It's not bad."

"I've heard worse," said Ilkar.

"Think it'll stand the test of time?" asked Sirendor.

"Well, we'll just have to wait and see." The Unknown lifted his goblet. "To us. To 'The Raven'."

The quartet clashed goblets, sloshing wine on the table.

"The Raven!"

A Blade to the Heart

Gaie Sebold

Lapscar, already doomed, approached his keep. He held himself rigid on the great scaled mount, massive shoulders back, head up. The torchlight flickered on his tusks and the claws of his raised hand. A chill breeze whispered through the rainy night, blowing about the cloaks of the guard on the battlements.

"What happened?" one muttered.

"Soul blade," said another. "They've sent for healers. Much good that'll do."

They looked down at their leader. Even among his species, who stood a head above most humans and could break a person's arm as a man might a twig, Lapscar was huge; his tusks five inches long, the muscles of his arms like boulders. Snarling, he eased himself from his mount.

None of his men dared offer help.

Lapscar looked up. The guards hurriedly looked outwards, over his lands, so long and well defended.

"Keep your eyes open, damn you." Lapscar's voice echoed in the dank well of the court. "We've driven them back, but you drop your guard and you'll be the first I come for, whether or not I remember your fools' faces. Stand *to.*"

The guard stiffened their spines. If they trembled, they hoped Lascar's sight was already dim enough to hide the fact.

The inner door boomed shut behind him.

"Soul blade. S'what finally did for…" the guard lowered his voice, "Bloom of Crimson. Mind, nothing natural could kill the Bloom."

The other snarled. "Shut it! You trying to bring more bad luck down on us?"

"You ever seen someone... after? You ever seen a wraith?" another said.

"No. Shut up about it."

"They're not going to let him turn *here.*"

"How they going to stop him?"

"They'll kill him, of course."

Killing Lapscar wouldn't stop him becoming a wraith. It would merely slow the process, and give them a chance to get the thing that had been their Lord out of the keep.

The first guard licked at a tusk thoughtfully. "Yeah. And who's going to do that? You?"

Lapscar kept walking. He had never noticed the cold; now the stone floor struck chill up the bones of his legs, reaching towards the chill spreading from his wound.

His courtiers were gathering - he thought. But other shadows, other whispers had been following him since the moment the soul-blade had struck. He swung his head, glared into the eyes of one of his councillors. No phantom this; Lapscar could smell his fear. "Don't crowd me," he growled.

"My Lord." Sweating, the councillor backed away.

Lapscar's grip was still iron. But for how long?

Around the councillor's face greyish vapours collected. Lapscar fought the desire to tear at them with his fingers.

He fumbled his way through the whispering darkness towards his throne, and hauled himself into it. Cold stone gripped him like a dead hand. He braced himself against it.

His vision cleared slightly. He could see his remaining sons, already eyeing each other, weighing strengths and weaknesses; his courtiers eyeing his sons. Suddenly he laughed, grating and terrible.

"Well, my vultures? Soon I'll be a thing to eat your dreams. You want to watch it happen? Get out."

He managed to hold himself upright until they had gone, then slumped, hand to his side. "Cold," he muttered. "So cold."

Lapscar tried to think. His rule had been brutal, but it wasn't strength alone that had kept him on his throne – they called him sharp as an axe. But now his mind was fuzzing over with ice-crystals.

Grimacing with the effort, he pushed back the dimness a little. *Think.* A soul blade turned a living being to a wraith, unkillable, susceptible only to powerful sorcery. Lapscar had never heard of a cure - only destruction, or banishment of the wraith to some grey realm.

The truth of soul-stealers was as ungraspable as their substance. No one knew whether they had countries, leaders, loyalties. They were drawn to battle; to certain victims. From some their blades sucked all the essence, leaving husks. Others survived, only to become wraiths themselves.

Lapscar's own father had been one such. Luckily for his family, the transformation had happened far from home. But perhaps their most famous prey had been the war-leader, Bloom of Crimson... Even unspoken, in the darkening fog of his own mind, Lapscar hesitated over the name. It tasted of blood and bronze, and rang with screams.

Footsteps brought his head up, his hand to his dagger. "Oh, Brug. Get out, didn't you hear me?"

The big stupid lump just stood there. "You're hurt. You want water?"

Lapscar ran his tongue over cracked lips. His tusks felt like old bone drying in a cold desert. "Yes."

Brug went. Poor fool. The only one who might be sorry at Lapscar's passing, at least he wasn't important enough for anyone to murder.

Of course if Lapscar returned in his new form, he would slaughter Brug with as little hesitation as he would step on an ant.

Without wincing, Lapscar lifted his armour from his breast and peeled back his tunic.

The wound looked like nothing. Barely two inches long. The blade had been narrow as a needle. But the feel of it… Lapscar closed his eyes, then wrenched them open in case someone should come in.

Already the flesh around the wound had a grey, insubstantial look.

Brug's heavy footsteps crunched through the gathering mists. "Water, Lord."

Lapscar took it, and drank. Cold water, at first refreshing, suddenly conspired with the dreadful cold rising from the wound. He went rigid, fighting the deep icy spread of it, knowing it was hopeless.

"Lord?" Brug said, distressed, "is the water bad?"

Lapscar forced his clenched teeth apart. "No. Go now."

Brug, always obedient, hesitated. Lapscar swelled with fury. Had even Brug begun to think he could be disobeyed? He, Lapscar, the Wolf of Gaen?

Before he could unlock his throat Brug said, "Forgot. Healer's come."

Not disobedience. Lack of brains. As he had several times before, Lapscar decided to let the fool live. "That was quick."

"Lord?"

Lapscar was suddenly uncertain. How long had he sat here, drifting into darkness? He pushed himself upright. "Has that skinny runt of a priest pulled his courage up far enough to come here? What did they offer him? My soul? Too late for that."

Brug wouldn't see the joke, but better a jest than a whimper.

Brug shook his head. "S'a woman." He paused a moment, pondering. "Still skinny."

Lapscar snorted. "Human?"

"Think so."

"Greedy, or desperate. Bring her. I could do with a laugh."

Brug opened the door. Lapscar saw the crowd gathering behind a small, cloaked shape. His lips drew back. "*Get out.* The healer can stay. The rest *leave.* Brug, to your room, and wait."

Brug's room was behind the throne; strong, fast, and too stupid for conspiracy, he was the only one Lapscar trusted with his back.

The others withdrew, slowly. Lapscar knew his hold wouldn't last much longer, and every effort drained him. But he would hold them, till the end.

The healer remained, a rock abandoned by the withdrawing tide. She was slight, as far as he could tell. Her hood framed a narrow, pale face. She stood quietly, hands folded, water dripping from her cloak.

"So," Lapscar said. "They told you? If you know your job you know that no crushing of herbs, no spell, no whining chant will change my fate one whit. There's nothing you can offer, healer, except some brief entertainment while I wait for night to take me."

"Perhaps there is something more I can offer, if you are willing to give what is needed." Her voice was low, a little rough around the edges.

"Hah, a price. I thought so."

"A high one."

"I suspected."

"Not gold."

"What then? Power? You think to rule here?" He choked on a laugh that turned to a gasping moan as the chill drowned him.

He opened his eyes to find her beside him, and tried to get his numbing hand to his dagger. *She crossed the room, while you gave in to it. A fine fate for the Wolf of Gaen, slaughtered by a wisp of a woman in the heart of his own keep.*

"I'm here to help, not harm," she said, completely unmoved by his snarl. "And how far do you think I'd get, if I cut your throat?"

"Depends who thought they might benefit," Lascar said, with the remnants of a grin.

"I know. Will you let me help you?"

"You can't."

"The Wolf of Gaen giving in to despair?"

"No. Reality. Besides, you never named a price. I'm a cautious fellow, I might lose everything on such a gamble."

"One way or another, yes. What is your life worth, my Lord?"

"Now we come to it. What do you ask?"

"Merely that you answer the question. That is part of the price."

Her eyes were a cool grey, the left pulled up at the corner by a small scar.

"Think before you answer, my Lord."

He held her gaze. The veils shuffled, clustering around his mind. "My name makes the earth tremble over a thousand miles of territory. I have cut my way here through rock and fire. I will hold it to the end."

"You have not answered the question."

"I…" The chills took him again, leaving him writhing helplessly, cold hissing in his veins. He arced his back, biting down so those outside would not hear him cry out.

Only when he felt her hand on his brow, burning like the sun, did a brief moan escape. With a shudder his muscles relaxed.

If anyone heard me whimper like a beaten pup, you are dead, healer. He shook off her hand.

"No one heard," she said. "And soon, you will cry out less. You will fight less. The cold will seem welcoming, even pleasant. The veils will wrap you like silk, and then they will lock like stone."

"You've seen this before."

"Yes. To live, you will have to fight as even you have never fought before, bleed as you have never bled."

Lapscar growled. "What do you know of fighting and bleeding, healer?"

"All any healer needs to know," the slightest of smiles quirked at the corner of her mouth, "and perhaps a little more than most. You have not answered my question."

"Ask me another."

"Very well. Who here do you trust?"

He snorted. "These are my people, bone and blood. I own them."

"But who do you trust?"

"To do what?"

"What purpose does evasion serve? Which of these your people, whom you own, bone and blood, would come to your aid for any reason other than fear? Which of them would stand by you if all your power was gone? Which would venture death for you, without your order?" She sounded almost angry. She, angry at him. Fury and amusement fought briefly, warming his blood.

"Sharp, aren't you? And you're right. Not a one," he said. "I hold what I hold by strength, and fear. It's always been enough."

"And that is why they chose you."

"My people didn't choose me, I took them."

"That isn't who I meant, my Lord."

He clenched his teeth on another chill. "The soul-stealers? What do you mean, they chose me? It was the luck of battle, and I was leading. That is what a chieftain does."

"I am aware of that, my Lord." Her tone was dry. "Soul-stealers recruit the strong. The hard, the tough, the fearless. Those who have built walls around their hearts."

Lapscar pressed a hand to his wound. His tunic moved unpleasantly beneath his palm. "I feel no wall. Just a damn great hole."

"My Lord is pleased to jest."

"What else am I to do? If you are only here to bandy words, healer, get gone."

"Words can be powerful, my Lord."

He opened his mouth to reply and again the dreadful whispering began, and he found himself speaking unknown words, crawling syllables skittering over his tongue. Greyness enveloped him. In it, things beckoned.

The cold will seem pleasant.

Damned if you'll take me that easy!

But there was a sensuous edge to the chill. A tempting emptiness.

"No!"

He was not sure if it was his voice, or another's. He felt dim warmth, grasped at it.

Not emptiness, not yet.

Already, returning to the world hurt, as though the shadows were weaving into his flesh, pulling away only with ripping reluctance. He opened his eyes, groaning. The torchlight seemed too bright.

The healer gripped one of his great clawed hands in both her own. Even through his pain her strength surprised him. Her hands were hard as a soldier's. "Stay with me, my Lord. I know it hurts, but you *can* fight."

"Done *that* all my life."

"I know. Believe me, I do."

Something fell on the back of his hand.

Lapscar looked at it. A drop of water, glimmering. "You *weep* for me?" He felt that he should be angry, but the anger would not come. *Who weeps for the Wolf of Gaen?*

He heard her draw breath, steadying her voice. "You will not weep for yourself, Lord."

"No." He drew his hand away, and rubbed the drop from his skin. Had it left a trace of warmth, or did he imagine it? "Nor will any other."

She looked towards the empty fireplace, rubbing her hands together. Perhaps touching him had chilled her. "Not one?"

"Well, Brug, maybe – for as long as he remembers my existence, which won't be long."

"Why him?"

"Loyal as a dog."

"And how did my Lord earn this loyalty?"

"What does it matter? The rest will squabble like crows over carrion."

"Is this what you built your demesne for?"

"You think I meant to get a soul-blade in my innards and see it all fall into the hands of fools?"

"Then why?"

"To get land, to hold it, to be strong – this is what it means to be a war-leader. And the strongest will follow me. Sooner than I'd hoped, yes. Perhaps I'll come back, and see how they're getting on without me." He tried to laugh. "They fear me now. How much more, when I am a wraith?"

"It pleases you to cause fear?"

He shrugged. "It works. *You* should fear me, little healer."

"Now, or later?" That wry note in her voice.

He laughed. "Both. What are you doing here? Did one of my enemies send you, to gloat?"

"No. Tell me about Brug."

"Why?"

She turned towards him, but the dim light and the hood made a mystery of her face. "That is the price."

He glared. "Words are worth nothing."

"Really? Words like; 'Disobey me again and you'll be hanging on the gatehouse with your guts around your ankles!'?"

He blinked. He'd used those words on many a raw youngster – and that voice! Low, deadly and completely convincing. If *he'd* been a raw youngster he'd have been damned near soiling himself with fear. Where had she found that voice?

"Or," she said, "words like 'The Wolf of Gaen?' Are they worth nothing? They were hard enough earned."

That was true, at least.

Tendrils of cold, growing through his flesh.

"And what do you gain if I tell you, healer? You can't live on words."

"On them? No. But by them, perhaps. Tell me about Brug."

"You dicker like a merchant."

She did not answer, pulling her cloak tighter.

"If you are cold, light the fire."

Eventually the logs caught. The healer held her hands to the heat. Lapscar thought he saw something like pain, but when she turned back her face was calm as still water.

The firelight could not reach the corners, where the whispering chill rose, thickening. Creeping out, towards him, over him.

"Tell me about Brug." Her hand on his, a small warmth.

"The others were pulling him about, spattering him with filth..." The picture in his mind was small and dull at first, gradually brightening. "I saw the size of him, thought, he can't even... even fight. Angered me, with his strength, he couldn't even defend himself. Knew he'd make a good bodyguard. Don't need wits for that."

"Tell the truth, my Lord."

"I am," he said, feeling the chill slide into his veins, muscles, bones. They would all dissolve. This heavy body would be nothing. His memories would be gone. He would know no weakness.

"Tell the truth."

She was persistent as a biting fly.

"I was angry," he said, barely caring. *It will wrap you like silk...*

"Tell me the truth, or you are a coward, my Lord."

Coward? "I pitied him!" The words gouged like chunks of stone. Brug's dull brown eyes, shining with tears, the ache in his own throat.

Suddenly Lapscar was wrapped in fire, a terrible heat scouring out from the wound. He howled, his spine bowing backwards, the arm of the throne cracking off, shattering on the floor. The chittering in his head rose to a grating skreel, unbearable, and died back.

"Well done, my Lord."

He opened his eyes. The healer stood in front of him, the tears in her eyes brimming with light. He felt drained. The fire flared brighter, forcing the shadows back.

"Damn you," he growled. "What do you mean, well done? Are you weeping for your failure? It's getting worse, and all you do is get me chattering about nonsense."

"What did you feel, my Lord?"

"Burning, woman."

"Yes, my Lord. Which will you have; the heat, or the cold?"

"What are you saying?"

"Those like you, my Lord, those who have wrapped themselves in iron and stone, can survive, as wraiths. Or you can fight. To fight..." she cleared her throat. "To fight you must embrace what you have denied. I warned you, the price would be high."

Lapscar looked down at his clenched, scarred hands. He had killed with them, often. "And if I will not pay?"

"Then you will become a wraith, my Lord. You shall become hollow will, empty strength. If you return here you will drain those who have fought beside you, caring nothing. You will steal Brug's essence and watch him fall, and because you are without weakness or feeling, you will know only a distant satisfaction. The choice is yours, my Lord."

"I..." The shadows were creeping out from the corners again. Up his spine crept the words of the skittering tongue, ready to spill from his mouth, weaving shadows around him. In a skin of shadows he would be invincible. The cold, like water, smooth and perfect, rose about him.

"Your name is Lapscar." The healer's voice calling, as though from the entrance to a deep cave where he sat alone. "Who named you?"

"My mother," he said, watching in a frozen fascination as the shapes of the shadows began to cohere. His hand moved to his wound again, feeling the dissolution of his flesh.

"What do you remember?"

Hands, worn with work. They had put food before him, stitched his wounds, caught him a cuff often enough, though unlike his father's blows they had never knocked him off his feet.

"Hands..." Oh, it *hurt*. A warmth that made his flesh dance with daggers. "Her hands..."

"Who was your first friend, Lapscar?"

Quiet, witch.

She would not let him go. "Who did you first trust beside you in battle?"

"Derl. Idiot. Got himself killed last year." The tears he had not permitted himself rose now, burning him like molten metal.

"When did you first see beauty?"

"In the leaves of a tree..." the dance of light and shadow, the grace of branches, in him like shards. He wept aloud. Her questions carried on, relentless, arrows with heads of fire. He battled for each answer; and each answer was an explosion of terrible heat. With each one the cold drew back a little, but with each he felt weaker, as though instead of blood his veins were filling with some dim heavy liquid.

Darkness and fire rippled against his closed eyelids, scarlet. The small hand still gripped his. "Healer."

"Yes, my Lord."

"Who named *you?*"

"My father. He called me Thelaine..." there was a pause. He felt her breath against his cheek as she murmured; "I was named for the little red flowers that grow near my home. Stay with me, my Lord. You are winning."

His instincts had not left him. "I hear something." Not the soul-stealers' whispering; a clatter and muttering at the iron doors. "They have come to finish me off, or try." He pressed against the arms of the chair, forgetting that one was gone, and nearly fell.

"Yes. Stay here." She moved towards the doors.

"Healer!" But he was too weak to rise. "Brug!"

Brug's heavy steps, a massive shape in the flickering darkness. Lapscar, breathing hard, clawed his way to his feet, using the broken throne, his vision hung with shadows. He could see only dim moving shapes.

"Help her, Brug. They will kill her. Don't let them hurt her..."

A Blade to the Heart

And with those words there was heat in him, dreadful, too immense a pain even to scream. Like a great iron vessel, heated too far, glowing scarlet then white-hot, something melted in Lapscar. Something, scalded in that heat, drew out of him, chittering with fury, a vile sensation like a leech pulling out of the gut. There was a feeling of collapse, of stone walls shattering, letting in the daylight. Then for a moment there was nothing.

Lapscar came back a little to himself. He could feel stone beneath him. He could hear the hiss of the torches, the harsher crackle of the fire. Brug's slow footfalls. He opened his eyes. The healer was at his side, calm as a priest at prayer. Brug stood next to her, grinning.

Lapscar looked at the great iron doors, but they were shut, and barred.

"What…"

"A moment, my Lord." She put her hand on his forehead. He closed his eyes again, feeling the small hard palm cool now against his skin.

He opened his eyes to see her smiling. "Well done. I do not know what finally drove it from you, my Lord, but I think we have won."

He coughed a laugh. "I feel as though an army had marched over me."

"Strength will return." She pressed a small bottle into his hand. "Drink this, it will help."

"What happened?" Lapscar took a swig of the liquid, astringent and sticky. "Did they try to come in?"

"Yes. We dissuaded them." She lifted her bag, slung it over her shoulder. "I assume there is a back way out?"

"What? No, wait. What is your price?"

"You have paid it, Lord. A little coin, if you wish, will feed me as far as the next town."

"Stay," he said. "We can use a good healer."

She looked at him, her face very still, her eyes on his. "To heal soldiers after battle?"

45

Lapscar opened his mouth, and shut it again.

She smiled. "I thank you for the offer, but I have work to do."

"More of the same."

"Yes."

"A moment, then." He moved, still slowly, to a chest that stood at the side of the room, and placed his hand on the lid. It was dark with age, carved with leaves and serpents. He opened the lid, drew out a leather purse clinking with coin, and stood in thought. Then he took out a small wooden box, of the same design as the chest. He brought them to the healer, placed them in her hands. The coin she tucked away without counting, but the box she held up to the torchlight. "This is beautiful."

He grinned. "A remnant of another life. I was a carver, once."

"You were a good one."

"Perhaps."

"Thank you," she said. "Goodbye, Lord Lapscar."

Strength was returning to him with the speed of his race and his own brutally honed constitution, but at once he felt oddly weakened. "Goodbye, healer." He hesitated, and said, "Thelaine. Thank you."

"My pleasure, Lord Lapscar." Her cloak swirled, and swift as a breath, she was gone.

Lapscar stood for a moment looking at the secret passageway through which she had disappeared. He shook his head, and closed the door. Then, Brug at his side, he went to the great iron doors and lifted the bar.

His war-council, his servants, his sons, backed from the opening doors. He looked at their wary, snarling faces, and felt a kind of sorrow.

"My Lord, is it you? I mean..." One of his sons, Gaflan, the eldest still living, looked his father over; hand to sword hilt, wonder warring with suspicion in his eyes.

"Aye. Me, as solid as ever I was." Lapscar held out his hand,

and his son, lip lifting over his tusks like that of a nervous dog, reached out and prodded it with the tip of one clawed finger. "Now, perhaps you can explain to me why you attempted to burst into the room while the healer was at work?"

A few of them looked at each other. Gaflan shifted his shoulders. "We heard cries. We thought the blade was taking you."

"And what happened?"

There was a peculiar, uneasy shuffling among them. Lapscar lifted his brows. "Well?"

One of his councillors stepped forward, clearing his throat. "It was the healer, Lord."

"The *healer?*"

"She…" the councillor, who was nearing seven foot, with tusks almost as fine as Lapscar's own and the scars of a score of battles marring his hide, bared his teeth. "Are you sure she healed you, Lord?"

"What do you mean?"

"Because she was no ordinary human!" The councillor hissed. "She moved like nothing I have ever seen. Pilsher is still unconscious," he waved a hand to the soldier lying slack-faced against the wall, "and Molik will be nursing his balls for a month." Someone – presumably Molik - groaned in agreement.

Lapscar felt something go through him, a strange, clear light. *I was named for a little red flower…*He walked through them. They eyed him suspiciously, drawing away, fearing his touch. "If any of you still think I am a wraith, I invite you to try a bout with me," he growled, clenching his fist so the great muscle of his forearm leapt up, quivering. "Otherwise, get to your duties. Gaflan, with me."

They went up onto the battlements. Lapscar dismissed the guards, though he kept Brug with him. He leaned his elbows on the parapet, and looked out over his lands. The clouds were drawing back, stars bright among the silvery wisps of vapour.

"Gaflan. Have you heard of Bloom of Crimson?"

Gaflan swallowed. When he spoke, his voice was unsteady. "Of course. But your deeds are greater."

"Rot, boy. My deeds may be spoken of for a generation, perhaps. But even you do not like to hear *that* name spoken above a whisper, and her deeds will ring in darkness for centuries. Beside them, mine are the tantrums of a child. She was the greatest and most terrible. You know what happened to her?"

"She was…" Gaflan cleared his throat. "She was soul-bladed, I heard."

"She would have been the most dreadful of wraiths, would she not? But no one ever reported seeing her wraith. Perhaps, like me, she survived…"

"I am glad to see you well."

"Are you, indeed? Well, you may yet have cause to regret it, boy. Go now." Lapscar watched his son depart, and grieved for something he could barely name.

"Lord?"

"Yes, Brug."

"The healer's gone."

"Yes."

Brug wrinkled his snout, and shrugged. "Healing's still here."

Lapscar looked at Brug, and smiled, a smile not without pain, but not without pleasure, either. "Yes. Sometimes, boy, you're sharper than my sons."

Some days later, Lapscar stood again on his battlements, surveying by moonlight the territory he had spent his life earning.

"You well, Lord?" Brug said.

"In a manner of speaking." Lapscar threw his head back, and laughed like a cracked bell, sending ravens circling up in the darkness, cawing their displeasure. "Saved and damned at a stroke! Ah, life is a comedy." He looked away, over the dark land. "I think she was alone, when it happened to her," he said. "And she fought. She won. The wit to realise how to fight, and the raw and bloody courage to do it! There's a soul worth fighting for.

She left me her name, at least. Perhaps I am a fool." He smiled to himself. "Oh, certainly I am a fool. But I can hope that she wanted me to find her."

"My Lord is leaving the keep."

"The keep will do without me." He ran his hand over the well-mortared stones, gently; brushed the dust off on his leg. "And I can do without the keep."

"Me too, then."

"If you wish. It'll be a strange life. But I could do with someone to watch my back."

Brug shifted his huge shoulders. "You always watched mine, Lord. Where we going?"

"Wherever we hear someone has been soul-bladed. I'm changing my profession."

"No more fighting?"

"Not if I can avoid it. It's not proper for a healer." Lapscar laughed again. "'All any healer needs to know, and a little more than most.' Damn you, woman. I'll find you if it takes me the rest of my days."

"She's only little. Can't have got so far, with those little legs."

Lapscar slapped Brug on the arm. "Let's hope you're right," he said. "We'll seek the little scarlet flower, and in the meantime, the Wolf of Gaen will try his hand at turning shepherd..."

A short time later, two figures left the keep by a hidden door, walking over the moon-silvered land and into another future.

Return to Arden Falls

A Tale of the Fallen Hero

Ian Whates

"May I buy you a drink?"

There are many questions I might say no to. This isn't one of them.

The man's timing was perfect. The Teller had just finished his performance, having spun an amusing yarn about a woodcutter's daughter and a lecherous Treemeister – those mythical mystical shepherds of the forest said to safeguard the wilds from harm. Utter nonsense, of course, but it made for a good story.

Having returned from the bar with my ale replenished, the stranger then assumed he'd bought my attention as well, claiming the chair opposite and asking, almost as soon as he had settled, "Have you ever been to Arden?"

My heart missed a beat but I managed to stay calm, raising my goblet and swallowing a settling mouthful while wondering whether any innocent-sounding question had ever been *less* innocent.

Only when the goblet was firmly back on the table did I reply, "Heard of it. There was a battle there once, wasn't there?"

"Yes, that's the place; a famous battle. Gerard himself fought there, at Arden Falls just north of the village. It's a beautiful place, picturesque, you know? To see it now you'd never guess that so many had died there. But, if you take the path from the falls back to the village, you pass this graveyard on your right, where the slain were laid to rest. Massive it is. They say that the dead dug their own graves at the very height of the battle, crawling in and pulling the earth down after them, just to escape the carnage."

"Really?"

Gods, how I hate these ridiculous legends. Arden Falls had been a grim and bloody affair, no question, but I didn't recall seeing any corpses leave of their own accord, crawling or otherwise. As for a graveyard... Bollocks. A mass grave more like; a pit into which the bodies were rolled after having been stripped of anything remotely valuable by the village folk and other opportunists.

The question troubling me just then, though, was who the hell this over-amiable fellow might be and how much did he know about me? Okay, that's two questions but, in mitigation, I had been drinking.

"I saw you fight earlier," he said.

A public duel, a pit-fight between me and a swordsman with twice my muscle and a tenth my skill, our bout squeezed in between one involving two malnourished 'Amazons' armed with knives and token wrist shields and a wrestling contest pitting a broad-chested giant of a man against a bear. The trifle I made by betting on the bear – no way anyone was going to risk a creature that valuable unless they were confident it could win – covered what I'd lost backing the blonde Amazon; I always have been a fool for a pretty face. As for my own duel, my opponent possessed all the characteristics of a former soldier: competent, precise, disciplined... and eminently predictable. I made sure the fight lasted just long enough to entertain the crowd, but the purse on offer wasn't sufficient to warrant stretching it out any further.

"You're good with a sword," my new-found friend told me.

"That I am."

"I want to hire you, to escort me to Arden."

Of course he did.

I'm not sure why I said yes – well, the money, obviously – but I'd avoided returning to Arden for all these years, so why the sudden change of heart? I think, on reflection, it was simply the right moment. To bury the ghosts, to say goodbye to friends and comrades I'd been too numb – both physically and mentally – to make peace with properly at the time.

Perhaps there were other reasons, but if so I prefer not to dwell on those.

Castor – that was how my new employer introduced himself. He was a garrulous bastard, but maybe some of that was simply to compensate for the fact that I wasn't. The journey to Arden took the best part of three days, during which I learnt pretty much his entire life story, while he learnt next to nothing about me.

Within the first hour of setting out I'd heard that he was originally from a small hamlet just south of Trilmouth. He was the youngest by an hour of twins and one of five children – four boys and a girl – his birth declared a curse and a blessing in equal measure. Twins were a rarity, for both to survive even more so; hence the positive portents. His mother, however, had been less fortunate, drawing her final breath at roughly the same moment he drew his first, which accounted for the 'curse' bit. Killing your own mother before you've so much as opened your eyes doesn't augur well in anyone's book. Personally, I reckon that outweighs 'oh look, twins; how lucky' every time, but what do I know?

During the first morning of our time together I also learnt that his father had been a blacksmith, teaching the trade to his sons, that Castor had no memory of one brother, who died in infancy, while his sister had perished of greypox on the cusp of her teens. That left three siblings: Artur, the eldest – who had inherited the smithy from their father – friend Castor, and his older-by-less-than-an-hour twin, Paulus.

Paulus was the problem. There seemed to have been some sort of falling out prompted by Artur's inheriting the family business, which caused Paulus to strike out on his own, settling in distant Arden. Castor had followed him. He clearly looked up to his older twin, which must have made the lad's death at the Battle of Arden Falls all the more difficult to take.

"I'd moved on from Arden by then," he said wistfully, without offering any explanation as to why. "I felt it though, the moment he died."

Whether you believe in all that rubbish about a special link between twins or not, one thing was becoming increasingly apparent: my employer was delusional. Not a problem – he was hardly the first such I'd worked for, and at least his didn't seem the dangerous sort.

"I never have been much of a one for the martial arts," Castor explained as the afternoon wore on. I hadn't asked; I hadn't needed to. "A bit of an oaf with a sword, in truth. Ask me to forge one and fine, I can do that, but when it comes to wielding it afterwards...?" He shrugged. "Hence my employing you. These are dangerous times."

True enough. I'm not sure the roads had *ever* been safe, but they certainly weren't these days. Castor had paid me a modest retainer with the promise of a more substantial fee at the job's completion. He let me know without quite being insulting that he wouldn't be carrying the monies with him, that they were deposited securely against our safe return. Anyone would think he didn't trust me or something, which was the first sign of good sense I'd yet seen in the man.

Turned out he hadn't been to Arden since before the infamous battle, despite his eulogising at our initial meeting, which, it emerged, consisted of embellishments built around memories a decade old and secondhand reports from others. Mind you, my own recollections of Arden were almost as old and by no means as pleasant.

We spent the first night under the stars, but broke our journey on the second at an inn, *The Butchered Stag*, where Castor encountered some competition on the conversational front, as the landlord insisted on regaling us with the tale of how the inn had acquired its name. To summarise: a horned larder of walking venison had been killed on this very spot.

"A giant, noble beast he was, majestic and fierce," the landlord insisted. "A prince among stags. His antlers take pride of place here to this very day."

He pointed to an impressive set of branching bones affixed to the taproom's longest wall. They did appear to be a little larger than the others mounted there, though not by much. The walls were festooned with the skulls and antlers of unfortunate plant-eaters, so numerous that I wondered how the patrons avoided impaling themselves when the inn got really crowded.

It was later that evening, as the two of us sat in a corner and supped ale together, that Castor dispelled any lingering doubts I might have had regarding his sanity.

"I've seen him, you know," he told me. "Paulus. His spirit comes to me in the depths of the night, begging for my help. He can't find peace. That's what this is all about. We have to recover his bones, so that I can bring my brother home and lay him properly to rest."

The subtle shift from 'me' to 'we' hadn't escaped me, but I let that one go, burying it away with my credulity. I asked instead, "And how exactly are you going to do that among so many fallen and buried?"

He smiled with the impregnable certainty of the self-beguiled. "Paulus will guide me, never fear."

I wasn't about to. The way I figured it, one bag of bones looks pretty much the same as any other. I had no doubt we'd come back from Arden with *somebody's* mortal remains, and if Castor chose to believe they were those of his dear departed brother, all well and good. Just so long as he wasn't expecting me to do the digging.

"Why wait until now?" I asked – a question I could just as easily have directed at myself.

"Paulus' spirit has only recently started appearing to me. I've no idea why that should be. Perhaps he's just now learned how to manifest, or maybe the torment of unrest has grown with each passing year, driving him at last to seek aid... At first I tried to ignore him, attributing these visitations to bad dreams, but they persisted, and his beseeching grows ever more desperate. My doubts have been satisfied. This really *is* Paulus' tortured shade. I *have* to help him, so that we both may find peace."

I kept my own counsel on the subject after that, resigned to whatever the morrow might bring.

In the event, what it brought was an ambush, though not until late in the day. By then we were close to Arden and, after three days in his company, I could happily have strangled my travelling companion. The opportunity to exercise my sword arm came as welcome relief.

Three of them, all mounted. One approached from behind, the other two rode out from a stand of trees directly in front of us: swarthy, grim-faced men, the sort for whom the word 'desperate' had been invented. No armour, no helmets: perfect.

The fellow to the left held a bow, mind you, fumbling with it as he attempted to nock an arrow while simultaneously controlling his horse.

I'm a great believer in seizing the initiative, especially when cornered. Without waiting for the would-be archer to get organised, or for anyone to issue whatever challenge they intended, I drew my sword and kicked my horse into a charge.

There's an art to fighting on horseback; you have to make allowance for the rhythm of your mount, adjusting to its gait and movement without consciously trying to. I've heard tell that the plainsmen of distant Yulgetthi are naturals at this, that they sit a horse before they can walk, think nothing of a ten year-old bringing down a desert grouse while riding at a canter, and that by the time they're twelve many can do a handstand on the back of a galloping steed, just for the hell of it.

Good for them. I, on the other hand, had to work at it. Long hours of sweat, toil, curses, chafed legs, blistered hands and aching limbs, not to mention bruises upon my bruises after being battered by staves, clattered into, and unceremoniously dumped from my saddle time and again.

Try sitting a horse and swinging a sword in anger without *some* degree of training and you're liable to end up struggling against your mount's natural motion rather than working with it. A cut will go too high or too wide, while any attempt at a decent thrust is more likely to unseat you than actually hit anything. Having an experienced horse helps as well, of course.

Not for the first time I had reason to be grateful for the zeal and dedication of my youth, particularly as the pair facing me gave every indication that they'd barely mastered climbing into a saddle.

My intention was to take them by surprise. Near as I could tell, it worked. Maybe the roar I uttered at the same time helped – I'm not above a touch of theatre when the occasion demands. An arrow zipped past as the panicked archer achieved some semblance of coordination, but it went well wide. I angled towards him on the basis that having fired the bow he wouldn't have time to defend himself properly. So it proved. I passed him on my right, which brought him in line with my sword arm while simultaneously placing him between me and his companion, hampering the latter.

One blow accounted for the first man, my blade cleaving into his unprotected face while he was still trying to draw his own weapon.

The force of impact nearly wrenched the sword from my hand, but I clung on, urging my mount into as tight and swift a turn as it could manage. Fortunately, that proved much tighter and swifter than my other immediate opponent, who was struggling to control his now panicked horse and turn it to face me. He succeeded well enough to at least muster some token resistance, blocking my first strike.

Not so the second, which slipped past his guard and between his ribs. I pulled the blade free and stabbed him again for good measure, though he was already going down.

My thoughts turned to the third attacker, but he had opted for a tactical withdrawal and was high-tailing it back the way he'd come. That left me with Castor, who still sat in his saddle but looked unusually pale. It was then that I noticed the blood seeping from between his fingers, which were clasped to his left arm just below the shoulder.

"The arrow…" he said quietly.

I cursed blind misfortune and abandoned any thought of going after the surviving brigand. The archer's shot had been so wild I hadn't spared it a second thought, but the arrow intended for me had obviously flown on to hit Castor, whom I was being paid to protect. That took a little of the shine off my magnificent victory.

"Sorry, I realise this isn't much," he said as I examined the damage, "but I've never been wounded before."

Wounded? It was little more than a scratch. The arrow hadn't even embedded, though it had dug a deep groove across his bicep in passing and the resultant cut was producing a fair bit of blood.

"You'll live," I assured him. "We'll have a healer take a look at this once we reach Arden."

After washing the 'wound' with water from the canteen, I returned to the two corpses, searching them for valuables.

Castor looked on with obvious distaste, asking, "Is that really necessary?"

"Necessary? No. But if I don't do it then the next traveller who passes this way will, and why should I let some stranger profit from my work?"

It didn't take long. For the most part the haul was meagre: the bow a sorry thing, not worth keeping and not worth trying to sell on. In addition there were two swords, one of which was shoddily made, a few knives – none of them the equal of those I already carried – some cheap oddments of jewellery, and little else. Apart, that is, from the coin; and therein rested the surprise. Each of the pair carried, if not a fortune, certainly far more than I would have expected given the state of their appearance.

Normally, brigands with this much money in their purses would have made a beeline for the nearest inn, determined to see how much ale and how many whores their funds would stretch to before they considered robbing again. Which made me suspect that this was more than just a random attack, that this pair had been hired to waylay my employer, but by whom?

The third man, the craven who had fled almost as soon as the fighting started? Perhaps.

I hung on to the coin and the better of the two swords, tossing everything else into the undergrowth and rolling the bodies in after. I would have preferred to round up the brigands' horses, which were likely to be the most valuable trophies of all, but Castor had to be my priority here; he was paying for my services, after all, and the way he was looking I wouldn't have put it past him to faint on me.

So we proceeded to Arden without further delay. Castor was quiet for once, possibly in shock. At least that gave me opportunity to reflect on the day's events and conclude that I might have accepted my employer's terms a little too hastily at outset. I should have held out for more. He clearly wasn't telling me everything, including why anyone would try to stop him from finding his brother's remains and how much of a threat that posed to me as the hired help. I decided not to confront him with any suspicions until I had a better idea of what the hell they might be; it did occur to me, though, that his incessant chattering might have served more purpose than I'd supposed, perhaps preventing me from asking whatever I *should* have been hearing.

We arrived at Arden shortly before sunset, approaching from the east and so failing to encounter the fabled falls which lay to the north of the village. Arden had grown since last I was here. Not so much a village now as a fully-fledged town.

We found rooms and stabled the horses at *The Green Dryad*, an inn I didn't recall and which, I suspect, had sprung up subsequent to the battle.

"Do you get many visitors coming through here to see the falls?" I asked the maid who showed us to our rooms. A homely girl with a pleasant disposition, she identified herself as Lisa when asked.

"Used to, sir, in the years immediately after the battle," she told me. "Not so much these days."

So the morbid glamour of visiting the site of the great battle was wearing thin with passing time, which didn't bode well for establishments such as this, built on the back of its attraction.

Castor was putting on a brave face but his strained expression smacked of martyrdom and you just knew he was weeping inside. Lisa must have sensed as much too, directing us to a local healer. "He's good," she promised, "and his prices are as reasonable as any."

Feeling somewhat responsible for my employer's misfortune, I considered paying for the healer's time with the coin I'd taken from the two brigands, though only briefly, reasoning that Castor doubtless had a damn sight more wealth than I did. With poultice secured over the wound and a foul-smelling elixir imbibed, we returned to the inn, where Castor declared himself weary after the long journey and announced that he was turning in early.

That suited me fine. I'd worried that he might want to see the falls straight away, without granting me proper opportunity to make my own peace with the place. If not for the shock of his 'wound', he probably would have done. I'm always grateful for small blessings.

I decided to walk rather than going through all the palaver of getting the horse brought from the stables and saddled again. It wasn't far, after all. A few folk passed me coming the other way, but the sun had recently set and evening would soon arrive to spread its cloak over the world, so I was hopeful. Company was the last thing I wanted when facing this place again.

I could hear the falls before I saw them. It wasn't a great roar such as they might produce in the rainy season, but rather a gentle murmur that crept up as you drew closer, so that initially you weren't certain if it was true sound or merely imagination that taunted the edge of hearing. Yet with every step the chatter of water grew louder.

The path brought me around a final knoll and past a small stand of trees and there it was: Arden Falls.

I'd expected instant recognition but that wasn't the case. The tumble of water was less than on the day of the fateful battle, though it still fell from a height of ten tall men, much as memory insisted, and the shape of the lagoon at the foot of the falls seemed subtly different, if roughly the same size. I suppose in the interim trees had grown, bushes had flourished in some instances and died back in others... It was unrealistic of me to expect that nothing would have changed, but for a moment the variances were sufficiently confusing to leave me searching for the instant connection I'd anticipated.

It *was* beautiful – a fact I'd never really had a chance to appreciate when last here. Ahead and to my right lay a small gravelly beach bordered by bulbous grey rocks that glistened with spray. A tree that might have been a willow bent forward to dangle frond-like branches just above the surface of the water, and that surface rippled gently as weak waves caused by the falls lapped against the rocks and rebounded. To my left an offshoot of the nearby forest met the water's edge, and in front of me stood the falls themselves.

A wall of rock, layered as if by a steady hand that had patiently set down level after painstaking level, each fractionally overhanging the one below. From the cracks between the layers sprouted a plethora of different plants, long straggly grasses predominant, and among all this verdancy small yellow flowers showed like stars against a night sky. Towards the centre, a dozen rivulets of white water tumbled over the top of the rocks, to spread into a milky veil that fell into the pool beneath.

This at least matched my recollection, and at last I knew that I truly was back at Arden Falls.

I walked onto the small beach, gazing out across the pool to where the white spume drifted up from the falls' disturbance. Reluctant memory stirred. The scene might have been tranquil, idyllic – the embodiment of summer and as natural a wonder as any man could ever wish to see – yet when I closed my eyes… I could picture the water red with blood and churned into rosy froth by the kicking hooves of war horses; bodies floating face down and peppered with arrows or facing upwards with agony frozen on their features and their bellies split open to let their guts spill out; I could hear the oaths and grunts of combatants, the clash of steel on steel, the screams of the wounded and the dying; I could smell again the acrid sweetness of charred flesh, the stench of human sweat and voided bowels. I could feel the exhaustion tugging at my limbs, my sword grown so heavy that I struggled to lift it, and I could recall with crystal clarity the resigned certainty that I would never leave this place alive.

For long moments I stood there, waiting for the ghosts to speak, but none did.

Eventually I opened my eyes, once more acknowledging the here and now.

I'm no saint, and have done things over the years that many would gladly see me hang for if they knew of them, but compared to the monster we stopped here at Arden Falls I was a prime candidate for deification. Malik the Magnificent he styled himself – that spoke volumes in itself. A self-proclaimed 'sorcerer' and a warlord of the vilest ilk, the atrocities committed in his name and at his urging made seasoned warriors quail and ensured his name became a byword for heinousness ever after.

Had he won that day, had he defeated us, the whole of the Free States would have been open to him and the world would have become a much less pleasant place than it is, of that I'm certain. If those of us who were there did nothing else to be proud of for the rest of our days, at least we had done this.

Dusk had fallen as I turned and made my way back towards the village. I'd barely set out when a voice called, "Hello?"

An old man sat by the road, a broken cane by his side.

"Are you hurt?" I asked.

"Twisted my blasted ankle when the stick broke. I wonder, sir, could you perhaps…?"

"Of course." I helped him to his feet, conscious of how frail he seemed. "You live in the village?"

"On the outskirts, this side of it; not far. And thank you."

To be honest, we'd have made better progress had I hoisted him up and carried him over my shoulder – he was light enough – but that would have been undignified, so I curbed my impatience and merely supported him as we hobbled and shuffled towards Arden.

We had reached a broad meadow bordered on three sides by trees and marked by an array of crosses, circles, crescents, stars and other religious emblems – some nailed to posts, others freestanding in the ground – when my temporary companion released his grip on my shoulder and said, "Thank you. I can make my own way from here."

"You live in the *graveyard*?"

"No, no." His smile seemed warm rather than mocking. "My home is in the woods just beyond. Taking a shortcut through the field of peace is simply the quickest way to get there."

"If you're sure…"

"Yes, quite certain, though your assistance has been invaluable."

I watched for a further moment as he limped slowly across the meadow, but he seemed to know what he was about, so I continued on towards *The Dryad*, intent on sinking an ale or two before I called it a day, and wondering whether that maid, Lisa, might still be around.

"Casts a spell on you, doesn't it?"

"Certainly does," I agreed.

It was the next morning and we were at the falls. A good night's sleep had seen Castor regain much of his customary ebullience. Lucky me. As soon as we had broken the night's fast, he insisted on heading off to view the site of his brother's demise.

I was grateful for the previous evening's solo excursion, which made the experience this time around... manageable. Mind you, Castor was so excited by the whole thing I'm not sure he would have noticed if I'd lain face down in the pool and drowned myself.

We stood on the beach. We stood on the rocks. We touched and remarked upon the clamminess of the cliff face. Castor then led me further along the road, past the falls. The path wound through woodland, climbing all the while, until eventually it joined the course of a narrow river. It didn't take a genius to work out where this was leading, and soon enough the trees drew back as we emerged at the top of the falls.

This particular vantage was new to me, and I have to confess the view was spectacular. To our right the river hurled itself off the cliff to plummet into the pool below. Looking further out, I gazed at tree canopies and the meadow of the graveyard, with the roofs of Arden beyond.

"Lend me your hand, will you?"

Castor evidently wished to take a step or two closer to the edge, and the rocks here were damp and treacherous.

"Be careful," I advised – less concerned for his well-being than for the payment I'd miss should anything happen to him.

"Oh I will be."

At his touch my hand grew unaccountably numb; a feeling that spread rapidly to claim my arm and beyond. I pulled free of his grip and stumbled back from the edge. "What...?"

He smiled; an expression of triumph and malevolence that seemed wholly out of place with my voluble companion of the past three days.

"Don't worry," he said. "A minor sorcery intended to incapacitate, not kill."

I drew my sword but the numbness had already progressed from my left arm to affect every limb. My legs buckled and the blade clattered from clumsy fingers. Castor stalked after me, like a predator fascinated by the futile efforts of wounded prey.

"If left unchecked the spell will eventually stop your heart, but you've no need to fear – I have no intention of letting it get that far." A figure appeared, presumably from among the nearby trees though I hadn't seen him arrive; a slender man with weaselly, pointed features and shifty eyes. "You remember Tryst, I'm sure, from yesterday's ambush." *The third man.* "A bit of theatre, that, to allay any curiosity you may have felt as to why I'd brought you along. We knew you'd see off the hired help, and if they *had* managed to injure you, well, we could have come straight here last night. It's primarily your blood we need, after all… The stray arrow wasn't part of the plan. Quite unsettled me to think how close I came to ruin courtesy of a freak accident."

One thing was certain: this might be a new self-possessed and confident Castor I was seeing, but he was still a talkative bastard.

"Why?" I croaked.

He continued speaking, either failing to hear me or choosing not to. "I spent years hunting you down you know, finding out what *really* happened here and then seeking the man responsible for killing my brother. Oh yes, that much of the story was true – the most convincing lies are always laced with a smattering of veracity, don't you think? My twin really did perish at Arden Falls, and he died by your hand, though his name wasn't Paulus. It was Malik."

Malik? Malik the Bloody Magnificent? I sought similarities, dredging my memories of that most despicable of human beings and comparing them to the man before me. Malik had been bearded, Castor clean-shaven, and the warlord had been stouter, more muscular… But the eyes, yes, I could see it in the eyes; the same coldness, cruelty, though I would never have associated such with the man who had journeyed beside me these past days.

"Gerard…" I said while I still could, my face growing as numb as the rest of me.

"Come, come, I'm aware of the official story, how my brother was slain by Gerard the Golden, but that's a lie and we both know it. A fiction intended to enhance the reputation of 'The Great Hero', to perpetuate his legend so that all of you might benefit. The famed mercenary band, offered all the best commissions because you were led by that mightiest of warriors, Gerard the Golden."

It hadn't been that simple. Gerard was there as well – the man was no coward, whatever his faults – we were both engaging Malik, who fought like a man possessed (and may well have been, if you give credence to such things). We were out on our feet, wounded, bloodied, exhausted… And if mine *had* been the fatal blow, what of it? I was more than happy for Gerard to take the credit. Why set myself up as Malik's Bane, a target for every scoundrel keen to make a name for himself? Besides, they'd thought me dead, my comrades, slain by the warlord's final thrust even as I'd killed him. By the time I'd recovered and put in an appearance the others had already settled on the story of Gerard's glorious triumph, which was fine by me.

Tryst grabbed me under the shoulders and dragged my unresisting body towards the trees. There, at the edge of the forest, hidden from view by the intervening rocks, a shape had been crudely drawn on a large flat stone. A pentagram… *Really?* Tryst set me down at its centre.

Castor followed, carrying my sword. "While we were at *The Butchered Stag*," he said, "you asked me how I intended to discover my brother's bones among so many. To give you proper answer: why bother with mere bones when I can provide him with a healthy living body instead; one that has so helpfully travelled all the way to Arden just for the occasion? Hm?"

I glared at him.

"My brother was unlike mortal men," he went on, casually wiping the blade of my sword on a cloth impregnated with goodness knew what. "He made preparation against unexpected setbacks such as this, ensuring his spirit would linger, awaiting recall, ready for the day Malik the Magnificent shall rise again. Who could have predicted his murderer would prove so elusive? Have you any idea how many survivors of that cursed day I've had to track down before I learnt the truth of what happened? All that wasted time…"

He seemed to have finished wiping my sword, stepping forward to peer down at me.

"As I said, it's your blood we need to start with."

He ran the edge of the blade down my right forearm. I watched, fascinated, as the flesh peeled back and redness welled out, to run down my skin and start to pool on the stone beneath. There was no pain, the numbness saw to that.

Castor stepped back, his arms outstretched, eyes closed. The world grew hazy, the rocks melted and warped. I blinked, striving to concentrate, to fight whatever was happening to me.

"Is he under yet?" That from Tryst.

"Almost," Castor replied. "It's time to begin." He started to intone something; a mumble too faint for me to discern.

"*Touch the tree*," a ghostly voice seemed to say.

That hadn't come from either Castor or Tryst. I sensed her then, a presence in this dream world that hadn't been with us in the real one. I tried to identify it but at first could discern no more than a nebulous sense of green and an impression of femininity. Concentration brought its reward, and slowly a form coalesced from the mist, resolving into a woman; a beautiful slender girl draped in green veils. Something about her struck me as familiar, though I couldn't place why.

"Touch the tree!" she urged again. "You *must* touch the tree."

I wanted to say *I don't believe in dryads* – for surely that's what she must be: one of the mythical wood nymphs said to assist the Treemeisters in their appointed work – but not even my voice would obey me. I was disappointed at myself for falling back on such superstitious nonsense in my hour of need and resolved to ignore the intrusion.

Castor's incantation had grown in volume, individual words now becoming clear: "Blood that claimed your blood…" I watched transfixed as his words took shape in the air between us, each letter etched in flame. "Muscle that powered the steel that untethered your spirit…"

"Ignore him!" the annoying girl said. "You must reach out to the tree. It's only a little way, but we can't help you otherwise."

Help me? How could a figment of my own imagining possibly help me?

"Don't give up! You can beat him. The strength of the forest is close, a power as ancient as the world and rooted in the very land itself; yours to call upon, but to summon it *you must touch the tree.*"

The world continued to grow stranger. Castor's outline was shifting, blurring. He became squatter, uglier, his forehead more pronounced. *Horns* sprouted from his temples and his eyes had become smouldering coals, while flames licked out from their corners to form eyebrows. Beside him, Tryst was transformed into a weasel in truth: a slender furry animal wearing a jerkin and a sword belt.

The transformations accelerated, and even this shadow realm started to fade.

Castor, Tryst, the dryad, all were deserting me, yet I wasn't alone, though I dearly wished I had been. A dark oppressive presence hung above me. Powerful, malevolent, *dreadful.*

"Yes, oh mighty Malik." I saw/heard the demon that had been Castor's voice say as if from a great distance. "Enter this, your vessel; fill his mortal form and *live again!*"

Malik, come to claim me after all these years.

Touch the tree.

I'm not sure if I heard or merely remembered the dryad's insistent imploring, but it fanned an ember within me, a lingering spark of defiance that refused to be extinguished without at least *trying.* Figment she might be, but my options here were limited. There was something I had to do. Oh yes, touch the tree. I couldn't see it but I knew it was there; the only presence still with me aside from the cloying company of Rot-in-Hell Malik.

I concentrated on that slender thread of hope, focusing on this solitary relief from my intended nemesis, who had begun to press down as if a great weight were settling on me. It wasn't so much my arm I moved then, as a lifeless rod attached to my left elbow. With some last vestige of will, I flopped that rod outward, so that my arm lay extended and an unfeeling knuckle brushed an exposed root.

Suddenly, everything changed.

The only way I can describe it is to picture a shutter being abruptly opened on a pitch dark room, so that sunlight bursts in to banish darkness into oblivion.

The suffocating presence of Malik was cast aside, flung violently away, and the numbness was flushed from my system. I could move again, feeling more energised and more *alive* than I ever had before.

I was on my feet in an instant, facing a stunned Tryst and a horrified Castor – both in human form once more. A tortured wail of "Nooo!" from the latter seemed to stir Weasel-face into action, but he was far too slow. I'm a blades man, always have been. They might have removed my sword but they'd left me my knives; big mistake. As Tryst's hand fell to the hilt of his own steel I reached quickly to the back of both my shoulders, where my throwing knives waited. I whipped my arms down and threw in one double-handed movement. Before Tryst could draw his blade more than halfway a knife had embedded in his chest, another in his left eye.

Castor regained enough presence of mind to flee, so rather than admiring my handiwork I drew another knife, which I flung with unerring accuracy even as Tryst's lifeless form hit the ground.

I missed.

Impossible. I could *never* miss at this range… unless my target was employing sorcery, of course.

I threw another knife, and this time watched as it veered away at the last instant, to sail out past the lip of the land and drop towards the waters below. Castor paused then, at the edge of the cliff, turning to face me and smiling. The cockiness he'd shown earlier was back. "Don't think this is over. You will pay for what you did and my brother *will* live again. This I swear."

I had another knife out, one of my final pair, but I wasn't going to waste this one by throwing it – I'd learned that lesson. Instead I stalked forward, the strange energy still pumping through my veins, dulling any pain and fuelling my determination to end this here and now, whatever Castor might wish.

The murder on my mind must have shown in my eyes because, for all his bravado, Castor took an involuntary step backwards... and caught his heel on something. For a protracted moment he stood suspended, arms flailing and eyes bulging as he fought for balance, teetering on the edge. Then gravity won out and he toppled backwards, vanishing from view with a forlorn scream.

I rushed forward, peering down to where his broken body lay splayed on the rocks close to the water. I then looked to see what had caused him to trip, finding an exposed tree root.

The energy that had sustained me throughout the confrontation chose this moment to drain away, evaporating as rapidly as it had arrived. I staggered back from the edge, lest I collapse and join Castor in his rocky fate.

The injured arm commenced to throb in agony now that the eldritch force had deserted me. I watched as blood ran freely down my hand to drip from outstretched fingertips, the wound having been given no chance to close with all the knife throwing I'd indulged in. I felt faint, disorientated, and wondered how much blood had already been lost.

My head throbbed too; in fact my whole body felt as if a troop of performing pixies were using it as a stage to dance upon. Standing upright suddenly required more effort than I could muster. The stony ground struck my knees, and I winced as the hand of my injured arm instinctively tried to take some of the weight.

Sitting, that would be good… or maybe lying down again.

She was there in an instant: the dryad, and beside her a man, looking old, wise, and benevolent, not to mention familiar. I recognised him at once as the old fellow I'd helped back from the falls the previous evening, though now he looked just as green-tinged as the girl.

I seemed to be slipping back into the hallucinatory state Castor had thrown me into during the aborted resurrection, which couldn't be good. If I were destined to die here there was something I had to be sure of first.

"Castor…?" I asked.

"Is dead," the old man said, his rich, deep voice promising all the wisdom of time itself. "His mad scheming will trouble the world no more, and the spirit of Malik the Magnificent is so weakened by today's failed attempt that it will be decades before he can try again, if ever. You did well."

If this was what doing well felt like, I never wanted to try the alternative.

"Now rest."

Soothing fingers touched my brow, but I wasn't done yet, and stubbornly fought to stay conscious. "You're a Treemeister, aren't you?"

"Am I?"

Riddles were the last thing I needed. "I don't believe in you," I said.

"Has anyone asked you to?"

"Am I going to die?"

"Not if we can help it. We tended to you once before and you're still here."

Suddenly I remembered. Intense pain, and this same man leaning over me, his face looming large as he lifted my battered body clear of tangled limbs and armour, of mud and blood and the dead… The girl/dryad was there too, tending me, caring for

71

me, healing me. How had I forgotten all this until now?

"So many deaths, so few we could help, but we did what we could," the Meister's voice seemed to say. Consciousness was slipping rapidly away. The last thing I recall was his saying, "You're not going to die, not today. You have too much still to do."

I came round in a bed. Not the softest of beds, perhaps, but it beat many of the places I'd woken up in. My right arm was bandaged and felt heavy, weak, while my head throbbed. Something sat on my forehead. Exploring with my left hand I found a poultice. It felt vaguely damp against my skin.

There came a gentle knock at the door. Lisa, the maid, entered bearing a cup. "I thought I heard you stirring, sir," she said. "Welcome back."

She had a winning smile, I'll grant her that. I wanted to respond but my mouth was unaccountably dry, causing me to swallow instead and lick my lips. I wondered how long I'd been unconscious.

"It's been a little over a day," she said, as if reading my mind. "I brought you some water."

I drank greedily. "What happened?" I managed to croak.

"They found you at the top of the falls, sir. They say you somehow cut yourself with your own sword. Do you remember that?"

I stared at her, seeing for an instant the dryad's face overlaying the maid's. Only then did the resemblance strike me: the fey creature from the falls had been an idealised version of Lisa. Doubtless that was where my addled imagination had dragged the image from. The realisation caused me to wonder just how far I could trust my own recollection of the previous day's bizarre events.

"No matter," she continued in the face of my silence, "I'm sure it'll all come back to you in time, sir. We've some broth on the go, if you feel up to a bowl."

"Please," I said automatically, without stopping to consider if I actually wanted any.

She paused at the doorway and hesitated, as though debating whether or not to say something.

"Yes?" I prompted.

"I just… Well, I'm sorry about your friend, sir."

"My friend?"

"The man you arrived with. He fell from the top of the falls. Broke his neck, or so I'm told."

"Oh. That's…" What exactly: a blessing, a relief, a cause for celebration? "…a shame," I finished.

She gave a quick smile, nodded in acknowledgement and then left. And if, as she turned away, her hair seemed for an instant to be limned in green as the sunlight from the window fell upon it, what of that? I was still woozy after all, and still recovering from the terrible ordeal so recently survived.

Whatever that might have entailed.

The Drake Lords of Kyla

Storm Constantine

The City in the Mists is reached via ten thousand shallow steps, which rise from the verdant farming valleys of the province of Tusk, up into the clouds and the land beyond. It is like venturing into the afterlife, or the secret country at the top of an enchanted ladder of vines: Kyla.

Halfway up the steps, where by now your lungs are hot with pain from trying to breathe the rarefied air and your limbs like the jelly-stars that cluster in the warm waters of the distant south coast, you will see a fairytale edifice looming out of the mists, taking on form, with its many floors, wooden struts and protective serpent carvings. Clouds of incense hang around it, unable to rise or fall in the thick air. This is The Last Inn Before the Mountains, the name of which is not entirely accurate, but for travellers conjures a delicious frisson of inevitability and danger. Beyond here – nothing of the world you know.

The mists of this land are clouds because here the land touches the sky. The clouds are not always there and when they are absent you might feel that the aching blue you gaze upon is truly Paradise. You will see things in the sky you have never seen before; creatures that fly without wings, daytime stars and birds the size of lions.

There is no entry into Kyla but for this one path. To the north it faces the cold ocean with cliffs thousands of feet high. The Black Mountains surround it on all other sides, but for this narrow passageway, the steps and then, beyond the inn, the throat through the mountains by water, the Old Path.

At the Last Inn, and the small village of Semum that straggles around it, you will first encounter the Lighurd. You will no doubt have been greatly anticipating this meeting, and your mind will be full of fancies about it. Then you will see your first two or three, squatting in the frozen dust outside the inn, the ground imprinted with the pattern of their hot, webbed feet. They might be playing knuckle-bone dice with a gang of guides, flaring their quills at one another, uttering the strange yet surprisingly lively croak that is their laughter. They were once dragons, this race. This is why you're here; you want to listen to them hiss of greater times.

It is not far to the ruins of Gyth, the City in the Mists, from the Last Inn; just a boat ride through the mountain tunnel and then on foot for less than two days. Guides there are aplenty, all eager for you to fill their purses – and they are not difficult to fill, this being a poor land, and you, of course, rich. Swarthy Sarks, black-and-yellow-skinned Meronnes, fey Fards; each of these native races are exotic and intriguing to travel with. But there are Lighurds too for hire, and who better to lead you into the whispering mists than the most ancient inhabitants of this lost realm? No, it was never really lost, merely forgotten, neglected. But that aside, your eyes might light upon a lone Lighurd, squatting apart from his companions, quills lowered and hanging long down his back, snake visage tattooed with mystic curls. You will glance at the gracefully long-fingered, clawed hands, the muscled thighs that might be scaled in turquoise, cobalt or deepest emerald. Never will you have seen a creature at once so primitive yet so magnificent. He might sense your interest and turn his long face towards you, gaze back with those golden snake eyes, nod once to indicate 'yes, I am for hire'. Your heart might pause then, as if you have won a great and unimaginable prize; a treasure from the past.

Despite what you might see, close up, of this incredible creature – the length and sharpness of his claws, the wide maw

The Drake Lords of Kyla

that might contain too many teeth – there is no need to be afraid. Lighurd guides – all male, for their females are rarely seen - will neither rob nor damage you. To the very few, for some unfathomed reason, they might even sell one of their whelps to take home with you. The stories of these young ones sickening and pining away from the Black Mountains are untrue. They will outlive you, and have to be bequeathed to your descendents or gifted to someone who might fancy such an ornament in their home. Lighurdkind can never be servants – *quite* – and no, I have not heard of them being taken as lovers. There is no such familiarity between our species.

So then, through me you know something of this land, its people, and you want to know what happened when I went to Kyla, how I came to acquire my companion.

I had been advised to travel there in the month of Pearly Rains, this being the most clement time to broach the ten thousand steps. I wanted to see Gyth, as every young historian does; it is an initiation into the mysteries of our calling, this distant, haunted tumble of stones. Not many can make the journey, its prime obstacle being the cost of the expedition rather than any physical difficulty. Kyla lies at the centre of the distant continent of Oort. Merchant ships from Tasmagore will offer accommodation for passengers, but not cheaply. The way is hard, the ocean tumultuous. My Order had paid for my journey, and also for me to be instructed in the language of Oort for a year before I left the University at Tasmagore. My tutors had given me certain tasks to complete, such as people to meet and ingratiate myself with, relics to secure, stories to record. My itinerary was full and I'd been four months in Oort before I even had the time to turn my thoughts towards the Black Mountains. By then, I had made my way slowly to Tusk and the lush Valley Below the Steps. Here I had been greeted by the mayor of Valley's Heart, become a guest in his sprawling wooden house. Foreigners visited these parts for only one reason; the desire to ascend. The inhabitants appeared amused by this. The mayor said to me, "Kyla lies upon our dreams. Yes, we go up there, but the Lighurd never come down *here*. The climb is long, the air thin, and there is not much left other than memories. If you seek memories, naturally the land will call to you."

I dreamed of it every night before I finally made my climb; my sleep buffeted by the scream of gigantic birds and oppressed by images of cyclopean remains that were stone, that were flesh, that were stone.

The journey too started like a dream. I was given a guide from Valley's Heart who would take me to Semum, since she had business there at the Inn. In fact, most transactions between the Valley and Kyla took place at this inn, Heartfolk not having much desire to travel further than that. The trade was mainly in relics; the Heartfolk would buy them with their own produce, and then sell them on to merchants travelling to the coast and beyond, to lands where the antiquities of Kyla were much prized.

My guide, Zharn, was a grand-daughter of the mayor. We set out just before dawn: Zharn, two grey goats with yard-long horns who would carry our belongings, and me. Zharn was short and stout; at sixteen years old a veteran of this journey. We were both dressed in the heavy, cream woollen tunic and trousers favoured by the Oorts, embellished with rich coloured scarves at the waist and with ornate embroidery at cuffs and hems. Our boots were of toughened goat leather, scored with spiritual symbols.

The climb began at a huge stone archway cut into the cliffs, and the first few miles were completed in shadow. There were no mists yet, just the murk cast by the overhanging rocks and the grey predawn light that didn't illuminate much at all. Zharn lit a torch, which she placed in a sconce conveniently attached to a horn of one of the goats.

After only an hour my thighs were hurting greatly, although we had now emerged from the tunnel of rock and the steps were far wider. We no longer needed a torch. Zharn grinned at my weakness but let us pause while she made a fire to brew us breakfast tea. The goats, hung with bells, tinkled as they chewed the tough, yellow grasses beside the path. As I sat, gratefully, and sipped the scalding sweet tea, I gazed at my surroundings: this wide and shallow stair, worn by many feet; how ancient it was. I could feel history around me, as if time was but an illusion. The era of the dragons is long gone; it has become merely legend. Few people really believe the Lighurd are the debased descendents of dragons, but rather that the stories of a dragon race grew up around the lizard people, who had perhaps once been a greater civilisation and had somehow lost it all. I had then no idea if this was true, but what was undeniable was that Kyla was full of mighty ruins. Whoever had lived there had been a great and powerful race and they had been physically huge, if the size of the ruins was anything to go by.

After the tea was finished, Zharn put out her fire and we set off once more. "Mistress Marala, we climb for nearly a day," said Zharn. "Don't expect tea every hour."

I managed a laugh. "I have travelled to many far lands, and have climbed mountains before. My legs will become accustomed to the ascent."

Zharn smirked; she did not believe me.

Strangely, the steps were busier than I thought they'd be. We came across merchant camps at corners in the path, where there were wide verges fragrant with herbs, and space for tents to be erected and rugs to be spread out in order to display wares. We passed other travellers, again predominantly traders, descending the path. Zharn swapped produce with just about everyone we met. She was particularly taken with a charming little black goat a Meronne boy wanted to sell her, but then hardened her heart because it was too expensive.

We did have to pause our journey a lot, because no matter how hardy I'd considered myself to be, the climb punished my body. By midday I could barely breathe. Happily, Zharn wanted to linger at every camp we encountered and examine the wares arrayed on the rugs. I bought a small serpent head fashioned in soapy, dark green stone; an unbelievably ancient relic. Zharn was scornful. "Mistress, you can pick those up by the dozen in Gyth. Why pay?"

But to me it seemed part of the adventure.

By late afternoon, having made good time, (so perhaps I wasn't as feeble as Zharn had feared), we reached The Last Inn Before the Mountains. I shall never forget the thrill of turning that final corner of the path, going beyond the last step and seeing the high, peaked roofs of the immense building rearing before us. It was surrounded by a wide veranda, crowded with chairs and tables, none of which matched. Here, guides, merchants, brigands and perhaps even slavers, sat together talking and laughing loudly, making flamboyant gestures, and clearly getting greatly drunk. The air was thick with the intoxicating perfume of incense and the fume of *makh*, which many of the company were smoking. Three musicians were making a racket upon strange stringed instruments I'd not seen before, comprising complicated webs of strings and delicate wooden struts. Another hammered upon a hand drum and yodelled. Altogether it was a scene of chaos. I didn't even think of Lighurds at that moment, let alone see one.

"It's not usually this busy," Zharn told me. "There was a fair held at Yee-Anan, the first town beyond the Old Path. It finished today." She grinned greedily. "They will have much to sell, and they are nearly all drunk. Why don't you get us a room for the night? I won't go home until tomorrow and I believe my lodgings were part of the fee."

"Of course."

I sidled up the crowded inn steps and between the haphazardly-placed chairs on the veranda, but no one gave me a second glance. Inside, I found myself in an immense, high-ceilinged room fashioned entirely from pale wood and again crowded with tables and chairs, most of which were occupied. The air was far muggier and hotter than on the veranda outside and the din even louder. A grill was set up in one corner, smoking voluminously, but issuing wonderful aromas of cooking spiced meat and root vegetables. Saffron rice steamed in great pans, smelling like incense. I realised how hungry I was.

Owing to the amount of guests in the establishment, I feared I'd have difficulty securing us a room, but the woman in black silk, who stood behind a high desk near the door, dealing with reservations, made no protest. I took one room with two beds to save money.

"Trading here?" the woman asked. Her long pointed fingernails were lacquered a very shiny obsidian hue. A band of black cosmetic was painted across her face, from which her eyes peered, shockingly white with inky irises.

"I'm a Historian from Tasmagore," I said. "I've come to view the ruins and... whatever else is found beyond the Black Mountains."

The woman grinned. Several of her teeth were studded with gemstones – blue and white crystal. "Need a guide, then. Or join a caravan."

"Yes, I will attend to this in the morning."

"Will keep my ears open for you," said the woman. "Here's your key. Room 38. Third floor." The key was small and black and seemed hardly a key at all, as if it would fit any lock in the building.

Zharn had been seeing to stabling the goats, and now shouldered her way into the inn. She grabbed my arm. "Let's go back out."

"Food," I said plaintively, pointing at the grill.

"There's better outside," Zharn insisted, "by the hot spring."

The atmosphere was quieter round the back of the inn. A dozen roaring braziers warmed the air. Some patrons, of both genders, were sitting naked in the heated waters of a bubbling pool in the rock, lit by a multitude of tiny firefly lamps that had been hung in the trees around them. Those languishing in the waters seemed faintly drugged; they spoke in low voices and their laughter was gentle. Nearby was another grill, and here a pretty boy was also cooking. Watching his careful, graceful movements was like observing a ritual being enacted; he clearly took his job seriously.

Carrying wooden trays crowded with dishes of beautifully-scented food, Zharn and I sat down at a table beneath a tree blazing with red and blue points of light. The subtle radiance dyed the girl's skin; she looked half supernatural. She smiled at me, uttered "welcome to the door step of Kyla," and then spooned a vast quantity of pale yellow rice into her mouth.

"It's wonderful," I said, gazing beyond her.

Ahead of us, to the north, against the star-sequinned sky, reared the mountain barrier that shut Kyla off from the rest of the country, but for the tunnel that pierced it. The Black Mountains were unthinkably old, the realm of gods long lost to human imagination, but not perhaps to the minds of Lighurds.

"I need to find a guide," I said.

Zharn nodded. "One will find *you*, don't worry. The inn hostess will have passed the word about you. Already they will be debating which one of them will slim your purse."

"Tell me of Lighurds," I said. "I didn't notice any here. I'd like a Lighurd guide."

Zharn wiped a long grain of rice from the corner of her mouth. "You foreigners are obsessed with them."

"Well, we've nothing like them at home. Tell me now, are they fierce, cruel, mindless, what?"

"They are men in serpent skins," said Zharn, "to be feared no more than any other man, and yet... They are different too, owing to the age of their race. There is no older species on this Earth, or so my grandmother told me. It weighs heavily upon them sometimes."

"What of their women? Do they look different to the males?"

Zharn nodded, took another mouthful of food and spoke through it. "If you are lucky, you might see one. They do not interact with humans greatly."

"And yet a man told me back in the Valley they will sometimes sell their children to foreigners..."

"That is true, though rare. Just because they are old and primitive does not mean they have no desire for their young to see the world. The humans who come here are rich and offer good opportunities for the youngsters of any race or species. That much you must concede."

"A good point," I said, although really it didn't ring true with me. The explanation was too mundane.

"But then," Zharn continued, suddenly appearing wistful, "I've heard there are people who can't bear the company of Lighurdkind in their homes, because some nights they keen for the vanished glory of their people, and the song is beautiful and terrible, capable of driving the most sensitive of listeners into the deepest melancholy. They are reminded of the futility of greatness, how glory is fleeting and nobility may be lost. Those long, scaled throats that hold no fire may burn a person with song."

"That is beautiful, Zharn," I said, somewhat aghast at her sudden eloquence.

She shrugged. "My grandmother says it to people."

Later in the evening, I was approached several times by individuals claiming they would be my best guide into Kyla. All of them, to my eyes, offered the promise of an intriguing journey, but I was waiting for something. You, of course, may have guessed what. He came to me as midnight drew near and a group of Roosha priests began to chant to the Goddess of Turning Days. Drunken inn patrons took up the song, as did the half dozen in the pool nearby.

"None of the cackwits here have my sense of the road," my latest applicant, a great bear of a Sark with a huge yet silky black beard, was saying to me. "I can take you to places few travellers see."

All of them had said that. Perhaps they did not all speak of the same places.

I nodded slowly at his words, somewhat intoxicated by the saffron-infused wine Zharn had fetched for us. "What is your price?" I asked.

"Too much," said an extremely sibilant, whispery voice behind me. At first I could not distinguish if it issued from a male or female throat.

The guide before me laughed good-naturedly. Whoever stood at my back was a friend of his. I could smell this person: dry, musky, hot.

"It is me she wants," they said.

The man narrowed his eyes. "And what interests you so much about her?" He glanced at me, pointing over my shoulder with a stiff finger. "I warn you. Don't be misled. He sees some profit in this."

I turned round, because not to do so would have seemed odd by now. He towered over me; seven feet of Lighurd. His emerald and black striped quills were very long and reached to his waist, many decorated with silver rings. On either side of his nostril slits, delicate tendrils drooped, rather like the whiskers of a cat fish. He spoke like a man, yet was not a man. It seemed preposterous he could speak the language of Oort, albeit in a struggling manner, because his jaw was not fashioned to utter it. He had no soft lips to form the words yet even so he spoke clearly. That always puzzled me.

"What is your price?" I asked him. Whatever it was I would afford it.

They called him Agouzi; this was not his real name. He came from a Lighurd settlement this side of the mountains; trader people, naturally. Zharn and I sat with the guide and his Lighurd friend, plus a few others who ambled over to join us, until at least two in the morning. Once our business arrangement had been finalised, Agouzi said nothing more to me, but I was aware of him constantly, also aware it was a feeling very similar to being near a person to whom you are greatly attracted, yet it was not that with him.

Zharn and I rose late the following day, both of us bearing the ill-effects of drinking too much alcohol at such a high altitude, after a long day's climb. As we ate breakfast in the vast room downstairs in the inn, I began to wish Zharn would continue the journey with me and even suggested carefully she might consider it.

"I can't," Zharn replied. "I have to go to the market in the Jade Hills tomorrow. Don't worry. You'll be quite safe. The Lighurd will look after you."

"They are... *trustworthy*, then?"

"Like all the people in this place, they know where their money comes from. Only a fool would hurt a traveller; they are walking purses, every one."

"So not even robbery?"

"A robbed person doesn't recommend a place to their friends," Zharn said. "Even less so if they are dead."

"I will bring you something back," I said. "From the ruins. You have been good to me, Zharn. I appreciate it."

Zharn shrugged. "We will hold a party on your return." She stood up. "Ah, here is your guide. Travel well, friend Marala." She bowed to me and departed.

And there stood Agouzi, regarding me inscrutably. His long black tongue slid out and licked the air.

"Would you take tea before we set off?" I asked, gesturing at the cups and pot on my table.

He shook his head, making his quills rattle. "We should begin," he said, "or we will miss the next raft to Yee-Anan."

I had already settled my account with the inn, so I only had to pick up my travel-bag to be ready. Zharn had instructed me not to buy pack goats before Yee-Anan, since it would be cheaper there; I intended to return with them laden.

Two dozen people crowded onto the raft that would carry us through the rock. A girl lit torches at each corner of the vessel even before we entered the dark. I sat next to Agouzi on a bench, pressed against him owing to the crowd. His body felt unnaturally hot. He seemed barely aware of me and did not speak. I found it hard to believe he was there beside me, like a myth come to life. I wondered what thoughts he had, or *how* he thought.

The tunnel beneath the mountains took two hours to traverse. There was quite a jolly atmosphere aboard the raft as the pilot's assistant, who had lit the torches, dispensed refreshments and then began to regale her water-bound audience with various recitals and songs. Lulled back into a half-doze by her lilting voice, I gazed dreamily at the tunnel walls; black rock occasionally starred with crystal veins.

When we emerged at Yee-Anan, and the pilot swung the raft up against the wide but sagging jetty, Agouzi politely suggested we might hire our goats and then continue our journey immediately. Perhaps he sensed I would be seduced by all the merchant stalls scattered about the town, which was really little more than a village. The buildings were old and low, sway-backed like geriatric horses. I pressed paper money into Agouzi's hot, clawed hands. "Buy us goats," I said, "and anything else we might need."

He bowed his head and loped off, switching his long tail in a manner that to me suggested faint irritation. But perhaps Lighurds don't express themselves with their tails in the same way cats do.

While I waited, I sat upon a tree stump near the jetty and shrouded my eyes with one hand to look around. The thin air sparkled with clarity and the smudge of a few clouds was high, high above me. I felt chilly, but not cold. The sun blazed without impediment. Beyond the flag-hung northern gateway to the town, I glimpsed a spreading vista of hilly plains, covered in gold and green lichens or grasses. Immense carrion birds sailed upon the air currents, uttering mournful cries.

Presently, Agouzi returned leading two black goats, each hung with four capacious panniers. Two of these baskets appeared to be full of supplies and camping equipment. I didn't expect any change from my money and didn't receive any. It was of no consequence.

"If the goats aren't enough, you may hire an Egni carrier later," Agouzi said. "The people of Kyla are used to transporting heavy loads."

"That depends on how successful my foraging is," I said, in what I wincingly realised was rather a flirtatious tone. "I hope you will guide me to places of wonder where I may plunder the past fantastically."

I realised then that when you are faced with a being who cannot physically smile or frown, lacking the fleshy facial tissue to do so, it is difficult to judge reactions and moods. Agouzi just stared at me. Perhaps he didn't have a sense of humour. I got to my feet. "Well, lead on!"

A rutted road led north, with thin straw-like grass growing like a stiff mane along its centre. People riding goats, slightly larger than our pack animals, trotted past us, waving hello. I wondered whether riding-goats might also have been a luxury I could have afforded. The natives of the area seemed to comprise mainly a short-statured, dark-skinned race, whose faces were almost invisible owing to the large hats, helmets and complicated veils and turbans they favoured. I had yet seen no Lighurds other than Agouzi.

"Where are your people?" I asked him as we walked, each on one side of the centre tuft of the road. "I thought Kyla was your land, yet all I see are these quaint little people, who are indisputably human." I smiled at him.

Agouzi cast me a sidelong glance. "It is the time of year," he said, as if that meant anything to me.

"I see... religious festivals, something like that?"

"Something like that," he replied. "Once we leave the main

road, you might see more of my kind. We might need to buy supplies from them, in between the Egni settlements."

"Egni being the... little people."

"Yes."

"People never speak of them when discussing Kyla; it is always Lighurds who are the topic of conversation."

"And you know little of either of our races," Agouzi observed, but not in a sharp tone.

"I'm surprised more people don't come here," I said. "It's so beautiful, so... unspoilt."

"They will stop altogether when the plunder is finished and everything is gone," Agouzi said.

"It's important to preserve the past." I was aware I sounded too defensive. "We learn much from it that helps us understand how we are now."

"This land is not your past," Agouzi said, without inflection.

I fell silent after that, sensing whatever I said would provoke similar answers that would, from any other mouth, sound sour and criticising. From Agouzi's mouth, it was difficult to divine his thoughts on the matter.

Conversation discouraged between us by my companion, we travelled on for the rest of the day in near silence. Occasionally, Agouzi would direct my attention to particular landmarks and tell me something of their history. Always ruins – sometimes just humps on the ground covered in lichen. My spirits fell, despite the clear, heady air; this land felt like the graveyard of all the species of the world. I felt too listless to reply to Agouzi's remarks or question him for further details.

We paused once to refresh ourselves at midday, but after building a small fire and preparing us tea and hot spiced rice, Agouzi wandered off by himself. He took his bowl of rice to a clump of rocks some distance away and there squatted to consume his meal, his back to me.

At sunfall, we came upon an Egni settlement and Agouzi suggested I take a room with one of the local families. This I did, and was somewhat revived by the cheerful tribe who offered me accommodation almost as soon as we stepped beyond the gate of their village. These people spoke a dialect I could barely comprehend, but they seemed happy simply to talk *at* me, and did not appear to expect responses. Chattering, they dragged me to their home and offered me vast amounts to eat and drink. I was very tired, and after eating collapsed upon the mattress in the attic to which they directed me and fell into the deepest of slumbers. Where Agouzi slept I had no idea.

In the morning, I was awoken by the family and given more food. Agouzi presented himself at their door minutes after I'd finished eating. I paid my hosts and we set out once more. Today we would reach Gyth.

Now the air was colder, and once a flurry of snow passed before my eyes, vanishing almost in an instant, as if the gods of the weather were teasing me. There was no one else up-on the road now, which surprised me. I'd expected a steady stream of plunderers, whose motivations would not be quite as noble as mine. The wind wove a lonely song, which was quite beautiful. Snow leopards, who appeared almost tame, lay, sat or stalked among the high rocks beside the road, observing us mildly. Sticks of incense the thickness of my wrist burned at intervals along the path, releasing a heavy perfume. I wondered if it was this that lulled the leopards.

Midmorning, Agouzi led us off the main track onto a tiny, twisting goat path between sharp black rocks. Here, tufts of a heavily-scented herb grew in the deep fissures, making the air almost narcotic. I could hear the bells of goats but could see none nearby. And now the mists came to claim us, stealing in like prowling cats, wisps that might be soft paws and tails, or hot carnivore breath. I mentioned none of these fancies to Agouzi, but even so he said to me, "The servants of Shah Mahra, the Great Snow Leopard, travel in the mists. They observe the hearts of those who come here."

"And do they judge?" My question came out sharp.

Agouzi laughed softly. "That is not their function. Look up there."

I raised my head and saw enormous dark shapes motionless in the dancing tendrils of mist. As I stared, these shapes resolved into the forms of two black granite leopards sitting erect, yet with their heads lowered; a watchful stance.

"We approach Tin gurra Lath, the gateway to Gyth," Agouzi said, "and here are its guardians. In years gone by, this was a city of towers so high their crowns brushed the realms of the sky. Its people rarely ventured into the lower areas and the towers were connected by bridges of golden ropes. It was called the City Above the Birds in the modern tongue."

In the silence that followed these words, I peered through the dance of the mist, and tried to imagine the ghosts of these towers around me, but all that remained were stumps; I could see that now. A graveyard of tumbled masonry stretched into the distance. Agouzi led the way over and through it, nimble on his long feet. I came more unsteadily behind, still giddy from the gift of the rock herbs. Occasionally, I would spy a face in the stones, the ripped visage of a tumbled statue, blind in surprise. But these were too big to pick up. Everything was. The fallen stones were mountains in themselves and cast thick dark shadows. I found the atmosphere oppressive.

"How far to Gyth now?" I asked, my voice unnervingly muffled.

"Beyond the gateway," Agouzi said, pausing ahead of me. He allowed me to catch up. "At the north gate of Tin gurra Lath lies the Queen's Step, or the wide road to Gyth. The two cities were almost one, except Gyth was on the ground."

Perhaps it was simply the combined effects of the rarefied air and the scented herbs that made me so dizzy, but I was finding it increasingly difficult to keep walking. Agouzi, now quite a distance ahead of me, again paused to wait. He appraised my condition and then, stooping down upon one knee, said, "climb upon my back."

And so I entered the city of Gyth like a child, riding upon the back of an adult.

The Queen's Step was not a long road and, once we emerged from the depressing stones of fallen Tin gurra Lath, the path swept down gracefully into a valley of golden grasses. Amid the mist, I saw trees with white bark and golden leaves, as if it were autumn, but the season was young. Nervous white deer grazed upon the grasses, pausing skittishly to observe our descent before bounding away, becoming one with the clouds around us. The Queen's Step was remarkably well preserved, each slab of its surface carved with different pictures. The images themselves were somewhat worn down but I was sure I could discern depictions of Lighurdkind upon them. As we drew nearer to the city, the mist rolled itself up, drawing back to reveal the mysteries of Gyth to me. "Set me down," I said to Agouzi.

It is difficult to describe what I saw. My first thought was that the city had been *scythed*, in that its buildings had been sheered away at the same height, as if with an immense blade. Even so, they remained gigantic, constructed from pale stone that now glistened in sunlight. This was a city of columns and turrets, of hidden walkways, narrow streets and wide plazas. Ceremonial ways – or roads I took to be as such – radiated from the centre to each point of the compass. Everything about the place seemed to whisper, "come, I am waiting to be explored. Look upon me. See my many ways, my empty palaces that are perhaps not quite empty, my temples blistered with the jewels of gods. Come to me now; immerse yourself within me."

Gyth was, without doubt, a goddess of cities. And I was compelled to run, again like a child, into the goddess' waiting arms. As I ran, the years seemed to peel back, and both Gyth and I became younger; the buildings became bigger around me. And my legs were pumping so fast I could barely keep up with myself; I would tumble into the city. And tumble I did, down the last stretch of the Queen's Step, over and over and over, as if I were trapped in a kaleidoscope, colours of sky and city and landscape blurring into one.

The sky is a queen's gown of stars, encrusted so thickly it is a blanket of light. I am lying on my back upon stone. I can hear myself panting and the beat of blood in my head. No, I am not lying, I am sitting. Images around me are shadows, yet becoming more distinct with every moment. Am I dreaming? I'm unsure, but I'm not afraid. I am where I'm supposed to be. I hear the tumult of many voices raised in excitement. From the ground beneath me comes a sensation of throbbing that is not quite a sound, but as I fix my attention upon it, so it becomes louder, more recognisable as sound; a deep and immeasurable moan. I'm reminded of whale song, but it is not that. Now, I see I am sitting with many others within a stone amphitheatre that is the size of a small town. My companions are Lighurds, all of them, who are far taller than Agouzi; they are true giants. They are dressed in garments of metal scales that emulate the gleam of their natural scales. Some have decorated their quills most fancifully with streaming or spiky ornaments. I am looking for females, but they all appear the same to me. How would it be possible to tell? I can perceive now, upon the cliff-like walls of the structure, great pipes or horns from which the immense moaning notes are emanating. This strange music stirs my blood, for I can tell it heralds an approach of some kind. Then, wooden gates at either end of the amphitheatre swing open in a slow, ponderous fashion. There is only darkness beyond them. The horns issue their notes a final time – a blast that shakes my very fibres – and then *shapes* lumber forth from the darkness.

These are creatures the size of cathedrals, taking careful steps with their surprisingly graceful webbed feet. I wonder if they are dragons, but then I'd always believed dragons to be beautiful, attenuated beings, at one with the air. These before me are incontrovertibly creatures of earth. Their hides are the colour of clay, although one is lighter in tone than the other. Their immense heads are reptilian but blunted, and have no quills like the Lighurds'. They are bipedal with legs proportionately larger than their arms, and long thick tails culminating in what appear to be natural spiked clubs. They face each other, clapping their clawed hands, shaking their heads, switching their tails. Above them, the horns boom once more, and around me the crowd rises to their feet, uttering cries. I expect the beasts to fight to the death, conjuring a greedy blood-lust from the spectators. No doubt they have placed bets upon the combat.

And then a lone Lighurd steps into the arena. He must be around eleven or twelve feet tall, yet is an insect in comparison to the snorting giants. They turn their heads sideways to regard him. Their mobile toes flex in the dirt of the arena floor. Is he a sacrifice? I don't want to see, convinced something terrible and sickening is about to happen. The Lighurd has copper and emerald scales, and is draped in a garment that appears to be fashioned of metal disks, yet it moves around his body like linen. He raises his arms and throws back his head, striding slowly towards the gigantic beasts. When he stands between them, he raises his quills, which surround him like a starburst. Crystal ornaments upon them capture the light of the sky and he becomes a being of starlight.

The beasts begin to circle around the Lighurd, very slowly. And now the crowd is uttering a crooning song, their lean bodies swaying as one in a sinuous dance. Someone next to me reaches for my hand and I see for the first time that I am Lighurd too; my hand is long and clawed and I am wearing a ring with an immense jewel, perhaps a topaz, on one of the fingers. I am singing too. I know the song. We are calling to the stars, to our ancestors. We are calling upon the wisdom of the Ahn Toth, these two immense beings before us. We have called them down from the Holy Peak to work their magic for us. They have travelled for over a week to reach us. They are the last of their kind.

The Lighurd in the arena is Kurra'Koor, the chosen one of our season. The Ahn Toth loom over him, weaving the air with their claws, drawing substance from it that I cannot see, cannot understand. They sing, too, and the sounds they make are tools to change reality. The starlight becomes an inferno around the body of Kurra'Koor. He can barely be perceived within it, and then it somehow falls and folds around him like a garment. A deity stands before us, clothed in light. Kurra'Koor's scales are of luminous pearl. Where once were quills are now spreading vanes or fins that gently float upon the air; unutterably beautiful. The crowd falls to their knees before this vision, myself among them. I feel a stirring deep within my being that is at once holy and lustful. I am also aware of a feeling of relief, as if some part of me feared this ritual might not work.

The paler of the Ahn Toth gently lifts Kurra'Koor with one hand as if he were a doll, only now he is no longer he but she, as is the being who holds her. She places Kurra'Koor upon her shoulder, where there is a convenient seat between knobs of bone-like protuberances. We will follow Kurra'Koor to the White Temple of Spring Flowers, and there our next generation will be created. For some time thereafter Kurra'Koor will bear eggs within the sanctum of the temple. Each one of us will have a son and we will know our own by sight. There is never any mistake over that.

I am given no more than this.

When I came back to true consciousness Agouzi was cradling me in his lap. One hot hand was on my brow. I felt the tips of his claws against my left temple. He was not looking at me but out across the city.

"Does it still happen that way?" I asked him.

He tilted his head to regard me, in the way the great Ahn Toth had done with Kurra'Koor.

"I *saw*," I said. "Kurra'Koor... the Ahn Toth,..."

"They were the last of their kind," Agouzi replied at last. "We had to learn what they knew."

"Were they... your ancestors?"

"In some ways," Agouzi replied. "We were certainly connected. Once the Ahn Toth ruled this land you call Kyla. They made us to survive them, but before they left the land there was much they had to teach us."

I struggled away from him, still awkward in my movements, disorientated. I was surprised he did not question me about what I'd seen, or *how* I'd seen, but then I was not surprised at all. "It was so unthinkably long ago. Your people... what happened?" I gestured at the ruins around me.

"Others came who coveted our land. They flew in above the mountains. There were wars. There always are. But as you said, that was long ago, and even the conquerors are dust." He stood up. "You must drink."

Agouzi fetched me water from our supplies, which I drank greedily, while Agouzi squatted before me, observing me, perhaps concerned my experience had made me ill. The sky seemed to be ringing like a vast bell, but perhaps that was in my head.

He did not owe me explanations. What I'd seen had been private, a racial memory of his kind. Why it had been shown to me particularly, I did not know. Yet still I had to ask. "You are all male until a certain season, then one becomes your queen?"

"We came down the Queen's Step," he said, as if this explained everything. Getting to his feet, he offered to me a hand. "Come."

By the time we reached the arena, or what was left of it, the moon had risen, blue in the velvet sky, surrounded by her starry court. The place was just a jumble of pale stones that dreamed of starlight. The Lighurd of the past were gone, aeons ago. Those who lived in Kyla now were very different. Did they still build? Were there fabulous academies hidden away somewhere, full of arcane astronomical equipment? Were the bones of the last of the Ahn Toth enshrined in some immense underground chamber, locked in by secrets and labyrinths, and guardians not of this world? I wanted to believe these things.

"Were you dragons?" I asked wistfully.

Agouzi squeezed my hand. "If that is what you wish." He threw back his head and uttered an ululating sound. For a while this echoed around the immense silent ruins, then other songs rose in response. My skin prickled.

"It is our *choice* now," Agouzi said.

And then they came over the broken stones, Lighurd maidens with their floating hair that was not hair, their almost feline yet serpent-like faces, their utter grace, their indescribable ancient beauty.

"I will give to you my son," Agouzi said. "Take him out into the younger world and tell him stories, show him wonders as is the privilege of your profession. He will tell you stories in return. When you are dead, he will bring your stories back to us." He opened his mouth, narrowed his eyes: a grin. "Perhaps even before that."

I managed a shaky laugh. "The children you give us, they are chroniclers."

Agouzi again narrowed his eyes in a smile. "We are intrigued by the follies of youth."

The ethereal Lighurd women had formed a circle around us now. Their light was not supernatural; their fish-fin hair merely snared the starlight and stored it.

One reached out to me and I took her pearly hand. She had chosen me in some way, and so had chosen Agouzi. "Can you be like her?" I asked Agouzi softly, "if you wish?"

"I *am* like her," he said. "Let the others take you, they will feed you. At dawn I will return to you."

The women took me to a bower among the golden-leafed trees. Here they bid me recline upon a bed of flowers and grasses and gave to me delicacies enjoyed by their people. The nervous deer were drawn to investigate and some of the women fed them. I lay back and gazed up at the firmament. Across it flowed an attenuated, graceful shape – a serpent of the sky that flew without wings. Or perhaps it was simply a flight of night-singing birds, like lace against the stars.

In the morning, Agouzi returned to me, as he'd promised, and I woke from perhaps the most refreshing sleep I'd ever experienced. The Lighurd women had gone, but they had left me gifts; a delicate stole of silver disks, a collection of tiny statuettes depicting goddesses and spirits of the land, four nets of fruit, two cooked birds, some steaks of a meat I took to be goat, spiced potatoes wrapped in muslin, and a flagon of golden liquor. Agouzi too seemed pleased with the food and drink they'd left behind.

We set out again, leaving Gyth behind, seeking out further remains even more ancient. You can see what I brought back with me – all these treasures. I travelled for three months with Agouzi among the vast ruins of Kyla. I found so many wonders, great and small, I had to buy another goat and hire two Egni as well. We climbed the highest mountain in the world, and at the top I shouted out my wishes for the future, since that peak is closest to the gods and they can hear you clearly there. We visited the vast catacombs that wormed through the mountain, filled with the tombs and creations of monstrous beings, the like of which I'd never seen before. Lighurds were more human in comparison. We visited a secret province few outsiders have ever been shown that is like the Garden of Creation, populated by a race of people so fair they must have been hidden away by the gods for their own protection. I have many stories to tell, but the one you really want me to finish telling is about the gift Agouzi gave to me, isn't it?

He was waiting for us as we returned to the ruins of Gyth. Poor child, he might have already been there for days before he spied us. He and Agouzi called to one another, long before I could see him with my physical eyes. He was like a smaller version of Agouzi rather than having the proportions of a human child. His quills were pale and soft and did not quite reach his shoulders.

"Leshi will have told him he is to go with you," Agouzi said to me as we approached his son. Leshi must be the Lighurd with whom he'd... well I suppose the word is 'mated'.

"Aren't you afraid for him?" I asked.

"No," Agouzi replied, again with his usual lack of inflection. His confidence could mean many things: he felt I was trustworthy, or the child was capable of looking after himself, or Agouzi could already see his son's future. I still don't know which of those it was. The young Lighurd's name is Ran'zar and I brought him home with me.

My employers were very interested in him, of course, and he was – and is – very interested in them. He has a great curiosity for the world, and is less concerned about our past than how we are now. Sights and experiences are like food to him. He knows the past of his kind – all of it, because I believe it is handed down as clear memories from one generation to another – but he will not speak of it to me. Not yet. As a child, he is more interested in his own desires and that is knowledge of us and our world.

Does he sing? Yes, all Lighurds sing, but I have yet to be driven to despair by the sound. He makes up songs in the evening about what he's seen during the day. But he is young, and for now I am happy he has innocence and a sense of wonder at the world. Only with the passing of time does history have more relevance to us.

Ran'zar will be less changed by his life here among us than I was from the brief time I spent in Kyla. I *will* go back. It's as if I have no choice in the matter. There is a secret life to Kyla that I am compelled to discover. No, not yet, but in some years' time. And I will see again the pale ruins of Gyth, the golden orchards around her and the white deer who graze there. I will take rarer paths into the mists, amid the shadows of great leopards and the creatures that swim in the sky. Led by ghostly bells, I will discover the most ancient of tombs and palaces, and the knowledge of who subjugated the Lighurd, who razed their cities, but did not quell them, who are now only dust. Yes, the land has crept into my blood and the songs still call to me from there, at night, in my sleep. I believe Agouzi knew how my vision in Gyth would affect me, and that was why he entrusted Ran'zar to my care. In truth, the child is *my guardian*, rather than the other way round. He will stay with me until death, as was promised. And when the time comes he will lead me home to whatever waits for me there.

A Tower of Arkrondurl

Tanith Lee

Alas, poor ghost!
'Hamlet' – *Shakespeare*

1

He had been dead so long, the Sorcerer, here. Yet the tower, tall and iron-grim, was still deeply feared and scrupulously avoided.

To come into that region therefore was to discover no human conurbation, not a single human dwelling, for miles. The woods flocked over the rise and fall of the land. But these even seemed empty of animal life or birds. Once he saw a white owl cleave the twilight with its wide-winged passage. Before suddenly it veered aside again. But the sun shone by day, and by night the stars; the moon rose, though she was thin as a nail's edge with waning. The moon... one second he allowed himself to dream of <u>her</u> – candlelight on amber hair – then closed the dream away.

Cyveth's horse was tired by now, the seventy-seventh evening of this particular trek. Tiredness was not unreasonable. Not only must the horse support Cyveth, but his personal baggage, which included a sealed casket heavily containing one of the reasons for the journey. When the horse spontaneously stopped, Cyveth allowed this. He looked out across the dusken countryside. Below lay a valley, already mostly smoored in shadows. Bridging the gap, a broad stone causeway stretched with, at its farthest end, a tower.

Cyveth recognised the tower at once. Aside from all else, he had been told of it throughout his current ride north. They had spoken, those that did, in forthright bursts, or in whispers, of Arkrondurl the Sorcerer. It was as if they *must* speak of him. As if to speak about him, one way or another, was like uttering a prayer, or – now and then – vomiting. Since these procedures relieved them, if only for a little while.

For minutes, or hours, they recounted his supernatural cruelties and murders, his evil games and horrendous raping scourges. Nothing they said of him was good. Nor ever dull. A new if freelance vocabulary had required to be coined in order to illustrate what he had done. The occasionally extraordinary descriptions had always made an implacable sense. By the time anyone, and certainly one such as Cyveth, reached this causeway and looked across at this tower, he must have become a *scholar* of Arkrondurl.

And Arkrondurl was *dead*. While, according to every muttered or shouted sentence, rumour, tale or inadvertent proof – the one-eyed man three days before, the *three*-legged man a month ago – death had only briefly interrupted, and then transfigured, the malevolent concentration of the Sorcerer. Flesh and blood he might no longer be, but intransigently vile and inexorably powerful he had remained.

Bats flickered now over the hills, like the paling-darkening blink of sudden eyes.

Cyveth dismounted, heaved off as much of his luggage as was needed, and left his well-versed horse to stand at ease. He crossed the causeway alone and on foot.

Beneath the tower he did pause to stare up at it, and saw with no surprise it was still, despite the intervention of decades, in full repair.

As he pushed open the metallic door, its hinges hardly creaking, he noted that after all, there were no living bats in the upper air. It was merely some disturbance of the dying light.

2

For things were not always what they seemed.

Cyveth had learned that years before. His father had been a magician of some ability, who used his talents mostly to entertain the crowds for money, or to process cures for illness or injury – generally also to make a living, but sometimes unpaid, from compassion. If ever Cyveth's father had committed any wrong act through his gift, Cyveth never either saw or subsequently heard of it.

Even so, there had been others in that trade. The tall thin man, for example, known as the Waspion. Or the shorter, plumper man known only as *Myself*. What *they* had done, or were said to have done here and there, was in itself a lesson, both in wickedness – and the human knack for uncovering it and awarding it great publicity.

Yet there had been warm and multi-starry nights in those southern regions of the past, times seated in the open, or in various secluded dens. And then the magical miracles were wrought – the horse which flew on the wings of a swan, the girl who walked – and danced – though the rock fall had broken her back twenty days before.

Sorcery was not only for villainy, or for gain and show.

Nor was the reality of the world formed from granite, merely *seemed* to be. The world's reality was *malleable*. And death, of course, was not the *end*.

3

Inside the tower was a hollow gut of stone, out of which a stone stair hauled itself upward into an overhanging stony enclosure that hid it. The coming of night was hiding it too, draping long thick curtains of shadow, veil by veil...

Lugging his essential gear, Cyveth took the stair and climbed into utter black.

But he was counting now. Formerly it had been on the thirty-third (twice), the seventy-seventh (five times), the ninety-ninth (once) step that a response took place. Not, however, here.

Moving on to the hundredth stair Cyveth nevertheless hesitated. Remarkably strong and well-conditioned, he was not yet either weary or winded. But a sensation – less caution than expectancy – caused him to halt. Despite this no reaction came. The tower felt empty – not of sentient occupancy, but of the presiding *unlife*, the un*dead*.

Presently, Cyveth resumed the climb. A hundred and one, a hundred and two, a hundred and *three* –?

And something *rolled* across his feet.

It failed to stagger him, physically or mentally. The ever-awareness of a number three, seven or nine in the equation could never be lost on the son of a magician.

The stair itself moved, then. It swung smoothly along and to the side, bearing him, primed and balanced, with it, and so into another wide gulp of open stony space. Which, as Cyveth was borne in on the magic stone carpet, bloomed up into ghoulish, greenish visibility.

Corpse-lights, the kind to haunt marshes, blossomed on all sides. They illumined like verdigris a high vault and the mathematics carved into it, the meanings of which were partly translatable by the visitor. Strange pillars, like misshapen limbs fossilized to basalt, strained up to support, or only clutch at, the ceiling. On the vacant floor was scattered a vague yet ominous type of dust, marked with indecipherable tracks, very narrow and broken, and always dimming out before they reached anywhere – or indeed before they had *come* from anywhere.

Cyveth jumped off the stair. He dropped his luggage on the dusty floor. It did not matter. If he succeeded, he would bear it out with him again. If he failed, he and it would simply remain to blend with the rest of the filth.

Along with all the other disparate training he had received, Cyveth had learned, from childhood, an actor's resonant and controlled voice.

"Greetings, if you are present, peerless and mighty Mage-Lord, Arkrondurl of the Towers."

Nothing stirred. Cyveth had not anticipated it would. As an actor, this was not the first and only time he had given such a performance. And though the setting of the stage might vary, the other leading actor must normally arrive on cue, despite the fact his *timing* was his own to choose. It was a law of sorcery as much as the theatre.

The curtains of gloom and gris green parted.

The master performer entered, from nowhere, and the silence rang with its deaf applause.

"Who speaks?" he inquired.

"I."

"I do not know you," said Arkrondurl the Sorcerer.

And Cyveth sighed. It was the only indication, infinitely misinterpretable, that an iota of his tension had left him.

"How," he said, "*should* you know me, Lord? I am nothing. While your golden name is fame itself."

Vanity. Playing to it might – did – often work. Fairly infallibly. And did so now.

"True," affirmed the hellish ghost. And flexing his long-fingered, pallid hands, Arkrondurl spun a brief episode of showy lightning round the space. "Yet, I am a revenant only. What need you fear?" Cat and mouse then, it seemed. Not quite unknown…

"I have heard the stories, Lord."

"Have you. *All?*"

"I have heard enough to freeze my heart and turn my bones to powder."

"And even so," said the Sorcerer, "you are *here*. Do you wish to become, yourself, a *story?*"

Cyveth laughed softly. "Perhaps."

Arkrondurl's long, pale face, intellectual and severe, ugly in its aesthetic elegance, terrifying in the sour and sadistic cant of lips and fleer of toneless eyes, now gelling in a kind of – pleasure?

105

Cyveth said, "For a nonentity such as myself, Lord, glory can only come through service to a far more dynamic being."

"Which being could that be?" (This was like verbal fencing with a flighty girl.)

"None other than yourself, inestimable Sorcerer."

"Let me show you," said the ghost, "a few small pictures; past events that have gone on here in my tower, as at other times in others of my towers. There are nine in all. Did you know this?"

"Oh yes, my Lord."

"It seems you have studied me like a book. It shall be your reward to learn a little more. See, then."

The lightning roiled again, and in the ropes of it, vivid and sudden, awful scenes splashed up in fragments, like splintered panes of coloured glass, each spiteful and foul enough to tear any eyes that looked on them, men and women – children – were caught inside the broken pieces; human creatures that suffered torture and obscenity beyond (beneath) description, and struggled, shrieked and died, in adverse tints, to a music of sounds that, in their turn, rent the hollows of a listening ear. Another man would have crumpled, puked, swooned; maybe died too. But Cyveth, if sufficiently white now to rival the ghost's bleached visage, stayed upright, motionless and quiet. He watched all, attentively. Although, of course, as with so much else, he had seen such stuff more than once before.

4

Nine – the number of the unholy lives of Arkrondurl. And the number of his towers, built, unalike yet siblings, and dotted all about the north and eastern map of the earth. In woods or a forest you would find them, on hillsides, as here, on mountaintops, on a tiny isle that stood up from a lake, on a rock that had set its foot deep into an open sea. One, so it was said, (and so at last it had been found to be) rose underground, far down in a cavern, where neither night nor day ever came – and glad perhaps they were to be excluded.

How he made the nine towers was easily comprehended: through sorcery. And in them, one by one, his nine separate mortal lives had followed each other, after certain accidents – when he had overreached his own perfidious cunning, or Fate, as once or twice it had, sent a hero wise and swift enough to tackle and destroy him. Through his nine lives, Arkrondurl, returning, had persisted on every occasion (until once more slain) in unspeakable power and ungrace. The whole span had amounted to three centuries. But then there followed his *alternative* existence, as exemplified tonight. A *ghost*. It was, always, a phantom in which the perverse and soulless expertise and sagacity remained, if anything enhanced by non-corporeality. His ghostly practices, they said, (they did not lie) exceeded those encompassed by him when simply living.

How had Arkrondurl managed, post mortem, to linger in the world?

They said, again, and some believed them, that no god at all would let *that* spirit through the gate of Otherlife. And even the demons of the icy pits of hell refused him. Only the long-suffering world, it seemed, had no say. And so he lodged on with her, abusing, as ever, his domicile, nor needing any more to pay the rent. A squatter unworthy of the name, as also of the name of man.

The stories and their trappings had been absorbed by Cyveth years prior to the evening of this call upon the ninth tower. He had heard tell of all of it and been at a loss. Until he learned, elsewhere, a mystery – which was itself the second half to another, the first portion being already known to him. Both were benign, though doubtless prodigious – and according to the majority of sources blasphemous and unforgiveable.

Till that second knowledge, the question had gone unanswered, the demand as to how to destroy a ghost, when exorcism (it had been tried with Arkrondurl so many ghastly times) had fearsomely failed.

For could there be any alternate way to render back to death that non-sentient being that would not, *did* not die? You could not rob the dead – of *life*.

5

The show of moving pictures was done.

Arkrondurl poised, another pillar – this one of poisonous salt amid obliging shadows.

"Well. And did you like what you saw?" The relentless voice probing, turgid with pride and satisfaction.

"Lord, whatever you see fit to do, in *my* eyes, has the gleam of gold and the brilliance of diamond. In my eyes, Lord – the only sin is to *deny* you."

Not all the self-in-love were blind. Arkrondurl, it would seem, had been, and was. Impassive and flaunting as a peacock he waited there, evidently grasping the idea that a gift was to be offered.

"My Lord," said Cyveth, "will you permit me to assist you?"

"*You.*" Arkrondurl laughed. "You... to assist – myself."

"In the most fundamental and servile manner, Lord. Solely that. May I detail my plan?"

"Amuse me. Do so."

Cyveth bowed low. And obeyed.

How many performances had he given in this role? Was he confident – as much so as any fine and tempered actor. Was he *word perfect*? Oh yes.

6

It was the Waspion who had disclosed the first secret to him. Cyveth, then just sixteen, and always curious, and – sometimes to a foolhardy degree – eager to learn, had risked half a day in the Waspion's uncomfortable company in order to be educated. Cyveth had also worked out a strategy with the Waspion, as with others one was ill-advised to trust. Cyveth pretended that he had only a slight talent in the magical arts. He could perform the odd crowd-pleasing trick, but had no aptitude for much else. In this way he had been shown, and so picked up, quite a number of skills. Then again, Cyveth was abstemious in their use. Magic both fascinated and perturbed him. As with fire, it could keep you warm and improve your diet, but you stopped short generally of burning down the house.

The Waspion was prone to drunkenness. He revealed the terrifying formula of the spell under the influence of black wine and red brandy. If afterwards he recalled what he had done, he did not allude to it, nor did Cyveth give any indication, let alone demonstration, of having found out anything unusual he could copy.

Of course also it had been obvious the gambit involved two processes. One could not be fulfilled without the other. The second and perhaps most needful of these Cyveth set himself to master some years further on. And that had been when first Cyveth heard of the Sorcerer Arkrondurl, his nine towers and nine lives and the enduringly indestructible problem of his ghost.

7

"Behold, Lord. Here in this box –"

The casket, about half the length of a donkey's back and the width only of a man's arm, lay out now on the dust. It was very plain, and its clasps of inferior steel had not yet been released.

(The ghost stood watching adamantly enough.)

Cyveth clicked his tongue – once, twice, three times.

The clasps scraped rustily from their sockets, the lid reared up, and fell back on the floor with a clatter.

"What is that?" Did the great Sorcerer not know? Surely – no, no. He did not.

"It is, inimitable sir, a man. Or, the body of a man in miniature. May I invite you, Lord, to examine it?"

"Why should I trouble?"

"Because, Lord, it might be worth your while. I could not dare suggest it otherwise."

For a moment, nothing. And then Arkrondurl gliding forward, gazing down.

Though less than the size of a year old infant, the male figure in the casket was in every and all ways adultly in proportion, and perfect. Had it been full-grown in stature and girth, plainly it must have been a figure of more than seven feet in height, wide-shouldered and lean of pelvis, muscular and formed – not well but *flawlessly* – with a complexion like fine bronze, hair black as death's river, and – for the eyelids stayed open – silver-eyed. So Arkrondurl had been, in youth, they said, at least in his colouring. The heroic and beautiful stature here possible was never his, except in illusion, through sorcery. The face too, no mistake – even at doll size – was that of an Arkrondurl not only young, and physically without fault, but of exceptional handsomeness. No mote of the sadistic, the debased or rotten had infected any aspect. Few women, or come to that few men, would look unmoved on such a sunrise of mortal gorgeousness.

"Very pretty," said the Sorcerer. His offhand tone would deceive only the most obtuse or silly. "But what does it *do?*"

Cyveth, showman, actor, trickster, mage, quietly and reverently told him.

"First, Lord, through my lesser and far subordinate art, I can make it grow to its full height and dimensions, strength and virility. Then, also through the one other huge secret I have learned, I will open it to receive your lifeforce, and your colossal intelligence. Beside which, my own meagre craft, or that of most, is like a sigh to a sound of thunder."

Arkrondurl turned on Cyveth then the blaze of his awful eyes. No more were they silver, but – a *nothingness.* Some colours were spectres never even born.

"And then – I shall live... in the flesh once more?"

Inside the voice was there the vaguest childish tremor? Or

not? Who could tell. *Cyveth* could. He had, before, unforgettably, heard these giveaways.

"You will live, my Lord," said Cyveth passionately and fiercely, "not merely as in the flesh you did, but to the extreme capacity your power, your genius and your knowledge deserve and have merited. So, lesser men must die to please you? Let them make room – make room for *choicer* men. You have *earned* this renewal, exalted master. *Let me serve you.*"

Only then did Arkrondurl toss towards him one slightly, playfully questioning look. "And your own reward?"

Cyveth laughed. "To live in legend. The wolf in shadow – blotted out – yet *there*. A mere human – who gave Arkrondurl back his life."

"You will be cursed. Perhaps sought and destroyed."

Cyveth shrugged. "But *not* forgotten."

It was now Arkrondurl who truly laughed. Inevitably, a repulsive noise. "Or *I* may kill you. You will know too much."

Cyveth lowered his eyes (another falsely modest and flirtatious maiden).

"Let us see," he said. And lifted the creature free of the casket.

8

Making the spell was, once the technique had been gained, comparatively straightforward, even rapid. And by now Cyveth was well-versed; he had performed it several times before. (The construction of the mortal receptacle – the miniaturized male figure – took far longer and was an act of many scenes, every version involving thirty-three days and nights. As with the ordinary miracle of conception, the creature must be securely planted and next grown, but this inside an alchemic crystalline womb, the nature of which was so bizarre it had, on each venture, startled Cyveth afresh.) But *now* – the spell was activated –

The quickness with which the figure expanded was epic. Within three minutes it had grown to the size of a twelve-year-old child. In three more it had achieved the fully-proportioned height and girth of a statuesque male deity. From its head the thick river of hair poured out. Within its open eyes moisture glittered; its lips parted to reveal the white and polished teeth of a healthy man some twenty years of age. By the ninth minute all was complete. If perfection had been merely obvious before, now it was overwhelming.

A god would *not* be shamed to put on such a physical garment.

Cyveth did not glance towards the Sorcerer. Cyveth, by now, had slight doubt as to Arkrondurl's reaction.

But when Arkrondurl spoke, the greedy lust anyway dripped from his voice.

"Yes," he said. "I will inhabit that. Never fear, I shall reward you. Now get on – make haste. *Rehouse* me."

Cyveth gave a cry of acquiescence.

He rushed to obey.

And as he drew, in palest light, the necessary arcane symbols on the ground, the walls, the air, and sprinkled there from pouches needful tinctures, smokes, sands, Cyveth held his own racing brain in check. The only danger in these final moments was that he might after all, though never before had he done so during the past teem of years, make some mistake. Less from carelessness than over-familiarity...

Far off in his mind as he worked, he glimpsed the sections of Arkrondurl's prologue. The heroes with swords who had come to slay the Sorcerer while he *lived*, some successful, most not. And the exorcists who had, all of them, failed. And the countless innocents and undeservers who had perished. And time itself. And eventually a hero who was not any such thing and his deed that, for the major part, could not earn him fame or lasting glory, being too unglamorous, and too subject to repetition. Or, seen another way, potentially too doomed, too *un*conclusive. For *this* 'hero' (Cyveth), was as yet young, and strong. But later... later... What then?

In the seventieth minute of his being with Arkrondurl, Cyveth grew still.

"Great Lord, all is prepared. There are three seconds of passage. In the first you will vanish. In the next you will enter he that waits to assist your avatar. In the third you will be within his envelope of flesh, anchored as any living man in his mortal frame. You will be *him*, and he – will be yourself. Your vehicle and your kingdom. Live long, and to the most entire scope you may, unsurpassable Lord, in this well-earned and apposite mortal life."

Arkrondurl, like a grinning scar on the grizzled sheen of the tower. An image made only the more disgusting by duplication.

And then the two words spoken.

The showman and trickster missing nothing, getting all right, as he must, and always had. Again word perfect. All perfect. Perfection.

A flash of flame, like that of an exploding star. Searing brightness, tumbling dark. Soundless cacophony. The deafening quiet.

Cyveth turned, slow and stiff as an ancient a hundred years of age. The ghost of the Sorcerer was gone. On the floor, the beautiful and full-grown man was stirring.

Wrapped in his own half-paralysis of horror, Cyveth watched, breath stopped, heart shuddering, all eyes.

A god, re-bodied, rising up in returning vitality, flexing and smiling, laughing as a lion roars – *No*. Not that. Instead – the creature on the ground – was writhing, rolling, foaming at the lips, its eyes wide and wild, noises spewing from its throat and nostrils, hands clawing – and now all of it, a composite chaos, leaping to its feet and at once falling down again, crawling, sprawling, mewling and screeching – slamming its handsome flawless skull against the stony wall over and over.

Cyveth swept up his magician's luggage, the emptied casket with it. A hero with a sword? The baggage Cyveth carried, *that* was Cyveth's sword.

Springing past the howling slathering mad thing, which did not somehow seem to see him, Cyveth reached the steps, jumped a perceived gap, and pelted down them. As he descended the length of the tower of Arkrondurl, and sprang out through the doors on to the causeway, the mindless outcry echoed on and on behind him, inside the stone. And while Cyveth ran back across the causeway under the star-prickled night, the notes of torment and despair continued, if anything more loud. The godlike body was strong. It could support an incredible amount, as it would be required to. Like the tower, the creature had been built to last.

Safely returned to the woodland on the causeway's far side, Cyveth found his horse. It was staring at the tower sidelong, less in fear than in a disapproving recognition. Which again was not unreasonable. Like Cyveth, this horse had witnessed eight times already an identical tumult.

Cyveth spoke the finishing word, the third of the spell – there must always be three (or seven, or nine).

Despite the lack of light – the starved moon was hiding in the trees – anyone might notice a peculiar change occur then to the tower. It appeared to have grown – solid. That was, solid all through, as if the mass of stone had knitted suddenly internally together. Not a window now or door, facing out. Inside, no staircase or space or vault or ceiling, no smallest hole or crack. A block of granite only. With, somewhere inside, locked, packed, trapped, the tortured and wailing new-gained body of the Sorcerer Arkrondurl, and the lifeforce of Arkrondurl. Which was in turn, doubly held, in body and in tower, *both*. It went without saying, had Arkrondurl been as he *had* been, flesh or ghost, he could have smashed instantly any prison, stone or flesh, to pieces. But Arkrondurl was not, *now*, as he had been. Why not?

As a living man, able once to be born and thereafter to return himself to life – if only eight further times – his ability had been virtually infinite. And as a ghost, his powers stayed incorrigible and supreme. Since the lifeforce, disembodied, and keeping still its personality, retained unimpaired the will and acumen of its physical former brain. If next this non-corporeal but vital force were reinvested in an unoccupied but viable fleshly form, it would at once control the new physical brain it had inherited. However.

9

As he rode the horse, at a regular yet peaceful pace, back towards the distant south, Cyveth allowed himself (at last, at last) thoughts of home.

Certain family members still lived there, in the mild warm lands, among the orchards and the vines, under a yellower sun and those nocturnal stars, burning thick as meadow flowers, and held up only by the low brown mountains and the faith of men. But he thought of *her*, too, free to do so (at last) – or for a while. She was the young woman he would marry. A year his senior, tall and slender, with hair like an amber waterfall. *Myself*, the other untrustworthy magician Cyveth had known in youth, had foretold such a lover and been proved, that once, honest and correct. Three future sons had been promised too, born without trouble, lucky and bold. Whether they might inherit showman's gifts, and the knack of learning sufficient magic, *Myself* had never said. Cyveth must trust that one at least would do. Or, failing this, that Cyveth might *find* another boy able and prepared to serve an apprenticeship, and, when Cyveth had grown old and lost the flair, who would agree to take on Cyveth's unavoidable, repetitive task. For of course, one could not lie to oneself, someone would have to do it.

While he lived and had his strength, Cyveth might well be called on to do it all again. And again. It might only be one single time, but he doubted that. It would be at least three times. Or seven. Or, once more, the full set of nine. Just as for the past many years he had done it, and ended only here, with the ninth tower visited, and the ninth undead version of Arkrondurl confined to his total internment. Again.

How to destroy the deathless undead? Make them *alive*. Yet an aliveness with a proviso.

Despite its faultless beauty, the alchemically fashioned male human body that had so lured – and captured – the ghost inside it, was in fact imperfect: it contained one invisible but pertinent omission. *A brain*. Certainly some of the vestiges of the organ were present, enough to allow consciousness, a type of sight, and of vocality, gesture and movement – but these nevertheless active only in their most crass and fundamentally useless capacity. Presumably the Sorcerer would have essayed some check of the creature, as it lay tantalizingly on offer before him, but any supernatural scan he had tried had been satisfied. For sure, he would have noted workable heart and lungs, stomach and other intimate inner areas, a skeleton and muscles of flexibility and endurance. For the brain, however, there was only a facsimilous shell equipped with feeble rudiments, a wheelless cart that no mind, small or great, could cause to move one inch. But it had fooled him, that self-enamoured monster, his evil genius *blinded* by self to all reality. So sure he was of the flawless case into which he was about to be poured – for he credited only his own ultimate triumph. And in he went, and behind him the door of flesh was slammed. And there Arkrondurl found himself, trapped in a body where he could enjoy no single second of sorcerous power, let alone individual governance. He would be now like any human thing whose brain and mind no longer functioned. While remaining always *mindlessly* aware, *mindlessly* awake, helpless, hopeless. Howling.

And the body was otherwise so healthy and virile. It could live for ten decades or more – unless, as had three times happened, in his transports of agonized physical uncontrol, the Sorcerer should accidentally kill it. Then, out the ghost would seethe again. Nor only one ghost, for like his lives there were nine of them, one for each tower.

These nine ghosts never remembered, it seemed, anything of

Cyveth – nothing of the trickster who had promised ideal rebodyment and glory, and instead condemned to hell-on-earth. Brainless, they had not kept the memory. And therefore Cyveth had been enabled to return and spring the cage again. (Cyveth, travelling these paths over, months and miles, listening to the gossipings of nightmare all heard before... Cyveth the jailor, himself perhaps also condemned – to his quest, forever.)

Or not forever. When old, weakened and exhausted – then his son, or some adopted heir, would take on the leading role. Three times, seven times, nine. Over and over, over and ever, for Hell's pit would not accept Arkrondurl and any sweeter Otherworlds were shut. Earth must imprison him, and men of earth, the men of Cyveth's line, see to the business.

Cyveth, riding south through the sun-petalled days, the high-roofed full-mooned nights, wondered how eventually he could come to tell his son about the quest and that he too would, ever after, be shackled to it. And Cyveth grasped it would be far harder, this telling, than going to see a tower of Arkrondurl and risking there everything in order to save the world. But he would do that, too. For though they mostly do not wish to, with no choice all mortal men one day must die. And perhaps, although this also they do not always wish, must return to life again.

WHO WALKS WITH DEATH

Jonathan Green

"Soth!" Jormungard cursed, gazing upon the scene in abject horror.

Even for one of his years and experience, the sight that greeted his unblinking eyes sickened him to the core.

Dead soldiers on a battlefield, who had met their ends with honour in mortal combat, their souls shriven, ready to be claimed by the raven's feast, that was what every warrior of Farrhold hoped for. Either that, or to die in a drinking binge such as was spoken of in the ancient sagas of the Farrmen.

But women and children, ripped to shreds, viscera strewn about the farmstead like Solstice garlands? No man of Farrhold wanted to see that – none but the depraved, cannibalistic cults of Namarr – and never was that more true than in the case of Jormungard of the House of Vanyr. The massacre of innocents was something he had hoped never to set eyes upon again.

"Soth?" his companion challenged him.

Jorm looked to the other man. Thorkill was squatting on his haunches, casting an experienced eye over the scene, hoping to pry its secrets from what the tracks and other bloodied signs told him.

"This wasn't the work of the worm god, although he will eat his fill this night. A beast did this."

"You're sure?"

"You were always handy with a sword, young master," the older man laughed coarsely, "and you know your way round a bow, but you don't have a tracker's eye do you? You never did."

Jormungard grunted. "That's what I keep you around for."

He had been a man these past five winters and yet still the grizzled veteran spoke to him sometimes as if he were a mere stripling. And he certainly wasn't that. He hadn't been that for a long time, not since he had sworn vengeance against the slave-servants of the death god for the slaughter of his family. It was such slaughter that he had never wished to see again, and yet here he was...

"You see this, here," Thorkill said, pointing with a hand thick with rings at a blood-filled impression in the ground, "and here?"

Jormungard forced himself to cast a critical gaze over the scene of the massacre once more, trying to see beyond the blood and gore, and faces forever frozen in shock and fear. He could see the prints, now that Thorkill was pointing them out. Whatever had made them was large, larger than a bear, and, more disconcertingly, the footprints looked to be closer to those of a man than anything else.

"What do you think it was?"

Thorkill breathed in through his teeth. "Of that I'm not sure."

"A troll," Jorm wondered aloud, "leaving its mountain fastness in search of food in these bitter months?"

"Maybe." Thorkill sounded unconvinced.

"You're sure this wasn't the work of... raiders?"

"Such savagery? I very much doubt..." Thorkill broke off seeing the look in the younger man's eyes. "You think Namarrans did this?"

"I have only seen savagery such as this once before," Jorm pointed out, the memory of his family's massacre overlaid upon this one in his mind's eye, crystal clear in every minute detail.

"No, this was the work of an animal. See these wounds?

They were not made by a keen-edged blade. They were made by an animal's claws."

Silence descended between them again as they examined the disembowelled bodies of the farmer and his family. An axe lay by the farmer's side, as did the purple-grey ropes of his spilled intestines. Whether the blood on the axe's blade was that of the farmstead's attacker or the farmer himself, it was impossible to tell.

The silence was broken by a cry, bestial and savage – a sound like death and rage and hunger – that rang out around the bowl of the valley. As one, the two men looked to the misted slopes above and then at each other. Thorkill held Jorm's gaze with a steely look, as much as to say, "Told you so."

The echoes of the cry faded but it was still several moments more before either of them spoke again, or Jorm's sword hand strayed from the hilt of his scabbarded blade.

They built a pyre from what wood they could find, and laid the family together atop it, their feet pointing west, their heads to the east, so that their departing souls might see the setting sun and know which way to go, to follow the fiery orb to the lands hereafter.

They stood in respectful silence as the flames caught hold, and watched as the sun sank beyond the far horizon. By the time they were done, night had fallen. And so, warmed by the bone-fire, the two men rolled out their bed-rolls and settled down to sleep beyond the ruins of the farmstead.

It was not until they were readying themselves for the off, with the return of the sun the next morning, that Jormungard saw the brooch, trampled into the blood-sodden earth, sunlight flashing from its polished surface.

"No!" He stooped to pull the object from the abattoir mud.

"I know this brooch."

"Whose is it?" Thorkill asked, hefting his pack onto his back and settling its weight across his shoulders.

"You know him too," Jorm said, passing his companion the bronze leaf. "It belongs to Sven of Skarrsgard."

"Sven of Skarrsgard? That drunken reprobate, who joined us in cleansing the Morrow Mounds of the half-dead that had made it their nest?"

"That's the one."

"The Morrow Mounds where we chanced upon that talisman wrought of star metal? The talisman that Sven insisted on keeping for himself."

"The very same. He saved my skin more than once that day, do you remember? And yours. He must have been here too."

"And judging by the way the brooch was trodden into the ground, he was either here before the attack commenced or he was here during it," Thorkill mused. "But I doubt he was here after."

Jormungard's expression was one of concern. "A man does not easily lose such a fine cloak clasp such as this."

"But it is something he might lose in the heat of battle."

"So he was here and faced the beast himself?" Jorm's complexion paled. "His body was not among the dead."

"Then there is hope for your friend yet," Thorkill said, "although he clearly did not slay the beast here either."

"No," the younger man agreed, "but who's to say he did not wound it, or that he is not running it to ground even now. Or that he has already done away with it."

At that moment the same animal bellow they had heard the night before boomed out across the valley. Mist still clung to the slopes rising above them like marsh-gas over the Daromarr Fens.

The beast still lives," Thorkill hissed. "Of your friend, I wouldn't like to say."

"Then we must hurry," Jorm said, his tone brokering no challenge.

Fog lay thick upon the peaks of the craggy hills as if it were a living thing that had claimed these lands as its domain.

But something else had claimed these marcher lands as its territory these last three months. The Doom of Farrenfell. The creature the superstitious folk of these ancient lands had named 'Who Walks With Death', Nam'karill in the old tongue. The bestial thing Jormungard and Thorkill hunted even now.

The tribal Marcher Kings might claim that these lands fell within the bounds of Farrhold, but out here, in the foothills of the Dragomyr Mountains, the truth of the matter was that in reality no man could claim dominion over so bleak and isolated a place as this.

These lands belonged to the Wyld, and the Wyld had hunted in the hills and valleys long before the Kings of Dromgarr and Farrenfell had braved the uplands in search of gold and precious timber.

The Wyld had been here before the Men of Farrhold and it was here now, in the form of its avatar, the beast, and it would dwell here long after Farrhold had joined the honour roll of lost empires.

"We're close." Thorkill stopped, sniffing the cold, damp, air. Jormungard inhaled deeply and caught the whiff of animal musk, of heaving flanks, gore-clogged fangs and malevolent intent.

"I know this place," Jorm said, his voice barely a whisper.

The shadow-shapes of menhirs solidified to become a cluster of standing stones, as a gust of wind dragged the clinging mist from the looming cromlechs.

"Yes," Thorkill agreed, breathing in through his teeth again. "I know these stones too" – he gazed up at the lofty megaliths – "although I do not think we have been here before."

The rising wind continued to clear the vapour from the top

of the crag, exposing the scree-slopes and hummocks and dew-dappled moss-covered earth beyond.

"No, we have not," Jorm said, his words quickening with apprehensive excitement, "but we have seen this place, from afar."

"After the cleansing of the Morrow Mounds," Thorkill said darkly. "I was so preoccupied with following the tracks through the mist I had no sense of the place we were in."

"Until now."

"Until now," Thorkill agreed.

Later, Jormungard would seem to remember that the mists darkened at that moment, as if the shadow of Namarr's hand had fallen across the ancient stones. What there could be no doubt about was that the shriek of carrion birds made him start, and even the steely Thorkill look round in surprise. Only it wasn't hill rocs, or even carrion crows that were suddenly assaulting their position upon the peak.

The figures came at them out of the persistent mist, between the stones, their ragged, feathered robes streaming out behind them, making them look like a murder of crows, screeching their avian war-cry.

Jormungard went for his sword. Thorkill's blade was already loosed from its sheath and ready in his hand.

They were confronted by a host of pallid faces, pinched with cold, dark veins throbbing beneath waxy skin, teeth sharpened to needle-like points. And the owners of those horrid faces clutched claw daggers in their bony hands.

Jormungard tensed as his mentor dropped into a fighter's stance, legs braced, knees bent, ready to meet the cultists' charge.

Namarrans, thought Jormungard, and his blood ran cold. He had been right all along. But knowing that didn't make him feel any better. All it did was to bring back the memory of that day, the one he had fought so hard to suppress; the scene that had greeted him upon returning home from hunting with Thorkill, his father's bondsman; the blood-splashed cobbles, the straw wet with gore, the courtyard gutters choked with viscera.

Thorkill met the leader's charge with a rising block. The man shrieked as his bear-claw dagger scraped across the cold steel of the huntsman's blade. He shrieked again as Thorkill swung his sword free and, two-handed, brought it round, the blade meeting the man's wildly flapping cloak and scraping against his ribs, its keen edge dulled by the coarse fabric with which it had become tangled.

The Namarran shrieked again, although with rage rather than pain, or so it seemed to the dumbstruck Jormungard. And then it was the cultist's turn to swing wildly at Thorkill as another of his number closed from the right.

With an impassioned cry of "For Soth!" Jormungard ran to meet the Namarrans' attack, his sword raised high, ready to be brought down in a sweeping slash at an exposed neck or unprotected belly.

A cultist met his furious, wild-eyed stare with a crazed, bloodshot gimlet gaze of his own, red-rimmed eyes sunken in the grey-ringed orbits of a skull-like visage. The cultist opened his black-lipped mouth wide and screamed in Jorm's face.

Jormungard had faced goblins and even an ogre in battle, but he couldn't help being unnerved by the cultist's inhuman shrieks. Channelling the blood-chilling fear he felt, as he stared into the face of one who had already given himself to death in mind if not in body, Jorm struck with his blade. But the Namarran was ready for him.

The madman raised his left hand, and the knife clasped within it. Jorm felt his arm jar as the blades met. He felt the power in the rangy man's taut muscles as the cultist trapped his sword between the bear-claw blade and the hilt of the dagger, twisting Jorm's arm round and down, even as he brought the second dagger, ready in his right hand, down in a stabbing motion towards Jormungard's own unguarded neck.

Moving just as quickly as the cultist, Jorm brought his left hand up from his hip to meet this second attack, unsheathing his own steel-edged dagger in one fluid action as he did so.

He caught the descending bear-claw in the prongs that flared from the base of the blade where it slotted into the hilt. Having halted the dagger's descent, he brought his now freed sword up once more. The muscles in his arm tenses and he grunted as he sliced the keen edge of the sword across his attacker's belly, feeling it meet resistance as the death-worshipper doubled up and fell backwards, his raven-shriek now nothing more than a gurgling death-rattle.

Jorm kicked the dying Namarran away, turning his attention back to Thorkill, who had despatched his attacker also and was already engaged in combat with another.

They had only been fighting for – what? – a few minutes? And yet Jorm could already feel the acid burn of effort in his arms. Sweat was running from his scalp and into his eyes, forcing him to take a hand from the hilt of his sword to wipe the saltwater away to clear his vision. But his own body was doing its part now too, the blood quickening in his veins, restoring strength to straining muscles, the natural instinct for survival strong within him.

They were still outnumbered, and worst of all the cultists had managed to cut them off from each other, as well as having them surrounded. Tactics and combat strategy seemed to count for little among the Namarrans, but a savage berserker approach to battle more than made up for what they lacked in terms of strategic thinking. All that mattered to them was the here and now, the brutal melee of the moment, another opportunity to feed their deathless master more souls. And if that proved to be their own, so be it.

The most dangerous opponent was one who had become heedless of his own fate.

Shrieking like carrion birds at the raven's feast, the cultists renewed their attack. They swept down upon the companions, as if on night-black pinions, raven-wing amulets and finger-bone necklaces rattling about their necks.

The bestial bellow cut through the banshee screams of the Namarrans, the lingering mist and the grunts of effort made by the beleaguered friends.

The beast came at them from out of the fog, wisps of vapour clinging to its massive frame, its fur as black as a moonless midnight and stinking of death, all muscle and rage and murderous intent.

Twice as tall as a man, and as broad across the shoulders as it was tall, the apparition put Jormungard in mind of one of the great apes he had heard tell of in far-fetched mariner's tales of the strange creatures that dwelt in the sweltering jungles of the south.

Slabs of muscle moved beneath the monster's pitted hide, and its arms were corded ropes of black meat that spoke of devastating strength. It was as if the night had taken on corporeal form, shadow given solidity, the bowel-watering terror of every man's nightmare made flesh.

The Namarrans scattered as the monster hauled its bulk between a pair of tilted standing stones, their crow-cries transforming into shrieks of fear. It seemed that, much as the crow-cultists were keen to send the souls of others to meet the lord of death, they were not so keen on meeting their god in person as readily.

Jormungard's heart raced. Namarrans pelted pell-mell towards him, offering only a desultory defence against his half-hearted attacks, both sides preoccupied by the appearance of the beast within the stone circle.

"Commit!" Thorkill yelled as he gutted a fleeing crow-man, drawing the keenly-honed edge of his blade across the belly of his fleeing foe.

Commit, Jorm thought. But to what? "The enemy of my enemy is my friend," he muttered breathlessly to himself. But which one was his enemy? The beast they had been hunting or the necrophiliac cannibals whose kind had slaughtered and violated his family, and who now threatened to take his own life in the name of the foul god of oblivion?

Jormungard quickly surveyed the killing ground bounded by the ancient, cracked and pitted stones, and made a tactical decision. Even if he took the beast to be on their side, and considered its presence akin to having another three men fighting for him, the Namarrans still outnumbered them three to one.

Hefting his sword in both hands, feeling the muscles of his arms sing now with the thrill of the fight, Jormungard chose his target and charged.

The Namarran's flesh was grey as ground-up bone meal, and hairless. The only colour anywhere upon his body was in the envenomed veins rising proud of his neck – and visible as the tracery of a spider's web upon his head – in the red-rimmed whites of his eyes, and the livid purple scar Jormungard could see describing a jagged path from the cultist's shoulder, across the man's torso, down to his left hip. The man's robe hung loosely open at the front, tied at the waist by a cord of glossy black hair – the man's own hair, if the stories Jorm had heard about the cult were true. The scar could have been an old injury – there was something about the parchment-cracked skin of the Namaaran's face that could have placed him at thirty, or forty, or even fifty – or it could have been a ritual scarring, the legacy of another of the cannibal cult's vile practices.

Bellowing a wordless war cry, Jormungard swung his blade. The cultist matched the blow with a sabre cat-fang dagger. He was fast and strong. The man pulled himself in close, bringing Jorm face to face with his enemy. He could see every detail of the unholy wretch's face, from the black veins pulsing at his neck, to the stabbing tip of his tongue thrusting between teeth filed to pike-like points.

Glancing past his opponent, for a moment Jorm's gaze met the berserker-crazed stare of the beast. Its chest and shoulders heaved, the creature's breath escaping its misshapen mouth in great snorting gusts. But in that instant it seemed to Jormungard that they shared a flash of understanding, both man and beast together. Or was it more than that?

Jormungard brought his knee up hard. The man doubled up, his grip on the knife weakening. It was a simple matter then for Jorm to finish the cultist with the dagger still gripped in his left hand.

Another came at him then, a crow-black cultist with a livid ritual brand-mark burned onto the left side of his face. In his bony hand he carried a club studded with sabre cat teeth – teeth not unlike those that filled the malformed jaws of Jorm's bestial ally.

Jormungard's blood was ablaze now and no longer frosted by fear. He blocked the cultist's wild swipe and caught the man's crotch with a sharp kick. As the man collapsed, Jorm brought his knee up sharply into the other's face, with bone-crunching force.

Another crow-cultist crumpled under the ministrations of Thorkill's blade, the cannibal's body suddenly as limp as a marionette whose strings had been snipped. Unleashing a blood-crazed roar, the beast tore a man in half, casting the bloody tatters of his carcass aside, spilling stinking offal across the churned mud at their feet as it did so.

With shrieking crow-men ranged all about him, Jormungard lost himself in battle, living only from one sword-stroke to the next parrying defence…

And then, abruptly, there were no more Namarrans left to fight; no more cannibals to kill. They had all been sent to meet the master they had so revered and feared in what had passed for their squalid little lives.

The three allies – Jormungard, Thorkill, and the beast – stood where they had fought, panting for breath, staring dumbly at one another as realisation dawned; not one of the crazed cultists had escaped them. Whatever the Namarrans' intention in luring the hunters here, it had failed – unless their plan had been to commit suicide by inviting slaughter at the hands of others.

But now Jorm's gaze lingered upon the hulking beast. It stood, with shoulders hunched, resting its weight on its fists, its massive barrel chest heaving, steam rising from its sweaty flanks.

The beast looked at him, and Jorm could not resist its furious gaze.

What he saw there chilled him to the core. He felt the same sense of kindredness that he had felt before when he first laid eyes upon the creature.

Was it that he saw something of himself in the beast, a darker, untamed side to himself that was slowly emerging as he continued to pursue his quest for vengeance? Or was it something else?

The mist was lifting from about the stones more quickly now, as if somehow the Namarrans' own dark nature had perpetuated its continuance before. A spear of sunlight pierced the dissipating haze, bathing the ancient stone circle in its golden radiance, and in that moment something flashed silver, grabbing Jorm's attention. It was something at the beast's throat.

The beast winced in the light and put up a shaggy-haired arm to shield its small, dark eyes from the sun. Jormungard sensed Thorkill tense, ready to fight again if a change in circumstance called upon him to do so. Jorm didn't move a muscle, his eyes transfixed.

At first he wondered if it was a collar of some kind; or was it a chain? The longer he peered at it, the more it looked like a chain.

Entranced, Jormungard took an unwitting step forward. The beast gave a grunting bark and shied away, taking its weight off its knuckles and rising to its full height, snapping Jorm out of his trance-like reverie.

Jorm froze. The chain had cut into the creature's flesh, giving rise to a raw, and clearly still suppurating, wound. And strung upon its gore-encrusted links, half buried in the meat of the monster's neck, was a disc of dark metal; a talisman.

He met the monster's gaze once more. There was something there, behind its unblinking eyes. Something akin to human intelligence.

"Sven?" Jormungard gasped. Unable to help himself, he

took another stumbling step forward.

The beast started, its black lips curling back to exposed blunted tusks, a guttural growl escaping its constricted throat.

Jorm tensed, his grip on his own bloodied blade tightening. Out of the corner of his eye he saw Thorkill take a step forward too.

The beast suddenly rounded on them. For a moment Jormungard thought they were going to have to put an end to the creature there and then.

Giving voice to another angry bark, the hulking beast turned and bounded from the circle of stones, loping away on all fours, chasing the departing mists from whence it had first appeared. Jormungard and Thorkill watched it go.

At long last, when all that remained of the beast's passing were twisting currents in the hazing fog, Jorm turned to his companion, a look of utter disbelief on his face.

"Did you see?"

Thorkill's eyes narrowed. "See what?"

"The chain! The talisman! The beast is… was…" Jorm faltered, struggling to find the words, a part of him unable to believe the truth he was attempting to utter.

"Sven of Skarrsgard?"

"Yes."

"Once, maybe, but not anymore." Thorkill's words were like an icy dagger to the gut. "The corrupting power of the talisman has changed him. Now he is Nam'karill, 'Who Walks With Death'."

Jorm looked from his mentor back to the enveloping mountain mists. If Sven was the beast, and it had been the dark power of Namarr that had changed him so horribly, reshaping his physical form, then had it been mere coincidence that caused the beast to arrive when it did, when they needed its brute strength and savagery the most? Or had Sven purposely led them to this place, at this time?

Had Sven witnessed the massacre of the farmer and his

family at the hands of the Namarrans? The injuries Thorkill had taken to have been caused by an animal's claws could equally have been caused by the cultists' bear-claw knives and sabre-fang weapons. Had the slaughter of those innocents in truth been the handiwork of the death-worshippers, as Jormungard had at first suspected?

Clearly enough of the man the monster had once been remained for the Sven-Become-Beast to understand that it could not break the Namarrans' power over it without the assistance of others, but also knowing that once that power was diminished, it might too have its revenge.

But Jormungard knew he could not leave things like this between them. Sven had become a creature born of corruption, altered by the death-dealing power of Namarr. He would never be human again, and the longer he remained an animal the more like an animal he would become, losing whatever semblance of humanity currently remained within his magic-warped mind. It could only be a matter of time before the beast killed again, and next time Jorm could not be sure it would only be death-worshipping cultists that fell victim to its untamed wrath and savage hunger.

No, he could not let his former friend go on like this. He owed him that much.

A mournful howl cut through the chill air and an icy breezy shifted the inconstant mists again. And there, atop a rocky tor on an escarpment above the standing stones, the beast crouched, its misshapen head thrown back, howling its challenge to the skies.

The Sven-Beast was waiting for them.

Jormungard, with the assistance of his mentor Thorkill, would meet that challenge, so he now swore. And when the time came, they would not be found wanting.

For to die in battle, meeting his end with honour and his soul shriven, that was what Sven Skarrsgard would have wished for. That was what every warrior of Farrhold wished for.

"He who hunts his enemies with vengenance in his heart walks with death.
And he who walks with death shall never find peace."

– old Farrmen saying

Skipping Town

Joe Abercrombie

"Maybe we should just skip town." said Javre.

"Oh no, no, no, not this time," Shev snapped back at her. "You can't just career through life leaving the wreckage of your mistakes behind you."

A silence as they hurried on through the shadows, Shev having to half-jog to keep up as Javre ploughed ahead with immense strides, brow furrowed in thought. "What is it that we've been doing this past year, then?"

"Well... we've... That's just my point! We can't *keep* doing it."

"I see. So we give Tumnor his jewel, and we collect the promised money, and we pay our gambling debts –"

"*Your* gambling debts," snapped Shev.

"And then what, we put down roots here?" Javre raised one red brow at the crumbling buildings, the rubbish-strewn street, a fish-stinking beggar hacking out diseased coughs in a doorway.

"Well, no. We move on."

"And what we left behind us tonight?" Javre jerked her head the way they'd come. "Would you call that wreckage?"

"I would call that..." Shev wondered how much this particular truth would stretch before it tore to bits. "A series of mishaps."

"It looked like wreckage to me. I mean, once the front of the mansion collapsed, you'd have to call that wreckage, no?"

Shev glanced quickly over her shoulder yet again to make sure no one was following. "I suppose an uncharitable speaker could describe it so."

"Then explain to me, if you would, Shevedieh, how your

way differs from mine, except that we leave town with less money?"

"We leave with less enemies as well!" snapped Shev. "I tire of dropping off a new score in every shit hole we pass through like a rabbit leaves droppings! Sooner or later I might need a good shit hole to pass through again. All the damn *enemies*. I wake up sweating, you know, in the night!"

"That's all that spicy food," said Javre. "I don't know how often I've warned you about your diet. And enemies are a good thing. Enemies show you make... an *impression*."

"Oh, you make an impression, all right, that I would never deny. You made a hell of an impression on those boys tonight."

Javre grinned a mass of white teeth as she punched one scabbed fist into one calloused palm with a smack like a door slamming. "I did, didn't I?"

"I'm a thief, Javre, not... whatever you are. I'm supposed to keep a low profile."

"Ah!" Javre raised that same red brow again as she glanced sideways. "Hence all the black."

"And it does look rather well on me, I think you'd have to agree."

"You certainly are a shadowy and seductive corruptor of innocent maidenhood!" Javre playfully jogged Shev in the ribs with an elbow and nearly sent her careering into the nearest wall, then caught her by the hand and dragged her into a crushing embrace, her cheek squashed into Javre's armpit. "We'll do it your way then, Shevedieh, my friend! Straight and true and morally upright, just the way a thief should be! We'll pay your debts, then let's get drunk and find some men."

Shev was still struggling to get a breath in after that elbow. "What is it exactly that you think I'd do with them?"

Javre grinned. "The men would be for me. I am a woman of Thond, and have grand appetites. You can keep watch."

"My towering thanks for the immensity of that honour," said Shev, slipping from under the weight of Javre's mightily muscled arm.

"It's the least I could do. You've been a fine sidekick so far."

"I thought this was an equal partnership."

"All the best sidekicks think that," said Javre, striding towards the front door of the Weeping Slaver, its sign hanging precariously from a rusting pole by one loop.

Shev caught Javre's arm and, by hanging off it with all her weight and digging her heels into the mud, managed to stop her taking the next step. "I have a feeling Tumnor will be expecting us."

"That was the arrangement." Javre looked down at her, puzzled.

"Given that he was less than entirely forthcoming about the job, it may be that he'll try to double-cross us."

Javre frowned. "You think he might break the agreement?"

"He didn't mention the traps, did he?" asked Shev, still heaving at Javre's arm. "Or the long drop? Or the wall? Or the dogs? And he said two guards, not twelve."

The muscles worked as Javre clenched her jaw. "He said nothing about that sorcerer either."

"Exactly," Shev managed to gasp, every sinew trembling with effort

"Breath of the Mother, you're right."

Shev breathed a sigh of relief and slowly stood, patting Javre's arm as she released it. "I'll sneak in by the back and make sure that —"

Javre gave her a huge smile. "The Lioness of Hoskopp never uses the back door!" And she sprang up the steps, raised one boot, kicked the front door splintering from its hinges and sprang inside, the filthy tails of her once-white coat flapping after.

Shevedieh gave brief but serious consideration to sprinting off down the street, then sighed and crept up the steps after her.

The Weeping Slaver wasn't the most auspicious of settings, though Shev had to admit she'd been in worse. Indeed she'd spent most of the last few years in worse.

Size it had, big as a barn with a balcony at first floor level, ill-lit by a vast round chandelier with smoking candles in stained glass cups. The floor was covered in dirty straw and a mismatched jumble of chairs and tables, a warped counter down one side with the cheapest spirits of a dozen dozen cultures stacked on shelves behind.

The place smelled of smoke and sweat, of spilled drinks and sprayed vomit, of desperation and wasted chances, and was very much as it had been three nights ago when they took the job, just before Javre lost half their promised earnings at dice. There was one clear difference, however. That night it had overflowed with scum of every kind. Tonight there appeared to be just the one patron.

Tumnor sat at a table in the middle of the room, a fixed grin on his plump face and a sheen of sweat across his forehead. He looked extremely nervous, even for a man perpetrating a double-cross on a pair of notorious thieves. He looked in imminent fear of his life.

"It's a trap," he grunted through his clenched teeth, without moving his hands from the table top.

"That we had gathered, fiend!" said Javre.

"No," he grunted, eyes swivelling wildly sideways, then back to them, then sideways again. "A *trap.*"

That was when Shev noticed that his hands were nailed to the table. She followed his glance, past a large brown stain on the floor that looked suspiciously like blood, and into the shadows. She saw a figure there. The glint of eyes. The glimmer of steel. A man poised and ready. Now she took in other tell-tale gleams in the dark corners of the inn – an axeman wedged behind a drinks cabinet, the nose of a flatbowman peeking into the light on a balcony above, a pair of boots sticking out from the door to the cellar which she deduced must still be attached to the dead legs of one of Tumnor's hired men. Her heart sank. She hated fighting. She wasn't bad at it, but she hated it, and she had the strong feeling she was going to be fighting very soon.

"It would appear," murmured Shev, leaning towards Javre, "that the scum who double-crossed us have been double-crossed by some other scum."

"Yes," whispered Javre. Her whispers were louder than the usual speaking voice of most people. "I find myself conflicted. Who to kill first?"

"Perhaps we could talk our way out?" Shev ventured hopefully. It was important to stay hopeful.

"Shevedieh, we must face the possibility that there will be violence."

"Your prescience is uncanny."

"When things get underway, I would be ever so grateful if you could attend to the flatbowman on the balcony just there?"

"Understood," muttered Shev.

"Most of the rest you can probably leave to me."

"Too kind."

And now the unmistakable tread of heavy boots and jingling metal echoed from the back of the inn, and Tumnor's face grew even more drawn, beads of sweat rolling down his cheeks.

Javre narrowed her eyes. "And the villain is revealed."

"Villains tend to love a bit of theatre, though, don't they?" muttered Shev.

When she emerged into the shifting candlelight she was lean and very tall. Almost as tall as Javre, perhaps, her black hair chopped short, one sinewy arm bare and covered in blue tattoos and the other in plates of battered steel, a gauntlet like a claw at the end, curving nails of sharpened metal clicking as she walked. Her green, green eyes glinted as she smiled towards them.

"It has been a while, Javre."

Javre pushed her lips out. "Oh, arse of the Mother," she said. "Well met, Weylen. Or badly met, at least."

"You know her?" muttered Shev.

Javre winced. "I must admit she is not an entire stranger to me. She was Thirteenth of the Fifteen."

"I am tenth now," said Weylen. "Since you killed Hanama

139

and Birke."

"I offered them the same choice I will soon offer you." Javre shrugged her broad shoulders. "They chose death."

"Er..." Shev held up one gloved finger. "If I may ask... What the hell are we talking about?"

The woman's emerald green eyes moved across to her. "She did not tell you?"

"Tell me what?"

Javre winced even more. "Those friends of mine, I mentioned, from the temple."

"The temple in Thond?"

"Yes. They're not so much friends."

"So... neutral towards you, then?" Shev ventured, hopefully. It was important to stay hopeful.

"More enemies," said Javre.

"I see."

"The fifteen Knights Templar of the Golden Order are forbidden to leave the temple except on the orders of the High Priestess. On pain of death."

"And I'm guessing you had no such permission to go?" asked Shevedieh, looking around at all the sharpened steel on display.

"Not in so many words."

"Not in so many?"

"Not in any."

"Her life is forfeit," said Weylen. "As is the life of anyone who offers her succour." And she extended her steel-taloned forefinger and drove it into the top of Tumnor's head. He made a sound like a fart, then dropped forward, blood bubbling from the neat wound in his pate.

Shev held her empty palms up. "Well I've offered no succour, that I promise you. I like a succouring just as much as the next girl, if not a good deal more, but Javre?" She worked her hand gently, making sure the mechanism was engaged, hoping that it looked like nothing more than an expressive gesture. "No offence to her, I daresay she'll make several men a wonderful husband some day, but she's not my type at all." Shev raised her brows at Weylen who, it had to be said, was much closer to her type, those eyes of hers really were something. "And, you know, not wanting to blow my own horn, but once I *offer* succour? I generally get all the succouring one woman can –"

"She means help," said Javre.

"Eh?"

"Succour. It's not a sexual thing."

"Oh."

"Kill them," said Weylen.

The flatbowman raised his weapon, candlelight glinting on the sharpened tip of the loaded bolt, as several other thugs burst from the shadows, brandishing a selection of unpleasant-looking weapons. Though what weapons look pleasant, when brandished at you?

Shev twisted her wrist, and the throwing knife sprang into her hand. Unfortunately, the spring was wound too tight, and it shot straight through her clutching fingers and thudded into the ceiling, neatly cutting the rope that held the chandelier. Pulleys whirred and the huge thing began to plummet towards them.

The flatbowman smiled as he squeezed the trigger, aiming straight at Shev's heart. A thug raised a great axe above his head. Then a great weight of wood, glass and wax crashed down upon him, crushing him flat, the flatbow bolt shuddering into the side of the chandelier an instant before it hit the ground with a shattering impact, taking two more thugs with it and sending dust, splinters, shards and candles flying.

"Shit," whispered Shev, standing stunned and blinking as the echoes faded. She and Javre stood together in the centre of the round chandelier's circular wreckage, apparently entirely unhurt.

He didn't raise his hand too often, but when he did Blind Crin, the God of Small Chances, was a hell of a patron god to have.

Shev gave a whoop of triumph which turned, as many of her

triumphant whoops did, to a gurgle of horror as an uncrushed thug sprang over the ruins of the chandelier with his sword a blur of hard-swung steel. She leaped back, tripped over a table, fell over a chair, rolled, saw a blade flash past, scrambled under another table, dust filtering around as someone beat it with an axe. She heard crashes, clashes, loud swearing, and all the familiar noise of a fight in an inn.

Bloody hell, Shev hated fights. *Hated* them. Considering how much she hated them, she got into a lot of them. Partnering up with Javre had not helped her record, in that regard or, at a brief assay, any other. She slid out from under the table, sprang up, was punched in the face and sprawled painfully against the counter, spluttering and wobbling and trying to blink the tears from her eyes.

A snarling thug came at her overhand with a knife and she jerked back at the waist, steel flashing by her and thunking into the counter. She jerked forward and butted him in the face, knocked him staggering with his hands to his nose, snatched his knife from the wood and sent it whirling through the air in one smooth motion, burying itself in the flatbowman's forehead as he levelled his reloaded weapon. His eyes rolled up and he toppled off the balcony and onto a table below, sending bottles and glasses flying.

"What a knife thrower," Shev muttered to herself, "I could have – urgh!" Her smugness was knocked out of her along with her breath as a man cannoned into her side and sent her reeling.

He was a big man of surpassing ugliness, swinging this way and that with a mace almost as big and ugly as he was, smashing glasses and furniture, filling the air with splinters. Shev whimpered every swear she could think of as she weaved and dodged, scrambling and jumping desperately, not even getting the chance to look for an opening, running steadily out of space and time as she was herded towards a corner.

He raised his mace to strike, broad face twisted with rage.

"Wait!" she wailed, pointing over his shoulder.

It was amazing how often that worked. He jerked his head to look, pausing just long enough for her to knee him in the fruits with all her strength. He gasped, tottered, dropped to his knees, and she whipped out her dagger and stabbed him sharply at the meeting of his neck and his shoulder. He groaned, tried to stand, then sprawled on his face, welling blood.

"Sorry," said Shev. "Damn it, I'm sorry." And she was, just as she always was. But it was better to be sorry than dead, just as it always was. That lesson she had learned long ago.

No further fights presented themselves. Javre stood by the chandelier's wreckage, her dirty white coat spotted with blood and the twisted bodies of a dozen thugs scattered about her. She had another bent over with his head wedged in the crook of one arm, and yet another pinned against a table by his neck at arm's length, kicking and struggling to absolutely no effect.

"Things must be going downhill." And with a twitch of her face and a flex of her muscular arm she snapped the first man's neck and let his body flop to the floor. "The temple used to stretch to a better class of thug." She dipped her shoulder and flung the other one bodily through a window and into the street, tearing the shutters free, his despairing squeal cut off as his head tore a chunk from a supporting pillar with him.

"The best I could find at short notice," said Weylen, reaching behind her back. "But it always was going to come to this." And she drew a curved sword, the long blade seeming to Shev's eye to be made of a writhing black smoke.

"It need not," said Javre. "You have two choices, just as Hanama and Birke did. You can go back to Thond. Go back to the High Priestess and tell her I will be no one's slave. Not ever. Tell her I am free."

"Free? Ha! Do you suppose the High Priestess will accept that answer?"

Javre shrugged. "Then tell her you couldn't find me. Tell her whatever you please."

Weylen's mouth bitterly twisted. "And what would be my

other —"

"I show you the sword," said Javre, and there was a popping of joints as she shifted her shoulders, boots scraping into a wider stance, and from inside her coat she drew a bundle, long and slender, a thing of bandages and rags, but near the end Shev caught the glint of gold.

Weylen lifted her chin, and did not so much smile as show her teeth. "You know there is no choice for us."

Javre gave a nod. "I know. Shevedieh?"

"Yes?" croaked Shev.

"Close your eyes."

She jammed them shut as Weylen sprang over a table with a fighting scream, high, harsh and horrible. She heard quick footsteps on the boards, rushing up with inhuman speed.

There was a ringing of metal and Shev flinched as a sudden bright light shone pink through her lids. A scraping, and a croaking gasp, and the light was gone.

"Shevedieh."

"Yes?" she croaked.

"You can open them now."

Javre still held the bundle in one hand, torn rags flapping about it. With the other she held Weylen up, her limp arms flopping back, steel cased knuckles scraping the floor. There was a red stain on her chest, but she seemed peaceful. Aside from the black blood pouring from her back to spatter on the boards in spurts and dashes.

"They will find you, Javre," she whispered, blood specking her lips.

"I know," said Javre. "And they each will have their choice." She lowered Weylen to the boards, into the spreading pool of her blood, and gently brushed her eyelids closed over her green, green eyes.

"May the Mother have mercy on you," she murmured.

"May she have mercy on us first," muttered Shevedieh, wiping the blood from under her throbbing nose as she approached the counter, dagger at the ready, and peered over. The inn's owner was cowering behind, and cringed even further as he saw her. "Don't kill me! Please don't kill me!"

"I won't." She hid the dagger behind her back and showed him her open palm. "No one will. It's alright, they've..." She wanted to say 'gone', but, glancing around the wreckage of the inn, was forced to say, rather croakily, "died. You can get up."

He slowly stood, trembling, peered over the counter, and his jaw dropped open. "By the..."

"I must apologise for the damage," said Javre. "It looks worse than it is."

Part of the far wall, riddled with cracks, chose that moment to collapse into the street, sending up a cloud of stone dust and making Shev step back coughing.

Javre pushed her lips out and put one considering fingertip against them. "Perhaps it is exactly as bad as it looks."

Shev heaved up an aching sigh. Not the first she'd given in the company of Javre, Lioness of Hoskopp, and she doubted it would be the last. "What's a girl to do?" she muttered. And she pulled the pouch out from her shirt, undid the strings, and let the jewel roll out onto the split counter, where it sat glinting.

"For your trouble," she said to the gawping innkeeper. Then she wiped her dagger on the jacket of the nearest man and slid it back into its sheath, turned without another word, stepped over the splintered remains of the door and out into the street.

Dawn was coming. The sun bringing the faintest grey smudge to the eastern sky above the ramshackle roofs. Shev took a long breath, and shook her head at it. "Damn it, Shevedieh," she whispered to herself, "but a conscience is a hell of an encumbrance to a thief."

She heard Javre's heavy footsteps behind, felt her looming presence at her shoulder, heard her deep voice as she leaned to speak in Shev's ear.

"Would you like to skip town now?"

Shev nodded. "Yes, I think we'd better."

145

The Land of the Eagle

Juliet McKenna

"... and the brass eagle stood proud on the highest pinnacle of the castle gate, overlooking the town grown up around the margrave's walls. Flying high on our flags, it was the token of our luck and so the eagle itself was carried into battle against the River Kingdom's army..."

Nedirin ducked his head to hide a yawn. He'd had a tiring day, herding obstinate goats in these gullies and thickets between the river and the uplands. Now that the herds were penned for the night with the dogs on watch, he wanted to wrap himself in his blankets and yield to his weariness. He'd heard old Thulle's stories so often that he could recite them in his sleep.

They all could, from the dog boys younger than Nedi to the grey-bearded herd masters as old as his grandsire. Their town had yielded to the men of the River Kingdom when Thulle was still a babe in arms.

If someone other than Thulle was telling the tale, the brass eagle had been cast into a charnel pit with the battlefield dead, or fallen into the river, or been stolen by the Paramount King's men to be thrown in their furnaces far away to the south, in their capital city where the ruddy brown Tane flowing from the upland plains met the pale silty waters of the mighty Dore. That distant river cut through grasslands bounded only by the horizon to east and west and by mighty forests to the south. So folk said but no one from Hatalys had ever travelled so far to seek their fortune and returned to confirm such stories of woodlands without end.

Still, listening to old Thulle was the price which Nedi must pay for a seat by the fire pit, and the weather was growing colder as the hazel and ash trees turned to autumn gold. So he hid his boredom and edged closer to the embers.

"If the eagle ever returns," Thulle continued, "Hatalys will be free."

That was the one thing which all the tales agreed on, though ever since he was small Nedi had wondered how that could happen if the bird had been melted down and turned into door knobs or buttons for fancy waistcoats.

"Give it up, for pity's sake," growled Uderil from the far side of the stone-lined pit.

Some of the men who had already forsaken the fireside for their bedrolls murmured agreement. Nedi's mother's youngest brother and his father's next elder were among them. They had promised to watch over him as he tended his family's goats while his father's broken ankle mended. They couldn't afford to abandon this last trip into the hills to fatten the billygoats born in the spring and now destined for salting and smoking after autumn's slaughters.

Uderil was still speaking. "I'll take the River Kingdom's grain and fine horses and black powder weapons to keep moor dogs from killing my goats over foraging for nuts and fruit and hunting hill elk with bow and arrow."

Seeing Thulle's eyes widen with outrage, Nedi gazed mute into the flames, keeping his face as blank as a freshly wiped slate. Antagonizing the spiteful old man was never a good idea. Nedi would wager his best gloves that Uderil's most highly prized goats would lose their bells and stray over the next few days or fall victim to stinking flux. Not that anyone ever caught Thulle wreaking such revenge.

"It's worth it, is it?" A new voice spoke up from the shadows on the far side of the fire. "Paying for black powder and lead shot carried a hundred leagues upstream? Paying tithes in coin and in kind to the Paramount King to feed and clothe the garrison who watch over us? Bending our necks to the justice of

148

strangers?"

"Getting our necks stretched, more like," Plore said quietly.

Nedi remembered his father and mother talking in low tones, sitting in their chairs on either side of the stove at home, the evening after Plore's cousin had been hanged. They hadn't realised Nedi was listening, crouched behind the curtain hiding the stair to the loft where he and his brothers and sisters slept, four to a bed. Nedi had got too used to sleeping alone in his blankets now that he was old enough to go herding goats with their father through the summer, only returning to the town each market day.

Plore's cousin had been a violent fool. His parents agreed on that. But did he deserve to hang for being the only man caught by the troopers after a drunken brawl where another bully had died? Any one of twenty men could have struck the fatal blow. Even the dead man's brothers and wife said so.

Father recalled the old margrave's lesser sentences. A man got a chance to mend his ways if he was punished with a flogging or a spell in the stocks or the pillory. But the new margrave had gone south and the castellan handing down judgements stamped with the Paramount King's seal only ever sent men to the gallows.

Nedi's mother was more distressed to hear that the hanged man's body had been given to the Horned God's temple, for the masked priests' secret rites before he was buried. Plore's family would have laid him out in a funerary gully, she wept, to be unmade by the beasts and birds of hill and valley to release his soul.

Nedi had crept silently back to the crowded bed, privately vowing to never fall foul of the Paramount King's garrison.

"Granted, there's bitter to go with the sweet." Uderil glanced at Plore, apologetic. "But we have to live each day as best we can."

"Do we?" the voice challenged. "Can't we make our own choices?"

"How?" Zanner, his mother's brother, sat up.

Nedi was startled to hear the hope in his young uncle's words.

"We look to our own lore," Thulle said robustly. "We all know that the eagle flew away when the Horned God's priests conjured monsters to break down the castle's gates. The king of the skies went to rally the beasts and birds to fight with our forefathers. Before he could bring them salvation though, the fools had surrendered for lack of faith!"

Along with everyone else, Nedi looked at Thulle. Only the crackle of burning wood broke the silence around the campfire.

Did the old man truly believe that the Horned God's priests had summoned up ogres to smash the city's defences? That griffins had soared up to the ramparts, rending the brave defenders with deadly beaks and talons?

"The eagle could win back our freedom, together with our own courage and resolve." The stranger walked into the soft orange light, carrying a heavy sacking-swathed bundle.

Uderil shuffled aside and the man knelt to begin unwrapping whatever it was. He was dressed much the same as everyone else; buff leather breeches and high topped boots to foil the thorn thickets, a leather jerkin over woollen shirts layered to keep out the cold. He had sturdy gloves tucked through his belt and a knitted cap warming his head. His complexion was weather-worn, his brows and stubble dark and his eyes brown, like everyone Nedi had known all his life.

The herdsmen all gasped as the last fold of sacking fell away. A statue shone golden in the firelight. It was an eagle rearing upright with mighty wings outspread and its head turned to one side. Flowing lines marked every detail of its feathers while carved facets gave the eye turned towards Nedi a piercing glint.

"The king of the skies has returned!" Thulle was so ecstatic that he almost fell into the fire pit as he scrambled to his feet. As it was, he brushed so close to the flames that Nedi smelled leather scorching. Tears glistening on his wrinkled cheeks, the old man dropped to his knees before the brass statue.

It was a sizeable thing, at least a cubit tall, with the bird perched on a square pedestal which had four stubby feet. Thulle stretched out a trembling hand only to snatch it back before his fingertips touched the gleaming metal.

"Where did you find that?" Uderil wondered aloud.

"How is that effigy going to restore our liberties?" Uncle Zanner demanded. "Who are you?"

"My name is Sincai," the newcomer told him, "and I believe this statue can help Hatalys regain its freedom if you men are brave enough to follow me to the town."

"We will follow you anywhere!" Thulle still gazed at the statue, rapt.

"Speak for yourself," Uderil snapped.

"Hear me out before you make any decision." The newcomer surveyed the assembled men. Even those who'd already fallen asleep were tossing aside their blankets, wide-eyed and open-mouthed.

"The River Kingdom has overreached itself." Sincai rose and tugged a long stick from the firewood piled close to the pit. He scraped swift lines in the dirt.

"Here is the Tane coming down from the plains and here is Hatalys. Here is the Dore, cutting the grassland from sunset to sunrise."

Then, to Nedi's surprise, he drew a second river joining the Dore far to the west.

"This is the Fasil and the town of Gotesh." Sincai dug a little hole in the ground where the two rivers met. "That has been a River Kingdom town for five generations but Hedvin and Bastrys —" he marked two more towns some distance further upstream on each river "— they drove the Paramount King's armies away in their grandfathers' day and the plainsmen have never returned."

He swept the stick across to the other side of his dirt map and scraped four rivers fanning out eastward from the River Dore. "You've heard tell of the Nalgeh Marsh? It's bounded by

151

three cities, Scafet, Julach and Avelsir. They have never fallen to
the plainsmen. The most westerly River Kingdom town is here –"
He stabbed the dirt a good way short of the sprawling marsh. "–
Usenas."

"What has this to do with us?" Zanner asked impatiently.

Sincai drew a slow circle around his map. Nedi saw the
stick's tip pass through the marks signifying Gostesh in the east
and Usenas in the west. It cut through the writhing line of the
Tane to the south and east of Hatalys. The triangle of land
between the Tane and the Dore, where the capital city ruled over
the bridges and all river trade up and down stream, was at the
centre.

"Here's where the River Mothar joins the Tane." Sincai drew
a second line coming down from the north. It met the Tane just
where the circle crossed the river. "Where the plainsmen hold
Mithess."

Nedi longed to visit Mithess. The town was only four days
travel down river by barge. Three days, so Uncle Zanner said,
when the spring swelled the Tane with snowmelt from the
mountains far beyond the high plains. When he was older, his
father said. If his mother agreed.

"Wait." Nedi's Uncle Isom walked forward to study the
scrawled map. "We're the only town outside that circle which is
under the River Kingdom's heel?"

Sincai nodded. "Anything beyond is too far from the
Kingdom's heart, as the folk of Hedvin and Bastrys showed and
so did the men and women of Scafet and the Nalgeh Mire. When
their people rebelled, the Paramount King's cavalry couldn't
arrive in time. Not before the townsfolk drove out all those
sworn to the Paramount King."

Sincai raised a warning finger as the men murmured
surprised approval.

"They let them leave with food for themselves and their
horses. They didn't put the River Kingdom castellan or garrison
to the sword or drag them to the gallows. They didn't ravage the

Horned God's temple or tear down the Sun Goddess' statues. They simply restored their old rites alongside the new."

He raised his voice over Thulle's muttered outrage.

"They chose trustworthy men to serve as constables to keep order in every district and to make up a jury for an assize at every third full moon, with a judge chosen by drawing lots among them. Merchants honoured their agreements with traders up and downstream. They proved that they did not need the Paramount King's rule to secure peace and prosperity so he had no excuse to send his cavalry against them."

"Good for them," one of the old men sneered.

"We could do the same," Sincai assured him. "Winter is nearly here. Drive out the castellan and his men and even if one of them sends a pigeon flying with the news, the Paramount King's army won't get here before the first snows fall."

"The castellan in Mithess could send his cavalry to join forces with the men we've thrown out," Uderil countered.

"As long as Hatalys men hold the walls and gates, all they can do is sit outside and battle the frosts," Sincai insisted

"While they wonder if Mithess' people are contemplating their own rebellion," Isom mused, "while their garrison's elsewhere."

"Quite so." Sincai grinned.

"The harvests are all in," someone beyond the fire observed. "Even if we couldn't go hunting for fear of the Paramount King's men, we wouldn't starve within the town."

"The storehouses will only stay full until the castellan starts sending barges downstream," Zanner said abruptly.

Nedi saw the men stiffen and glanced at each other, grim-faced. Nedi remembered the hungry days at the end of last winter when the snows and the river ice had endured for a full half-moon longer than usual.

Even the thriftiest bakers had run out of flour so there was no bread and the men couldn't hunt or fish to ease their wives' struggles to eke out their pantries' dwindling supplies. Old

Mistress Tigad, who ran the dame-school where Nedi had learned his letters and numbers, had been found dead and cold in her bed.

"Who are you?" The question was out before he realised he had spoken aloud.

Sincai smiled. "I'm the man who's spent these past eight years sneaking out beyond the walls to search every nook and gully for the place where the eagle must be buried, after hearing my grandfather's tale of his father carrying it away for safekeeping."

He looked at the rest of the men. "My family name is Dorsin. We're leather workers and we live around the Aspen Gate."

"I've sold hides to a Rever Dorsin," Uderil said thoughtfully.

"The eagle wasn't carried off. It flew away." Thulle was still gazing, entranced, at the statue.

No one paid him any heed. Uncle Isom looked at Plore and Nedi saw something pass unspoken between them.

"What do you have in mind?" Isom asked cautiously.

"Men were hanged for talking treason in the old margrave's day." Plore tossed another log into the firepit sending up a shower of sparks.

Sincai nodded. "We cannot debate and discuss our plans in the streets and taverns. Word will get back to the garrison and the castellan will send ten men to seize each one of us. We need to strike as unexpected as lightening and in as many places as we can. Let the garrison try stamping out ten different fires when twenty more have sprung up before the first is quelled."

"Fires?" Thulle looked around with unnerving eagerness.

"No one will be lighting real fires, you old fool," Uderil said scornfully.

"Just kindling a lust for freedom in people's hearts." Challenge shone bright in Sincai's eyes.

"Fine words," Uderil observed. "What do you actually want us to do?"

"Raise a cry for Hatalys and the eagle," Sincai said promptly. "Rouse everyone to come to the castle and see it for themselves. Then we'll tell the castellan and his men that they're no longer welcome. If they come out to confront us, they'll be outnumbered and we can drive them to the gates. If they hide behind the castle's walls, we bar the gates to keep them inside until they've emptied their store rooms. Then the price of food and drink will be leaving the town."

"Why should we be the ones to start this landslide?" Zanner demanded.

"Who goes around the town more unnoticed than goat herders and their wives?" Sincai grinned.

He was right, Nedi realised. Day in and day out, men too old to endure these hills drove freshly purchased beasts to each district's butchers, from the tender and sweet-fleshed kids to the aged nannies destined for the stewpot. The women sold milk and cheeses from door to door each morning, leaving the dogs and younger children watching over the milking flocks grazing around the town walls.

"The townsfolk will laugh in our faces," one of the grey beards prophesied.

To Nedi's surprise, Sincai shrugged. "Then what have you lost? What have you risked? Calling folk to come and see a marvel isn't treason. You won't even look foolish when the mockers learn that the eagle is there for all to see."

Uncle Isom raised a hand. "How do you propose to get something that size back up onto the gatehouse pinnacle?"

"We need someone who can climb." Sincai looked around the fire. "That's my other reason for coming out here."

Muted laughter eased the tension a little. Goat men were well known for their surefootedness. They had to be as nimble as their charges, given the beasts' perverse ambition to scale the steepest crags in search of forage. Come the winter, when the snows penned everyone up within the town, Nedi's father and uncles mended leaking roofs and rebuilt unsteady chimneys.

Abruptly he realised that everyone was looking at him. Despite the heat from the fire, Nedi felt chilled to the bone.

"The lad's the best climber here." Thulle's unblinking gaze was profoundly unnerving.

Nedi silently cursed his own readiness to help the old man rescue a cragfast goat the day before last.

"The garrison would just think some lads were larking about," Uderil observed slowly.

"I couldn't!" Nedi's voice rose embarrassingly and he swallowed hard. "Not without my father's say-so."

"Your father would agree in a heartbeat." Plore looked steadily at him and Isom nodded.

Zanner grinned. "You'll be up there, back down and away before any River Kingdom man can find a foothold."

"If we're to do this, let's do it sooner than later." Plore rose to his feet.

Half the other men joined him, their faces eager in the firelight. Did that mean it was agreed? Was there to be no show of hands? No further discussion? Nedi wanted to ask but the words froze in his throat.

"If we leave now, we can be at the gates by daybreak," Sincai said swiftly. "You can go and wake your wives and all spread the word."

"We'll tell your father and mother," Isom assured Nedi.

"If they forbid it, we'll come at once to call you down," Zanner promised.

"We'll keep the goats penned until you come back," one of the greybeards announced. "The dog boys can cut fodder and shovel shit for a few days."

Nedi saw the other men were already rolling up their blankets and securing their few possessions in the bags which each herder carried. He rubbed a shaking hand across his face and felt the prickle of bristles. So much for his pride in those. At the moment, he'd give anything to still be a smooth-faced dog boy.

"Come on, young hero." Sincai was at his side. "Don't you want to be the man who restores the eagle to Hatalys?"

Nedi supposed that would be something, since it seemed he had no choice. He gazed at the statue. Thulle was wrapping it in the sacking again, as gentle as a man swaddling a baby. "Who's to tote that weight back to the town?"

"I will," Sincai assured him.

Nedi looked up at him. "Where did you find it?"

Sincai grinned. "In the last place I looked."

Before Nedi could press the stranger, Isom came over. "Your father will be proud of you."

And that was that. The rest of the night passed more quickly than Nedi could have imagined. The men all knew the path and then the familiar road and the air was cold enough to turn muddy ruts sufficiently firm for them all to find sure footing. The moon rode high in the sky, round and full, to light their way.

By the time the sky paled, the town's walls cut a jag-toothed line of darkness across the horizon. Nedi was stumbling with exhaustion but he still kept pace with his uncles at the head of the straggling column. Though his fear of falling behind and being lost on the road was fading, dread at what was to come took its place.

Someone cried out from the rearguard, chagrined "The gates won't unlock till dawn!"

"They'll open to me," Sincai shouted over his shoulder.

Nedi caught a glimpse of his face in the strengthening light. The stranger had carried the eagle's great weight all this way yet his pace was unflagging, his certainty undimmed. Nedi began to wonder if this madcap plan might actually succeed.

Reaching the gatehouse, Sincai knocked with a brisk triple rap on the porter's door cut into the great double oak gates.

Like every boy, Nedi knew that opening the gate was completely forbidden between the dusk and dawn horn calls from the castle. Get locked out, their mothers warned, and you'll be cold and hungry all night, if the moor dogs don't eat you for their own supper.

But the porter's door opened up and a man greeted Sincai with a fervent smile. He ushered them all through the portal before locking it securely again.

The goat herders quickly dispersed, each man heading for home. Zanner clapped Nedi on the shoulder. "We'll meet you at the castle. You need not climb if your parents forbid it."

Before Nedi could answer, he hurried away to catch up with Isom.

"What's the matter?" Sincai murmured.

Nedi turned to see the gatekeeper drawing Sincai close to say something in urgent low tones. Nedi couldn't make any of it out.

"Let me take that." Thulle had been following Sincai so closely that he'd been all but treading in the younger man's footprints. Now he reached out to slip the rope sling supporting the sack-swathed eagle from Sincai's shoulders.

"I'll take the boy to the castle. No one will look twice at an old fool like me."

Sincai let the old man take possession of the bird before looking intently at Nedi. "There's something I must attend to. Can you see this through without me?"

He's asking me, Nedi realised with nervous pride. Not old Thulle. He nodded jerkily, his mouth dry and not just from the long night's journey.

"Come on." Cradling the eagle in his arms, Thulle forced the boy onwards like a grizzled dog herding a young billy goat.

Nedi didn't need any old man chivvying him. He knew the quickest routes to the castle through the town's back alleys, up the sloping streets to the highest point of the wall-girt hill. More than once, he glanced over his shoulder to see Thulle labouring under the eagle's weight and had to slow to let him catch up.

All the while, the daylight was strengthening. Nedi saw the first signs of households waking; threads of smoke from chimneys and upper shutters unlatched as chamber pots were emptied into the gutters below.

The castle's gates were still firmly bolted when they arrived in the cobbled square in front of the ancient stronghold. Twin towers, as round as a drum, stood on either side of the peaked arch of the gate. Above the iron-bound oak, the wall linking the towers stretched upwards high, as sheer as any cliff. Rising like steps on either side, the stonework rose to a pinnacle above the wall-walk which circled the castle's battlements. The highest point was the plinth where the eagle had once stood.

How was he supposed to get up there? One slip and he would plummet to his death. Nedi turned to Thulle. "I can't —"

He gasped as Thulle's knife prodded his belly. The old man had set his burden down and drawn the long, square-ended blade that every goat man carried to hack a path through brush or to cut fodder.

"You will," Thulle assured him.

"Or you'll gut me?" Nedi cried, incredulous. "Who will carry the eagle up then?"

"I'll say a cavalryman killed you." Mad cunning lit the old man's eyes. "While the townsfolk raise a hue and cry, I'll slip inside and go up the stairs."

He was, Nedi realised, quite crazy enough to imagine he could succeed.

"So climb," Thulle snarled, "before your fool of a father arrives or your uncles."

Could he yell for help, Nedi wondered, if the castle gates opened? Not before the old lunatic killed him.

Trembling, he studied the angle between the curve of the closest tower and the wall spanning the gateway. The stonework had been coarse when it was first built and long years of rain and frost had crumbled the mortar away. Moss outlined useful ledges and tufts of yellow grass were seeded here and there. Nedi and his friends had climbed just such weathered stretches of the town wall when they'd been supposedly herding milch goats in the pastures.

"Take it up!" Thulle jabbed his arm with the blade.

Nedi felt a sting like a wasp. Had the lunatic drawn blood? "All right! All right!"

He grabbed the loop of rope and slung it over his shoulder. The eagle wasn't as heavy as he had feared but it was still a substantial burden. He worked his other arm through the second loop to pull the lump of sacking tight between his shoulder blades.

"Let me look for the best route," Nedi snapped as Thulle advanced his menacing blade again.

He contemplated the round towers. They were only two storeys tall, albeit high-ceilinged within. If he could get as far as the top, he could climb up the stepped side of the stonework rising behind the wall-walk easily enough. It wasn't so far. Not as far as he had climbed before in the hills, at least a few times.

Nedi reached for a handhold on the gatehouse wall and found another on the side of the tower. As he pulled himself up, he wedged his toes into convenient cracks. He was grateful for his sturdy boots, though he knew his mother would scold him for scarring the leather.

More handholds presented themselves. Nedi climbed as quickly as he dared to get beyond Thulle's reach, pressing himself close to the masonry.

"You have two hands and two feet. Keep three of the four firmly planted all the time." He recalled his father's words when he'd first been sent up a crag to chivvy a young goat who saw no need to be penned for the night.

Moving more slowly as he climbed higher, the cold stones numbed Nedi's hands. Perversely though, his fingertips felt scoured raw. He should have put on his gloves.

As he stopped for a moment, his foot slipped on sodden moss. The eagle on his back swung sideways, nearly dragging him to his doom. The ropes cut deep into his shoulders, agonizing. Heart pounding, Nedi scrabbled desperately at the masonry. Finally his boot caught on some foothold.

Breathlessly, he tested its strength. Would it bear his weight?

He clung to the stones with one hand and forced his other toe deeper into its own crevice. Snatching for the next handhold, he pulled himself upwards.

Someone exclaimed below in the square, only to be cut short by a warning murmur from a handful of people. Nedi could not look down. He wasn't even sure he could climb back down. He had no choice but to continue with this madness even though his arms and legs were trembling with exertion and fear.

Nedi pressed his face against the cold stone and craned his neck, trying to see upwards without fatally unbalancing himself. He was heartened to see he was closer than he had imagined to the dubious safety of the tower's crenellations.

He could hear baffled voices within the tower. Narrow windows overlooked the approach to the gate and along the length of the castle wall to either side. Nedi guessed that more windows overlooked the courtyard within the gate. The garrison had woken up. What would happen when someone roused the castellan?

Was there someone already up on the tower roof keeping watch? Nedi couldn't see. Would he get to the top only for grasping hands to drag him onto the leaded roof, demanding to know what he was doing?

Then they would seize the eagle and he would have risked his life for nothing. Thulle would never forgive him. Whatever Sincai and the others might say, the old madman would cut his throat one dark night, Nedi was sure of it. Or the castellan's men would throw him off the tower to fall to his death, smashed and broken on the cobbles below.

He began climbing faster regardless. He must climb up onto the gatehouse pinnacle as soon as he possibly could. His only hope of safety was getting higher than bigger and heavier men dared to climb.

There was no one on top of the tower. Nedi hauled himself up and toppled forward between the upthrust masonry to land painfully hard on his numbed yet aching hands. The eagle's weight bore down mercilessly between his shoulder blades.

He scrambled across the tower roof. The stepped facade of the wall spanning the gateway seemed impossibly narrow. How could he hope to do this?

How could he turn back? Hearing shouts in the castle's courtyard, Nedi looked down to see men pointing upwards. He unslung the eagle from his back and looped his arms through the ropes again so that the ungainly bulk was held against his chest. He began climbing up the stepped stones rising behind the wall-walk on his hands and knees, even though the wall itself was barely wide enough.

He kept his gaze fixed on the next step and then the step after that. If he slipped, he would try to fall sideways towards the gatehouse's outer face. He might just land on the wall-walk. Capture and a broken arm or leg would be a fair trade for his life.

Nedi reached the top, breathless and sweating despite the cold air. Agonisingly careful, he sat astride the last stone below the plinth and gripped the wall with his knees and ankles. The sacking-wrapped bundle sat safe within the circle of his arms as he clung onto the plinth for added reassurance.

Now he dared to look down. Outside the castle, he saw a crowd with their pale faces turned upwards and hands pointing just like the garrison men. They had all come to see the eagle returned. So Nedi had better oblige them.

He began picking at the ropes with his sore, cold fingers. His breath came faster, harsher, as he broke his nails on the knots pulled tight by the eagle's weight. Finally the hemp yielded and Nedi could unwrap the coarse sacking to reveal the eagle's head.

Close to, it was crudely made. Rough edges on the cast metal hadn't been filed smooth. The incised lines marking its feathers were uneven and incomplete. Its head and beak looked more like a crow than an eagle and Nedi had never seen any real bird spread its wings in such ridiculously rounded fashion. Its legs were slightly different lengths with clawed feet seemingly melting into the square pedestal.

The crowd below began cheering nevertheless, as the strengthening sunlight struck golden fire from the brass. So now Nedi had to secure the thing in its plinth. He could see the four holes where the brass pedestal's stubby feet would hold it secure. He held on tight with his knees and feet as he lifted the eagle up.

His arms burned, already so tired from climbing. Nedi was seized with terror. He wasn't going to be able to do this. At the last moment, with his last despairing effort, he lifted it a little higher and further. As his strength failed, the pedestal's brass feet slid into their sockets.

A triumphant cry rose up from the crowd below the gate. Newcomers were swelling the tumult. Now pots and pans clashed loudly together, punctuating a rhythmic chant.

Rough music. Nedi had heard it a few times. When a man persisted in beating his wife. When a mother let her children go hungry and barefoot. When some adulterous couple dishonoured their vows and their spouses. When remonstration had failed. When help was rejected or abused. Then the clamour would start. It would last night after night until exhaustion wore away defiance and the guilty sneaked away with nothing but the clothes on their back.

Did the River Kingdom men understand? Did they realise that the Hatalys folk were telling them to leave? That they would brook no refusal? Nedi looked down into the castle's courtyard and shuddered so violently that he almost lost his balance. He clung to the stone, pressing his cheek against the eagle's plinth.

The garrison had drawn up in serried ranks. They were loading their hackbuts with black powder and lead shot. Nedi saw faint wisps of smoke rising from the coiled lengths of alchemist's twine which each man would clamp in his weapon's serpentine lock. Uncle Isom had shown him how a pull on the trigger snapped the curved lock down to ignite the priming powder in the flash pan. That prompted the black powder in the iron barrel to fire quicker than blinking.

Nedi was aghast. The cobbles would run red with blood.

Why hadn't the older, wiser men foreseen the castellan ordering his men to fire on the crowd? Was Uncle Isom going to be killed? Uncle Zanner? Where was his father? Was his mother among the women drumming on cookpots with their ladles?

Raucous shrieks closer at hand suddenly deafened him. Nedi was completely surrounded by fluttering wings and screeching birds of every size and colour. Had they been startled from their roosts by the noise?

As he ducked the countless scratching talons and piercing beaks, he froze, astonished. All his terror of being so high above the ground, all his fears for his family's fate vanished like morning dew. He could see the eagle despite the swirling cloud of birds. Only it wasn't the rough-hewn brass effigy which he had carried up here.

The golden metal bird was a thing of beauty, precise in every lifelike detail. It perched, wings raised and angled, ready to plunge from the sky to seize some unsuspecting prey. Its hooked beak gaped. Its eyes shone bright as diamonds. It turned its head to look at Nedi with a fierce hunter's gaze.

The other birds swooped down to fill the castle courtyard. The garrison men shouted and cursed, flailing with their hands and hackbuts. It did no good. From hedge sparrows to crag crows, the birds clawed and pecked and shat all over the River Kingdom men and their weapons.

When the flock dispersed as suddenly as it had appeared, the courtyard was deserted. Nedi saw that the men had fled back into their barracks. Some had held onto their weapons but more had let the precious hackbuts fall to the ground. Powder spilled over the cobbles along with lengths of alchemist's twine, all now soiled and useless.

Someone had opened the castle gate! He saw the townsfolk crowding into the courtyard. Soon the men were banging on the doors all around. The garrison emerged with their hands raised in surrender. A knot of richly clad River Kingdom men were swiftly surrounded by Hatalys' leading craftsmen and merchants. They broke into several earnest conversations.

Nedi looked down outside the castle again. The crowd was still growing. More and more people were coming to see this marvel and to join in the triumphant cheering.

They were pointing up at the eagle. Now it looked just the same as it had done when it was first revealed. It didn't matter. From that distance no one could see it was ugly and crude.

Nedi contemplated the effigy. Had he imagined the living bronze's magical beauty? No, he hadn't. He could go to his deathbed as an old, old man, quite sure of what he had seen. Though he didn't think he would tell anyone. Not and be mocked for a fool like Thulle.

Firstly though, if he was to live to be a greybeard, he must get safely down from this perilous perch. Nedi considered his options and decided to climb slowly and carefully down to the battlements and wait there until someone came to show him the proper route through the castle.

It wasn't until he was safely on the wall walk that a profoundly unnerving thought struck him. If the eagle's magic had summoned the birds to overwhelm the garrison, did that mean the rest of Thulle's tales were true? Could the Horned God's priests truly conjure up monsters?

Nedi looked up at the eagle and a golden shimmer blinded him. For an instant he thought he saw the bird transformed once again. As he blinked, he fervently hoped that was a promise of the eagle's aid, if the River Kingdom's masked priests could really call on such sorcery and try to reclaim Hatalys for the Paramount King.

All Hail to the Oak

Anne Nicholls

Kataljid ran towards the scream. All that stood between her and its source was the high wall of the mansion that was her gaol. Vines clotted darkly on the garden-side of the smooth marble. Somewhere outside, lonely footsteps echoed in the late-night citadel. They halted at that frightened shriek.

Kilting up her robes, she scrambled up to the top and reached instinctively for the sword that should have been hanging at her waist. But of course guests of the Empire – or hostages – weren't allowed weapons, not here in the capital itself. Surprise would have to be enough. From within the foliage Kataljid scanned the moon-shadowed square.

Three youths surrounded a fourth, a boy shorter than she was. She couldn't see him clearly. One lout stood stolidly on the boy's feet, trapping them. Another, built like an ox, held their victim's arms behind his back. The third darted in from the side, thrusting a burning brand at his head. Sparks fizzed along his black curls with a stink of burning hair. The youth hated himself for that scream, she could see it in the way his face worked. Wait! It was Salrivos! Her gut contracted at this threat to her only friend. She was so focussed on him that she didn't notice a figure hiding behind the dried-up fountain.

Kataljid leaped and screeched a war cry. Not until she was plunging through the air did she realise the one with the brand was the empress' son but it was too late. She was among them.

Shocked, the Rovalans were easy prey. The massive one at the back tumbled, pulling their victim down. The fat one in front lost his balance, crashing onto Salrivos' ribs. She heard the crack of bone.

But the third, Prince Torturer Herricus, stumbled back, keeping his feet more by luck than judgment. It took him a heartbeat to remember his firebrand and bring it into play.

By then she was inside his reach. Inside the stench of musk and sweat and jasmine. She slammed her elbow into the prince's throat. Flames whisked past a handspan from her eyes. He toppled, haloed by a shower of sparks. His head rang against the flagstones, a horrible sound. She was already somersaulting over his body while his friends were still groaning. The fat one scrabbled for a jewelled dagger. Kataljid kicked him under the chin and swivelled to face the emperor's boy but he was scrambling away, calling for his slaves. New footsteps now, running towards them, and shouts of alarm.

Dragging the rescued lad free, she hauled him into the souk. Salrivos had half-fainted with the pain. It took all her strength to hustle him along. At last she crouched behind a stack of trestles and yanked him down. He tussled but she got one hand over his mouth and held him until any sound of pursuit faded in the night.

"It's all right, you're safe now," she said finally, releasing him.

He shoved her away. "You stupid mare!" he gasped. "I'll never be safe again!"

Kataljid goggled.

"You don't get it, do you? Saved by a girl, and an acorn-eater at that! Things were bad enough before but the prince and his gang will really have it in for me now. I doubt you'll last the night. Go *away!*"

"Acorn-eater?"

"You figure it out. If the prince doesn't kill you first." He limped off into the darkness and she could have wept. Another hostage, he'd been the only one who was genuinely kind to her at the empress' reception that had finished scant hours before.

Her heart sank. "You're welcome," she muttered, and turned

her mind to the formidable task of finding her way back inside the Lion Mansion, preferably without Princess Nalix realising she'd escaped in the first place. Which, considering the height of the walls, the soldiers at the lighted gates and the wreck of the silks the princess had made her wear wasn't going to be easy. "Remember your position" would be the least of it.

Princess Nalix, roused from her bed by the guard who caught Kataljid sneaking in, grimaced with such fury her make-up cracked. The tirade she launched scarcely covered the sound of a man sniggering from her rooms.

"Remember your position": that was why her guardian cancelled all the getting-to-know-you rides and picnics for the next three months. The tale had got out, of course. Rovalan gossips were quick to tell how a cowardly hostage in the heart of the citadel needed saving from a single acorn-eating thief. Apparently Prince Herricus had stayed up late debating with his tutor, sorry not to have been there to impale the intruder, doubtless some lower-city scum. Thankfully her name wasn't mentioned.

As the days lengthened into sweltering summer, Kataljid was forced to spend her time cooped up with Laratus, the princess' chief eunuch. Who despised her. Instead of parties she got lonely lessons in deportment, manners, poetry and heraldry. On top of grammar, history and dancing with stiff old tutors who looked like they had a spike shoved up their –

She barely stopped the thought in time to keep it behind her teeth. Prince Herricus and Salvrivos weren't the only ones she'd offended, goddess alone knew how. Now she wasn't even allowed to play ball with the guard-captain's daughter, the only other girl in the Lion Mansion anywhere near her age.

Chewing the end of her stylus, Kataljid gazed blindly out of the window, recalling the day the galley had brought her here, wondering yet again how everything had gone so wrong.

It had started that first day when she was green off the boat, when they hustled her to the Guests of Empire Reception. Her Rovalan had been halting. She'd missed half of what people said to her, and most of what happened around. How she'd blushed when one of the dainty girls hissed, "Lumbering barbarian!" in a mock whisper that carried across the throne room. The girl - the empress' daughter, it turned out - giggled, and so did the group round her. Glaring at them, Princess Nalix chivvied Kataljid away, but the sniggers broke out again at their backs. It was the princess' furious tirade back at the mansion that had driven Katalid to take refuge in the night-scented garden. Where she'd heard a scream that had lost her any chance of an ally in this hostile heart of Empire. She was fifteen, a humble disciple of the goddess, never meant for the lethal dance of politics. Was it any wonder she set out to fail her lessons when all that awaited was the bearpit they called a court?

At first sight of the capital Kataljid's jaw had dropped open. The eunuch who'd been rowed to the last port to begin her 'taming' cleared his throat. His name was Laratus, and he nagged from dawn to dusk. As the galley passed the lighthouse, sunrise painted the city on the cliffs in gold and red and black. It towered above her, a bewildering sprawl of buildings spilling down to the sea. She'd never imagined there were this many people in the world.

Kataljid clamped her jaw. She stared down at her short, shaven-headed tormentor, well aware of his intentions: to groom her as quickly as he could for life as a marriageable pawn. No doubt Laratus would be freed as a reward. While she practised stumbling around in their stupid flowing gowns, the crew laid bets he'd stay a slave for a very long time.

"Don't gape, my lady," the eunuch said. "It doesn't do to look as if you don't belong."

But Kataljid knew she didn't. They could dress her in satin and wind her hair with pearls but this hive of palaces and commerce was nothing like her wild homeland. Here the highest point was not a mountain but The Castle. So many emperors had forced towers and turrets onto the place that it seemed crowned with spears. It hung brooding over its reflection in the blue waters. Kataljid's hand twitched to where her sword was no longer at her side. She stifled the motion but Laratus had seen it.

"Have no fear, my lady. Your slaves will protect you."

She arched a blonde eyebrow. "You mistake," she said, in clumsy Rovalan. "I was trying decide where I go first, Theatre of Acarius or hunting in the park."

"A good recover, my lady, worthy of one much older than yourself." Before she could protest he added smoothly, "In fact you will go to the Lion Mansion so that Princess Nalix can see you properly attired for the empress' reception. See that?" He pointed to a line of tiny coloured flags onshore. "They set it up the instant we rounded the lighthouse. That means it's to be this afternoon. You must be the last to arrive."

Kataljid seldom traded on her rank but she'd had enough of the unsufferable old prune. "I am a princess, Laratus," she said carefully. "I decide for myself."

"Indeed, my lady, but here you are one princess among many. No doubt you will wish to refresh yourself before entering the citadel." He turned away, all solicitude, and beckoned slaves to take the girl in hand. She'd never felt so insignificant.

The mansion turned out to be a fortress with Lion mosaics everywhere. A lot of them seemed to be made of gold. Kataljid had thought her father's feasting hall was big but the Great Hall overwhelmed her. It had colonnades and side-aisles, a minstrel's gallery and a dais. Which held so many statues and paintings that she felt trapped in a giant's jewel-box. She was afraid to move. It hadn't been half a day yet and already the princess' shrieks of, "Be careful! That screen cost two talents" or "Don't you know that vase is a personal gift from the emperor?" had her on edge. Yet again she emerged from behind a screen in her latest change of robes and squirmed beneath Princess Nalix's contempt.

"Well, Candis —"

"Kataljid."

"I told you, child, from now on you are Candis. What civilised person could get their tongue round that tangle of grunts?" The princess pinched her painted mouth and walked around her, twitching aside the folds that hid the Lion sigil. "I suppose that will have to do. All the other hostages arrived days ago."

"I couldn't help the storm!"

"Hush, child. We cannot keep the empress waiting any longer. And do *try* to keep that — that *acorn-eater's* accent under control." She swept out to the forecourt where a line of guards surrrounded a long box on poles, and climbed into it. Laratus shoved the newly-named Candis in after her.

Acorn-eater? She didn't know that word. She'd have to find a bilingual scribe to tell her what it meant. There was nothing she'd ask of that eunuch, not even a translation.

Kataljid hated the confines of the litter. Trapped within its carven screens, her keeper's perfume was stifling. When she went to open one, Nalix said sharply, "No, no, Candis. It does not do for you to show yourself to the populace." Almost under her breath the older woman added, "At least not until you've stopped behaving like an ape."

Kataljid seethed. "Did you say something?"

"Did you say something, *your highness,*" Nalix corrected.

A dagger thunked into one of the screens. As the litter lurched into a lumpen run the door fell open. Kataljid almost tipped out onto the cobbles. Amidst shouts and the clash of steel Princess Nalix clawed her back with surprising strength. One of the bearers slammed the panel shut. Gasping and hauling herself to a crouch, Kataljid tried to peer out but she was jolted too much. All she glimpsed was a thin man sinking beneath a tide of swords, shouting she didn't know what. Then the litter rounded a corner.

"What was that about?" asked Kataljid, groping for a knife she'd hidden under her sash. It wasn't easy. The litter was at a steep angle. She heard shouts and the bearers panting like bellows because they were climbing the last part of the hill.

"Nothing," Nalix snapped, hanging on to a strap. "Hand over that knife. Or do you want us arrested? We're nearly at The Castle. Sit properly and for the gods' sake straighten your stole. It's covering the emblems of our houses. If you must hide your little nut-tree that's up to you but don't, please, obscure our Lion."

"That's not a nut-tree!" Kataljid protested. "It's the Shield of Oakland."

"Which, you'll notice, is beneath the Lion of Empire. Ah, we're here."

The Castle towered over the citadel, much as Kataljid felt she towered over the swarms of Rovalans. Passed by gate sentries and hall sentries and sentries at various doors, the litter finally bumped to a halt. Kataljid, peeping through the carvings, saw only a segment of the courtyard. From somewhere out of sight she heard the scrape of swords drawn from scabbards. She jumped out, crouching, ready to defend the princess with her life.

And heard a crowd gasp then ripple with laughter. It echoed, shocking pigeons into noisy flight. The honour guard resheathed their weapons. Princess Nalix stepped from the litter, straight-faced. The amusement died.

Everyone on the steps behind straightened from their bows as Princess Nalix stalked through them to the pavilion at the top. Hot-faced and feeling gawkier than ever, Kataljid was righting her headdress when Laratus scuttled up.

He adjusted Kataljid's robes, all the time darting looks at a woman in red who waited under the Lion canopy. Everyone else stood in a great fan-shape with her at the focus. The rubies on her tiara shook with suppressed hilarity. Laratus stifled a groan.

Kataljid blew aside a stray lock of hair and raised her chin.

Red-faced, she said in halting Rovalan, "Enough, Laratus. I'll not apologise for my training. It saved my life in hunting."

"But it's going to make life in Rovala a tad awkward."

Kataljid wanted to shrink so she didn't stand head and shoulders above everyone else. Instead she drew herself up and swept past the eunuch. "You always have to have the last word, don't you, Laratus?"

But her haughtiness failed. At that exact moment the courtiers shouted, "All hail to the Lion!" and the eunuch dragged her into a bow.

That was when she first saw him. Oh, not the emperor. He sent his regrets but Princess Nalix had already told her not to expect him at a presentation of minor hostages. Guests. They'd be met by Empress Haladra and her son, Crown Prince Herricus.

On the top stair Kataljid stopped. Princess Nalix chivvied her towards the crimson-robed empress, who was her much-younger half-sister. Beside her, looking away to hide his mirth, stood a youth dressed in cloth of gold with sigils of the Lion House. He couldn't stop his shoulders heaving.

No, the boy ahead of Kataljid in the reception line was the one who caught her gaze. Not only was he good-looking, he seemed as nervous as she felt. He was wreathed in cheap scent that tried to copy the prince's musk and jasmine. His looks were exotic, and he was dwarfed by the gaudy courtiers. At first his shortness made her think he was younger than she was, then she saw fuzz sprouting from the neck of his tunic. His curls were the darkest she'd ever seen, his skin a warm gold. When he turned to stare curiously around, his guardian elbowed him and he snapped almost to attention. A flush stained his neck. He polished his sandals on the back of his legs. His guardian, probably a general if all that gilded armour was anything to go by, nudged him crossly. The boy moved forward as though his feet weren't quite connected to the floor. His bow to the imperial family stopped just short of grovelling. His patron nodded, making the gilded feathers on his helmet flutter.

The very last in the queue, Kataljid waited her turn. Stares pressed in on her. The whole court was just dying for her to make a fool of herself again. She wobbled on the wretched high heels. When it was her turn, Princess Nalix and her royal sister smiled at one another like sharks.

A steward announced, "Kataljid, heiress to the throne of Oakland."

Prince Herricus craned his head back and drawled, "What's the weather like up there?" His mother jammed her elbow into his ribs. It didn't stop him and his two cronies chortling behind their hands. Apparently they were Lilixar and Belden but she didn't catch which one was which. One was flabby, the other all muscle and no brain.

The empress offered her condolences on the death of Kataljid's elder brother. Kataljid felt a quiver of optimism – would Haladra be an ally against her guardian? – until she realised a scribe prompted the remarks from a scroll.

That set the tone for the Guests of Empire reception. A few guests dropped a patronising word, perhaps thinking of Oakland's riches in timber, gems and aurochs, riches she now stood to inherit, however reluctantly. Riches in a kingdom she'd never been trained to rule. If only her big brother hadn't died. She missed him fiercely.

Some though, the ones closest to Prince Herricus, turned a cold shoulder. Others giggled and didn't speak to her at all.

Not the exotic lad, though. Kataljid was standing alone on the balcony when he sauntered across, short but beautiful, and said, "You look lost." She smiled a welcome. He shot a glance at the prince and got a nod before smiling back. After that he was charming.

His name was Salrivos and he'd lived here as long as he could remember. They talked until the sun went down, and he didn't mock her accent once. When slaves carried out incense to keep off the insects he said in flawless Rovalan, "Don't worry.

It's not so bad being a guest of the empire. Anyway, I'm the youngest son. I doubt my life would last very long if my brothers laid eyes on me. No, my home's with General Adraius and Lady Adraia."

Clearly he'd expected her to gasp in awe but she shrugged and shook her head.

"You know, of Eagle Mansion?" He pointed to the silver bird embroidered on his tunic above some emblem she couldn't make out. Salrivos went on, "I wouldn't even know what my mother looks like if they hadn't sent a portrait." His tone was as level as if he were discussing a discarded shoelace.

Surely he must be pretending not to care? Perhaps it was to save face. This was only her first day here, the thirty-seventh since she'd left home, and already Kataljid was swamped in homesickness. How much worse it must be for him! To hide her pity - and secretly because she felt awkward looming over him — she leaned on the balcony. Down below lamps began to shine through the dusk. Dim twinkles answered them from across the bay.

Laughter brayed from the crowded hall. Kataljid was sure they were talking about her. But Salrivos was nice. She decided he must like her, at least a bit. Her name sounded like music from his lips, or perhaps the wine had gone to her head. She almost screwed up enough courage to ask, "What does *acorn-eater* mean?" but a flunky came to whisper, "Prince Herricus' compliments, lordling, and why are you wasting time with that blond troll when you could be losing a fortune to him?" The slave hadn't meant her to hear.

Salrivos pulled a face. Without a word he scampered to the royal brat. Feeling abandoned, Kataljid wondered if he did like her after all.

That same night she'd spoiled everything by rescuing him. From the Lion Emperor's son.

"Shoulders back, Candis!" Laratus said in exasperation. "I've had enough of this pretence of yours."

For the last eight weeks she'd thwarted his plans for 'taming' her. The eunuch's dislike couldn't have been plainer. The feeling was mutual. As for forcing her to mince around with an empty jar on her head, what was the point? Her stupidly high heels slithered on the marble. She barely caught the pot before it smashed.

The ferocity of the eunuch's hiss belied his servile posture. "How do you expect to walk elegantly when you won't stand up straight?"

"I don't have to carry water," she snapped back. "I'm not one of your peasants."

"Any of whom would be more graceful than you are." He dripped his acid in perfect Rovalan, his drawl even more pronounced than his mistress'. Kataljid was sure he was more of a snob too.

She lifted the pot back. It wobbled the other way. The sudden prick of tears caught her by surprise. Instead of these dreary humiliations she should be back in Oakland helping with famine relief. Homseickness throbbed like a wound.

Eventually she mastered herself. "I'm sorry to disappoint you, Laratus, but my strengths are healing and hunting, not learning how to simper at courtiers who either hate me or want to use me."

"So use *them*, Kataljid." For once he didn't call her by her Rovalan name. Instead he reached up and put the jar aside, then took her hand in his soft ones and drew her over to a bench. "You have a homeland, a family." He swallowed. "All this posturing I'm trying to teach you, it's not just for me. It's to protect you at court. Don't you realise? This is training for another sort of battle so stop pretending you're useless. Are all Oaklanders cowards? Are *you* a coward?"

She tried to leap to her feet but his grasp was surprisingly strong. Also he allowed a foreign accent into his voice. At first she suspected mockery and her eyes flashed, but it was different from the sound of her tongue. Softer, with furred gutturals.

"Please, Kataljid. Sit by me." She perched as far away as she could get. He patted her arm and said gently, "I know you heard those fools on board betting on us. You think I'm only pushing you because I want my freedom. At the start, that was probably true."

"And now?"

"I saw you that night after the hostages' reception, remember? No, of course you don't. You didn't see me. Too busy rescuing your ungrateful young princeling. That was some war cry! I was on my way back from a poetry evening and saw the imperial brat up to his tricks."

"You did? Wait a moment. Why didn't *you* rescue that boy? I thought you didn't want me getting into trouble."

Laratus dropped his humble mask. Sourly he pointed to the Lion brand on his temple. "Remember my position, mistress."

Of course. He was a slave. In Rovala that was lower than the low. It didn't matter that he ruled the Lion Mansion, the personal aide to Princess Nalix herself. He was still a slave. They'd already taken his manhood. If he laid a finger on a noble they could have him beheaded. Or if he even looked at one aslant...

And yet he'd touched her. He had quite literally put his life in her hands. "You *do* have courage, Kataljid, or at least you did back in the spring. You acted not out of self-preservation but because you still believe in fairness. You were quick. Clever. You're not stupid so stop pretending you are."

"But I don't want to be with people like that!"

"But nothing. You have a job to do. Your people expect it. The drought in the north has weakened your country along with all the others. It's playing right into your enemies' hands. The wolves are out there laying ambushes and you've been hiding in here –"

"I'm not hiding!"

"So you don't have the first clue what they're up to. They're up in court right now, manoeuvring to get the biggest cut when your land is conquered." Abruptly he walked away, then stopped, not turning. "As mine was."

The first Kataljid knew of the Great Corn Riot was the smoke drifting through the windows of the Lion Mansion. It added an unholy tang to the bright autumn breeze. Coughing, she let go of the scroll she'd been conning and went to close the shutters. She'd learned a lot in the last month, not least that pigs ate acorns. Pigs, halfwits and peasants. And ignorant barbarians like her.

From the window she saw fires scattered across half the city. All at once flames burst from the corn exchange. She was already casting aside her stupid skirts when the *whomp!* of the explosion broke over her.

Fastening her breeks, Kataljid leaped down the stairs and flew across to the gates. Guards barred the way with their spears.

"Princess Nalix's orders, m'lady. Food riot. It's not safe out there." That was Captain Camadus, of course, the one who'd forbidden his daughter to talk to her. To stay calm Kataljid thought of the cartoon she'd drawn of him so she could singe it when he vexed her. The caricature of Nalix was down to a fragment.

"But the fires!" Kataljid shouted. "People are burning to death down there!"

Distant screams tore through the dusk. Briefly the captain closed his eyes. "It's 'ard, miss, very 'ard, but a slip of a girl couldn't do nothing about it any more'n I could."

"I've got my medicines. No, don't turn away! I trained as a healer before my brother died. I was never supposed to be the heir."

"But Princess Nalix –"

"But nothing! She's loyal to the emperor, isn't she? Which makes her responsible for his people while he's... indisposed." She wasn't going to make the mistake of saying the Lion Emperor had been suddenly taken drunk. Again.

The captain winced when he heard another scream, this one

a child's. He scratched his cheek, clearly torn. Laratus scuttled out of the dusk, hissing, "You can't go! You're responsible for making the best match you can for your people. You can't do that when you're dead!"

Kataljid dragged him out of earshot. "Laratus, you don't understand! It's the magic of our realm. Our kings are tied to the land and our queens are healers. When people are in pain it stabs me like knives. Even if you tie me down, those screams will cut my flesh. See? It's started!" She thrust her arm at him. Blood trickled over her wrist. "Please, Laratus, I *have* to help!"

The eunuch looked at the drops pooling crimson on the ground. He nodded permission. Triumphant, she whirled, not quite managing to hide the scissors from her medicine pouch. The eunuch thoughtfully watched her go.

Kataljid was glad when fresh bandages arrived. The litter-bearers carried them, and salves, and the juice of the poppy, right into the lamplit temple where she worked alongside the priests. To her surprise, Laratus had brought them himself. Or rather, he'd accompanied the bearers and a batch of Lion guards to protect them from the masses. He ordered the burly men to assist with the groaning wounded, and poured a drink for Kataljid. "With my very own hands, I hope you'll notice. You should be honoured."

"I'd like to see you do it with anyone else's."

"Very droll, my lady. Princess Nalix has realised what a help we could be to the emperor's subjects."

The blond girl was coming to realise how obliquely the eunuch spoke. Equally circumspect, she replied, "I'm sure the empress will be suitably grateful." Layers of debts and obligations hung unspoken between them.

"Good girl!" Laratus said with a wink. Then he heaved a sigh and put himself in charge of organisation. With the corn stores gone any food merchant's stores had fallen prey to looters. The death-toll below the citadel was appalling.

Kataljid straightened her shoulders and walked tiredly back to a new group of scorched and mangled commoners. For a moment she felt their pain less keenly as she suppressed a small, selfish smile. However much she pitied these poor half-starved folk, now she was in Nalix's good books she wouldn't have to spend another three months mewed up after all. Then a father ran in carrying a screaming baby. Stomach roiling, she rushed to dress its burns.

Two nights later she attended the viewing of moonflowers on Lady Adraia's pond at the House of the Eagle. It was her second ever expedition to a Rovalan great house. Salrivos would be there, and Herricus. She'd looked forward to this and dreaded it in equal measure. When the imperial party arrived she bowed and joined the chorus of "All hail to the Lion," hoping the prince wouldn't spot her.

Luckily the garden shadows hid her when she was presented to the lady. Also Princess Nalix's supporters now included her in their chit-chat. With Laratus' lessons in mind, she didn't allow their smiles to fool her. Empress Haladra deigned to thank her on behalf of the emperor, which was an excuse for a self-serving speech. Luckily Herricus was too busy flirting to pay attention. After that the empress' followers oiled around her. Shared looks of triumpth told Kataljid she still wasn't catching all their verbal barbs. Nor did Salrivos show any sign of recognition though she caught him watching her once or twice. Protective of his cracked ribs, he moved stiffly, hanging around Prince Herricus and his toadies, begging for attention like a dog begs for crumbs. She remembered them well and now she knew their names. Belden the Belly, Lilixar the strong one and the loathesome Prince Herricus. Recalling his firebrand, she pulled her veil further across her face.

Nevertheless, after three months with only tutors to talk to and slaves who were too scared to respond, it was exciting to be at a party. Even if it was a party with screechy Rovalan music.

Girls clustered round her, chattering like parrots, and boys showed off to catch her eye. Kataljid hid her grin behind her veil. Also, as long as her height didn't give her away, Herricus was unlikely to notice her. It seemed he liked a flagon or three. Like father, like son. Just in case, she sat down as soon as she could. Two stone-faced matrons plonked down either side to keep watch on her. They were poor relations who breathed at Nalix's whim.

At moonrise the white lilies opened. Their perfume was intoxicating. Literally. Laratus had warned her to breathe through her veil. Being unused to the scent, the hostages would be drugged more readily than native Rovalans. "This is your next test," he'd warned her. "Don't succumb to licentiousness. Don't swoon at what you see. And don't let a certain Lion cub catch you on your own."

As the evening wore on, the rustles and sighs from the shadows vied with the music. Licentiousness indeed. Kataljid sat uncomfortably where she'd been told, between Princess Nalix's dependents, either of whom could have repelled a cavalry charge with a single glance. At least they weren't openly mocking the foreigners drugged into passion. She wished she'd never come to this party.

A Rovalan maiden threw her arms round the prince's neck and tittered, "Just look what's going on behind those palm trees, your highness. To think they're hostages! Your imperial father is saddled with worthless acorn-eaters."

"Acorn-eaters," slurred Belden, more than a little drunk himself. He obviously assumed only true-blood Rovalans were sober enough to hear. "Since they're dim enough to set the corn exchange alight, what else can —"

"That was some fool in the army who didn't know flour can explode," retorted Lilixar.

Herricus slapped them both. "Shut up, you morons!" he hissed. "Do you want the rabble blaming us for them starving?" Much louder he said, "It's for their own good. Rationing's a sensible policy."

"Yes, for acorn-eaters," chuckled Belden, unabashed.

"There is one difference between acorn eaters and hostages," announced Lilixar with the air of one lumbering towards a punch-line.

Herricus joined his cronies in the chorus. "The ones at court don't eat acorns 'cause they live off Rovalan banquets. Now shut up, Ox."

The words came to Kataljid as though from far away. Gazing dreamily beyond the dark, petalled waters, she thought of the hills of home. Then recalled the swathes of horse-bones on the steppes below where the people had slain their herds because there was neither grass nor corn. It hadn't been so bad in Oakland where snowmelt trickled down the mountains. And her father's kingdom was all that stood between the starving Empire and the weakened hordes?

A hubbub pulled her from the moonlilies' thrall.

"Enough!" cried Lady Adraia. The Rovalans fell silent. A wail from inside the house pierced the night. Ignoring a couple writhing in the shrubbery, the lady and her husband Adraius hurried to the empress' side.

Princess Nalix snapped her fingers at her chief attendant, who sped to find out what was happening. A sense of wariness racked Kataljid. It broke the moonlilies' spell. Upset by the distant weeping, she would have gone to help if the dowagers hadn't clamped her on the couch, hushing her whispered pleas.

In suspicious silence everyone waited for the empress' messenger to come back. Guests and Rovalans drew apart into separate muttering clumps. The last of the hostages came out sheepishly straightening their clothes and asking, "What's wrong?" Whom they chose to approach was interesting now she'd learned the sigils of each house and scion. And which house sponsored each hostage from all the kingdoms of the world.

Salrivos visibly hesitated between a group of foreigners and the knot of Rovalans round the prince. He was still dithering when Princess Nalix upstaged her imperial sister. "Apparently a mob is burgling its way up to the citadel. They claim it's because they have no food."

Annoyed, the empress spoke over her sib. "Gentles and guests, General Adraius and his good lady open Eagle Mansion to you until the rabble is put down."

"Oh come on, Haladra!" begged a duke who'd bedded her not a week ago. "We can't stay here. We've got homes to defend!"

The empress raised her brows so high, cakes of white paint fell from her forehead. General Adraius declaimed, "The empress and Prince Herricus *are* the Empire. Any *loyal* man's duty is to stay and defend them."

Startled, the duke bowed and retreated. None of the cliques would take him in with treason hanging in the air. Even his child bride drifted away.

Thinking of the looters, Kataljid found herself hoping Laratus would be all right.

Perhaps the randy princess wasn't immune to the moonlilies after all. Nalix held a whispered argument with her sister. No doubt she was thinking of her treasures in the hands of plebs. Too worked up to notice Haladra's stare, the princess only shut up when her entourage thinned.

Kataljid wished she was out of this wasps' nest but her keepers kept tight hold of her. Men of the Lion Guard patrolled the mansion's walls alongside the Eagles. Kataljid realised she had no choice but to stay put.

Unfortunately, as the duke passed her, the wind caught the hem of his cloak. It knocked her headdress askew. She stifled a gasp. The problem wasn't air on her burns. It was the cruel glitter in the eyes of Herricus, and the way he nudged his friends. Hovering beside them, Salrivos looked away.

Now she was glad she was sitting between her stone-faced guardians, because she was trapped in Eagle House with the prince, and goddess alone knew how long for. Kataljid determined to stay awake.

It was a long night on a hard pallet. A mob roaring "We want bread!" had broken into the citadel. Kataljid could hear them being slaughtered just outside the fragrant garden.

By dawn the rebels were defeated. The last shreds of revolt were pinned in the smoking city below.

A slave burst into Nalix's room, a redhead branded with the Eagle. The slam of the door jerked Kataljid from her doze. She glanced round wildly in case it was the Prince of Arson but the slave-girl clapped her hands and proclaimed, "All hail to the Lion! The empress' actions have saved the citadel. In the name of the emperor she bids you return to your homes and prepare."

Kataljid grabbed the girl's sleeve as she passed. "Prepare for what?"

The slave prised Kataljid's fingers from her arm. "Civil war, of course."

It took Kataljid a moment to realise the slave had actually touched her. By then the redhead had slipped away.

No one could explain how the litters had got broken. The empress commandeered the only decent one. Princess Nalix almost managed to grab another that was just about whole but Prince Herricus stared her down. That too was new, thought Kataljid, seeing the surprised look on her guardian's face. Evidently Herricus' star was on the rise. She wondered uneasily how he'd managed that.

It was a sorry procession that went back to the Lion Mansion. Walking down the steep streets in stilted sandals was well-nigh impossible. Crossly, Nalix commanded her captain to slice the heels off with his scimitar. The exposed wood skidded under Kataljid, who grabbed wildly to save herself. Unfortunately her fingers tangled in Nalix's stole. The elderly princess crashed to the cobbles. Her scream abruptly ended. Kataljid tried to reach her. A smell of oil assailed her nostrils then her head rang against stone and everything went black.

Out of the darkness came a whine like the hiss of a sword whipped through air. Only this sound didn't go away. It got louder and louder, drawing Kataljid into a whirl of pain. Concussion. She opened her eyes but the blackness didn't go away either. A smell of dank cave was the only sign she hadn't gone blind. And a hint of... cheap musky jasmine?

"Princess Nalix?" she croaked, but there was no answer.

Dizzily she crawled around her prison. Suddenly her outstretched hand met nothing. For endless moments a dislodged pebble tumbled through the blackness. Trembling, she drew back to safety. It took a long time for her heart to stop pounding.

At last she nerved herself to inch along the rim of the abyss. Soon she collided with a wall. She followed it around in a ragged half-circle. With each frustrating touch she was more certain there was no door. Nor could she feel a ceiling. Maybe they'd dropped her down by a rope.

Creeping into the middle, she found her guardian. Whose robes were sodden with blood. Princess Nalix would blackmail no more men into bed, not without the heart that had been hacked from her chest.

Kataljid tried to scrub the metallic stickiness from her hands but it clung. Fighting down panic, she slumped against the rocks as far from the corpse as she could get. If she hadn't broken Nalix's leg would her guardian still be alive? No, came the recollection. The cobbles were slick with oil. But she'd still hurt a daughter of the Lion House. Why hadn't they executed her yet? And if they'd murdered Nalix, why hadn't they killed her at the same time?

"Kataljid?"

She thought her mind had generated the voice but it called again from far below. Opening her eyes, she saw a faint spot of light coming from the void. A torch! Almost she called out but only her captors knew she was here. There was nowhere to hide.

Brighter grew the light, throwing shadows into relief. Kataljid hid in a crack, grasping a rock as a weapon. Then the flames leaped over the brim and a slave climbed into her cell. The Eagle brand on his temple seemed to flutter its wings in the uneven light. Behind him came a bald man marked with a Lion.

"Laratus!" Heedless of the prohibition against touching slaves, she threw her arms around her mentor. He hugged her back. The front of his tunic was stuffed with pieces of metal that stuck into her. "What's going on?" she asked him.

"Revolution. Haladra's seized the throne. My guess is she's poisoned the emperor. She's going to share the throne with Herricus. They're blaming you for Princess Nalix's death so they can demand compensation from your father. A herd of your Oakland aurochs should be enough to keep the army on their side." He turned, lighting a second torch at the one that was guttering. "Come on. We've got to get out of here."

Kataljid could have smacked her head at her own stupidity. If she'd had the courage to explore the edge of the abyss, she'd have found the steps hacked into the rock. She tucked her skirts under her belt and clambered down. As soon as they were trotting along the safety of a tunnel, she panted, "How did you know where I was?"

Laratus indicated the Eagle slave. "Vetrus came to tell me."

"You saved my baby, princess," Vetrus said. "The one with the burns on his chest, remember? He'd have died if not for you."

She stammered, "I – I'm glad he's all right. But how –?"

"I'm one of Salrivos' body-slaves. Prince Herricus sent his friends to make sure he'd followed orders. I was the one who brought them wine. Salrivos said he'd stashed you in the general's larder but begged them at least to tell him why. Then Belden said didn't they want a bit of fun in revenge? They're just waiting for Lilixar."

Almost at the end of the passage Vetrus pressed a stone in the wall. In response a block pivoted, revealing a roughly squared room stacked with weapons.

She chose a sword and shield, battered but serviceable. Laratus cuddled a crossbow that took three bolts at a time. There was enough padding down the front of his tunic that he'd never be able to draw a full-sized bow. Poor frightened eunuch, clanking with every step. Why hadn't he just picked up a breastplate? Vetrus himself, a wiry man with bony features, chose a sling with a pouch of lead shot.

A hinge creaked somewhere.

"Ssh!" Vetrus hastily pulled the slab to. From the tunnel, light burst through the narrow gap and the jingle of military harness came echoing closer. It all but masked excited whispers. Voices she knew. Lilixar the ox, Belden the lard-arse... and pretty-boy Salrivos. The fugitives scarcely dared breathe. Hastily they doused their torch in a pot of sand.

"What?" gasped Salrivos, having to take two steps to their one. "I'm s'posed to marry that acorn-eater?"

They carried on past the hiding place. Belden snapped, "Yes, you moron! Weren't you listening?"

"I would if anybody ever told me anything."

"Oh stop moaning, you little squirt."

Now the voices were receding. Noiselessly Kataljid opened the secret panel and dodged after them.

"Listen, squirt. You marry the bitch, Herricus executes her for treason, you pretend you've escaped with her baby –"

"What baby?"

"I don't know! Any one we can lay hands on. Then you can be regent to it when you get to Oakland. Call up our troops and suddenly you're a king."

Too angry to think straight, Kataljid tore herself free of Laratus' grip and followed as closely as she dared. She needed their light to see by. The lads' voices were distorted now as they climbed up the chasm wall. She hung her sword down her back and recklessly set her toes in the first crevice. It was much harder when their torches bobbed so high above. She strained to hear

Lilixar's words drifting down into the darkness.

"Then you bring all that meat on the hoof to pay off the army so they don't join the rebellion. Everybody'll love you. What've I forgotten, Bel?"

"Then oh dear the empress has an accident and Herricus takes the throne."

"Yeah, King Salrivos, you'll be the new emperor's right-hand man."

They were scrambling into the cell now. Belden, the last, slapped the short hostage on the back. "Remember who your friends are when you've wooed your acorn eater, eh?" Kataljid clamped her lips and hung silently, keeping her eyes just above the rim.

Lilixar ignored the byplay. Stomping over the old woman's body, he stopped, then whirled, waving his torch into every dark corner. "Where the fuck is she?"

Belden seized Salrivos. "Yeah, you toe-rag, what have you done with her?"

"Nothing!" Sal couldn't have looked more desperate if he'd tried. "My slaves left her right by the princess."

"Can't have done." Lilisar punched him. "What are you up to, you snivelling little prick?"

Kataljid realised how stupid she'd been. There was no other way out. They'd be climbing back any moment and she was one against three. She felt her way down, feet slipping in her hurry. Her pulse pounded in her ears but she managed to regain her footing before she dropped into the abyss. If the prince's clique hadn't been rowing they'd have caught her. At last she reached the ledge.

But they still had a torch. Their descent was much faster. Kataljid hopped on one foot then the other, ripping off her sandals, then fled ghostly up the passage.

She just made it back to the secret armoury before the prince's coterie turned the final bend. Through the crack in the door she watched them. Belly Belden was in front. Lilixar the ox frogmarched Salrivos along behind.

Laratus shot his bow. The three bolts fanned out. One took Belden through the throat and their torch flew out of his reach. Another sliced Lilixar's shoulder but the third clattered uselessly against rock.

Belden fell, clawing at the blood bubbling from his neck. Lilixar threw Salrivos towards the attackers and backed off, kicking the torch away so he was less of a target but the Eagle slave rolled a handful of shot and Lilixar slipped. His head crunched against the wall and he slid unconscious to the ground.

Salrivos scrambled to a crouch. His black eye didn't seem to trouble him. He spun his sword in a glittering pattern and advanced. Laratus was feverishly reloading his crossbow. The passage was too narrow for Vetrus to use the last round in his sling. All that stood between them and freedom was one slightly battered youth.

Kataljid edged forward, seeking an opening. Salrivos drew a dagger.

The fallen brand lit their faces. "You!" he gasped, then noticed her sword and buckler. "But –"

"Get on with it, you conniving murderous bastard." She lunged in a feint. He resisted the lure, parrying with insolent ease. Skilfully he let her wear herself out against his ever-dancing blades. Short though he was, Salrivos outclassed her. His grin was a taunt.

She jumped back, panting. "It's not going to work, you know. You'll never win Oakland. You think it's just like the empire, don't you? Well it's not. At home kingship doesn't pass down through blood so your random baby can't get you the crown."

"So? A new line's got to start somewhere." A flick of his wrist and a silver star spun towards her. She ducked. It sliced a hank of her hair before clattering on rock.

Kataljid rolled into his legs, counting on the constraints of the tunnel to stop him taking a swing. He didn't bother. Tossing the dagger from a throwing hold to a thrust, he bore down. He was faster than anyone she'd ever seen. She kicked out ferociously, connecting with his leg. Salrivos screamed and fell, blade shattering on the floor. Like his ankle. He clutched the white bone as though he could push it back under the skin. Whimpering, he collapsed. "Don't hurt me!" He grabbed at her robe. "Please, Candis. I don't know what you heard but I wouldn't have done whatever it was."

She tore free. If Salrivos hadn't been so focussed on her he would have noticed the secret panel swing open again.

"Please, Candis, please!" Sweat sparkled on his ashen cheeks. "You've got it all wrong! I was going to run away with you where we'd both be safe." Then he cast another star.

His ruse had bounced back on him. Salrivos hadn't given a thought to the magic of an Oakland healer. Kataljid felt his agony as though her own bone had fractured. She would have fallen but for her sword. It deflected the star but she overbalanced.

Three bolts leaped from a crossbow, their impact hurling Salrivos across the passage. A slingshot caught him above the heart. His beautiful face went slack.

With his death the pain vanished, at least the pain in her leg if not the one in her heart. Now she heard a battle in the mansion beyond.

"Sounds like our side's winning," said Laratus.

"Maybe." Vetrus gave a feral grin and swept up the fallen torch. "But let's take the back door just in case."

Down through the maze of caves he led them. In parts the caverns were so vast they were lost in shadows, in others horrifyingly tight. As they wriggled through a fissure Kataljid felt the weight of the mountain pressing down at her in the dark. Ahead, their torch guttered and fear gripped her. Chanting mantras to the Goddess, she strove to quell her mounting panic. To be lost down here in the endless night...

But Vetrus found another brand, which lit them until they

found themselves staring up at ripples of sunlit water. Reflections on the roof of the cave, she saw as she and Laratus caught up. A lake, salty and turquoise and gold, lapped right to the mouth of the cave. Which was below sea level, lit by the rising sun.

"Lucky it's not full tide yet, eh?" The Eagle man grinned. "Best get going before it is." He dived in. After three deep breaths he jacknifed, plunging deep. For a moment they could see his body arrowing underwater, then the brightness swallowed him. They had no way of knowing whether he'd safely reached the other side.

"Can't! Can't!" Laratus wrapped his arms around himself, teeth chattering. "Can't."

Kataljid threw her arm over his shoulders but something sharp pierced her breast. She shoved him away, her pained cry echoing above the splash of the waves.

Still clutching himself, Laratus toppled in. Kataljid peered anxiously but he didn't come up.

She launched herself in a shallow dive and turned back to search the dark waters. Bubbles rose into the light like drops of frothing gold. She followed them down into blue dimness.

Her groping fingers found him. She yanked at his arm but he weighed more than an aurochs and she couldn't budge him. The eunuch flailed, frantically trying to pull something out of the armhole of his tunic. A goblet spun away, startling a small fish.

Kataljid batted off his hysterical clutch and unbuckled his belt. Jewels tumbled in slow motion, a shimmer of metal and colour that sank into the sand. Laratus grabbed after them but she dragged him to the surface.

"Leave it, you idiot! I'll come back when I've got you out."

"Not that much of an idiot, then," the eunuch grinned as the vessel he'd chartered swept them out beyond the headland.

"Only to swim wearing a talent of bullion." Pretending to adjust the voluminous shawl over her head, Kataljid nudged him companionably. She had to make sure the crew didn't see. After all, a slave wasn't supposed to touch one of the noble class. "I have no objection to actual treasure. I just don't like my friends drowning."

Beside them, in the shade of an awning, Vetrus leaned up from his couch and called to his servant, the girl with the blue eyes of the north. "Wine for my companions, if you please, and fruit juice for my son."

"And some dates," mumbled his wife through a mouthful of spiced lamb.

The slave in the headcloth was unusually tall for a Rovalan, and beloved of the baby recovering from horrific burns.

Once on the shores of the northland, Kataljid stopped pretending to be a slave. With the empire in turmoil, it was safer for them all to be travelling traders. The fortune she'd gone back for was easily enough to buy a waggon, goods and guards, and Laratus still had sapphires and rubies to spare.

As they reached the foothills, Vetrus and his family turned aside. They wanted to join the uprising, but first they had to leave the baby with relatives in their tribe. Besides, the profits from this journey would help fund the rebels. All of them were determined on that.

The waggon trundled into the distance. Kataljid and Laratus rode up towards the pass. She was sad to see them go but the further she penetrated into Oakland, the more excited she grew.

After miles of hairpin bends, they reached the saddle between the last two peaks and paused to gaze down into King's Vale. Beneath them the fields and forests were more brown than green, crippled by the drought. Except around the lake where she had learned to swim, back when her brother Torgil was still alive, and her little brother Astwin was scarcely out of the cradle.

A frigid drizzle began. Testily Laratus fashioned a blanket into a hood. "I knew it. It always rains in the barbarous north."

She laughed. "Call this rain?" Inhaling the precious scents of home, she kicked her mare down the slope. "Come on, Laratus!

You haven't seen anything yet."

It was dusk when they passed the Temple of Healing. Kataljid felt both comfort and pain. Three years she'd lived there, learning the goddess' work and making friends. All she'd ever wanted was to be a healer, right since she gave acorn-cups of 'medicine' to her dolls. But now she had to be a monarch in waiting.

A villager spotted her riding by. "It's the healer princess!" he cried, and people flocked around. Food, dry clothes, fresh mounts; they could hardly do enough, and all the time they laughed and bantered with her. Laratus hid his surprise. "Spent too long in Rovala, old son," he muttered to himself, and tried not to show his distaste for sheep's cheese.

Kataljid revelled in hearing her real name and speaking her own tongue. They spent half the night talking to the abbot while a runner sent for the Oak patrol. At dawn she stepped out into the chill air of home, and discovered yawning and grinning made a painful combination. When the Oak guards clashed spears on shields she almost dislocated her jaw. Laratus cringed back but Kataljid, first wondering and then eager, ran forwards.

One of the patrol threw aside a winged helmet and ran to meet her.

"Lerica!" "Kataljid!" they squealed at the same time, jumping up and down in delight.

Best, though, was riding up to the Oak Hall and seeing her little brother toddle towards her, dragging their father, who forgot all about kingship and openly wept as he hugged her. Kataljid swept Astwin up to ride on her shoulders, and laughed delightedly at his merry eyes. Then did a double-take. The moppet was wearing a coronet of oak-leaves.

"Is he –?"

"Yes, love." Her father squeezed her. "He's starting to show the Power of the Land, thank Goddess." He stopped questioningly as tears rolled down his daughter's cheeks. "Or have you changed your mind? You want to rule now?"

"I'm just so happy!" she sniffed. "Studying at the Temple has always been my dream. And I'm sure you'll teach him to be a much better monarch than I would." Arms around each other, the king and his family turned to go inside. Then she turned back. "Hurry, up, Laratus! You're not supposed to keep kings waiting, remember?" But she laughed as she said it, and held out her hand to him. A free man, he took it.

What did it matter that the welcome feast was meagre? She knew Oakland went without to help the starving on the steppes. It was enough that her father's hall was bright with torchlight and warm against the frosty wind. Her family's joy was tangible.

As real as that of Laratus, when King Olleyrand ordered his slave-mark bleached, and granted him a fiefdom. The eunuch didn't even wait for her to translate. He bowed so low his hat fell off. "All hail to the Oak!" he cried, and gave a broken speech of thanks. Kataljid realised he'd listened as well as taught.

At midwinter a messenger burst into the hall, snowflakes billowing around him. He shouted, "Sire! The delegate from Rovala has just arrived!"

King Olleyrand stood, eyebrows raised. "At this time of year? Must be more desperate than I thought."

Kataljid stood back out of sight. She watched the man stride, Eagle-crested robes aflutter, into the throne-room. Even his gilt armour couldn't make him anything but a short foreigner with knees blue from the cold. He was one of the two people present who didn't know the saying 'too stupid to wear breeks in snow'. Laratus, in his cosy local outfit, had learned the lesson for himself.

Translator trotting at his side, the general strode into the circle of light before the throne. When he snapped a fist across his chest in a salute, snowmelt dripped from the plumes on his helmet. "All hail to the –" He looked around the crowded hall and swallowed. "… to the Oak. Such sad news about your

195

daughter's treachery, King Olleyrand." The translator interpreted automatically, then quailed as he realised what he'd said. Bearing bad news to people in power didn't make for a long life.

Anger surged around the hall. The general shot a hasty glance at the thanes behind but went doggedly on. "It grieves me to bring you tidings of her treachery and death. She slew her guardian and members of the Lion House. The emperor demands compensation. A thousand head of aurochs will be the initial tribute."

Laratus whispered in Kataljid's ear. Haughty as Princess Haladra herself, she stepped out of the shadows.

"You?" the envoy gasped. "Here?"

"As you see, General Adraius, rumours of my death have been greatly exaggerated." Her Rovalan was perfect, which was just as well as the translator covered his face in horror. "Far from committing murder I was abducted. I was lucky to escape your civil war."

The Eagle shifted uneasily. "A... a minor disturbance, child."

"Minor? Perhaps you don't realise how far the news has spread. New warlords are carving out territories left, right and centre." She spread her hands. "And as you see, I am alive to refute your claims."

Despite the winter chill General Adraius began to sweat. He waved a hand to dismiss her, and gazed imperiously at the king. It would have been more potent if he hadn't been trembling. "Sire, Emperor Lalixir has proof of the murders your daughter committed. As she is alive she will form part of the blood price for her crimes. That may mean you pay less tribute next year."

Kataljid chuckled. "Nice try. Lalixir just wants to buy off the army because he doesn't trust them. Besides, he's too busy fighting all those uprisings to waste time on me. Now hear my father's terms for your tyrant."

She glanced at King Olleyrand, who nodded and asked her to translate. She wasn't about to let the unhappy interpreter water things down out of fear. "I pity your people," the king said, "but whom the gods destroy I should not succour."

"Oh, father, how terribly unjust." To make certain Adraius had got the message, she said it once in each tongue. When the king winked she fought to suppress a giggle because she knew what the next play in the game was. It had all been planned out long before because they'd known this day would come. "But surely, father, if the empire made a sacrifice to our goddess, she'd allow us to give them a little charity?"

Straight-faced, Olleyrand thanked her for her pious suggestion.

The spectre of famine and unrest in the empire loomed over their negotiations. At last the general spent a fortune on a thousand head of aurochs, Oakland to see to their transportation. He didn't seem to notice no one actually mentioned a delivery point. As they'd suspected, he was Rovalan enough to think the capital *was* the empire.

Laratus wrote out the agreement with the interpreter hanging over him. King Olleyrand signed it in blood. Cursing under his breath at acorn-eater customs, Adraius nicked his palm to add his name.

Kataljid snatched the parchment from his grasp and smiled. There was a distinct glitter in her eyes as she blew the signatures dry. "Of course Oakland is happy to help the empire in its hard times. We will split our deliveries equally between every province."

Adraius blanched. "But – but –"

Olleyrand smiled coldly. "My housecarls will see you safely to your camp, general – ah, Agriljus, didn't you say? The emperor wouldn't want anything to happen to you before you get home, now would he?"

Doubtless afraid to face Lalixir, Adraius ignored the slight. Besides, the tall warriors who filled the hall suddenly pressed in on him. He must have realised then that he would never see a copper of what he'd looted from rebel towns.

Two days later, Laratus happily checked off the wagonloads of payment. His new gold tooth glinted in his smile. Tomorrow he'd start a short break on his estate.

The estate he owned as a free man of Oakland. It was right next to the healing house where Kataljid looked after her patients.

But first Laratus was going to play horsey with his fosterling Atwin. The eunuch was part of a family at last.

Sword and Circle

Adrian Tchaikovsky

They were shouting for her. At first she thought she heard her name in the tulmult: "Ineskae! Ineskae!" but that was her sodden imagination. The roar was a wordless demand that she turn up and bleed for them. Out there was a makeshift amphitheatre, just a hollow in the ground. Its uneven sides were lined with a raucous, leery crowd who wanted to be entertained by her death.

There were almost no Wasp-kinden amongst the spectators, that was the shame of it. The Commonweal had possessed a tradition, once, of stately and mannered duels between skilled masters. Like so much, it had not survived the war. What the Wasps had brought with them was a taste for blood and brutal violence, and these conquered locals were latching onto imported ideas with a will. Why not try to emulate the winning side, after all? Centuries-old traditions had not stopped the armies of the Black and Gold.

She drained the jug, harsh grain spirit searing her throat. The sound of individual voices blurred in her ears so that the mob of them, gamblers, brigands, fugitives and deserters, became like a wave of the sea that ebbed and flowed in its own living rhythm.

"You need to go!" someone shouted in her ear.

"I need to drink!" She was already swaying: a wizened woman of the Mantis-kinden, lean and leathery as dried meat, every feature withered as a prune. Her wild white hair floated about her head like a cloud, and her eyes were red-rimmed. Her people had a reputation as peerless killers. It was a reputation she was trying hard to undo, but so far it had proved insoluble in alcohol.

When she took a step forwards, she stumbled, then wheeled around glowering as though someone had tripped her. Had it not been for that accursed badge, nobody would have taken her seriously.

They were not taking her seriously. They were laughing at her. She realised she had lurched forwards just enough to be nominally before her opponent. She was supposed to be fighting.

"Grandmother." Her opposite number was a broad-shouldered man of the Dragonfly and he had one of their long-handled swords down by his side. "Perhaps you have come to the wrong place. This is a fighting circle. For fighters."

Hoots, jeers. Had her badge lost its power at last? Was that why they were so deservingly derisive?

No. She realized that her dishevelled, stained robes were hiding it. With a convulsive twitch of one hand she freed it from the folds, presenting the device to her enemy and to the mob. The sword within the circle blazed in gold from left breast and the catcalls and mockery died in patches. She turned one way and the other, feeling the world swim and the ground tilt beneath her feet.

"Yes!" she shouted out. "Look at it! It's right there!" She tried to point, but ended up jabbing herself painfully in the chest.

"How dare you?" came the voice of her opponent, the nameless Dragonfly warrior. "How dare you steal such a thing and defile it?" He had been in the war, she guessed. To him, the Weaponsmasters' order was an ideal that had somehow survived his people's defeat.

She deserved every drop of his contempt, but still she slurred out, "Didn't steal it." The charge of defiling she did not bother to defend.

Then he was at her, just a simple cleaving stroke aimed at ridding the world of this offence to dignity. She tried, she really *tried* to stand and take it, but the badge was a harsh master. The badge would not let her.

She had come to the circle without a blade, but it was in her hands even as her enemy swung, the grip familiar as breathing: a Commonweal sword like his, five feet from point to pommel, and half of that haft.

She struck halfway through his swing, the blade dragging her tired old arms with it, no messing about with ripostes, but making the parry itself an attack. She ended in a high guard, commanding the middle line, point jabbing at his face. Convulsively, he tried to force her sword aside, because he was far bigger and stronger than she. It took the slightest rotation of her wrists to angle her blade inside his own and, in pushing her sword across himself, he cut his own throat. It was a miserable death for him, a miserable show for the audience, a wretched failure for an old woman who wanted only to die.

Die with dignity, she reminded herself, but that ship had sailed long before, carried off on a tide of cheap spirits.

Later, sitting with a bowl of something clear as water and harsh as defeat, she sensed someone approach her from behind. There had been a time, shortly after the war, when she had put her back to corners to deny the assassins their due. These days she sat with her back to open doors whenever she could. Surely *somewhere* there was a killer competent enough to rid the world of her?

Not this one, though, and she turned and rose in one smooth motion, holding the drink up at arm's length, bringing the blade down in a smooth strike to bisect her enemy's left side from his right. Except the sword was not in her hands, or anywhere in evidence. *Always the fucking thing knows best.* She was left in a guard as perfect as an illustration from a manual, save that her hands were empty. The boy she faced was barely twelve. He had a name, she recalled.

Eshe: a malnourished Dragonfly-kinden child, hollow-cheeked and hollow-eyed. She could not remember where she had got him from, or why. He had just been there, one morning, getting the fire going when she woke on the cold ground. He was just another of the ten thousand orphans the war had churned out.

"Please, Weaponsmaster, we must go." He was so deferential to her. It was as though he saw someone else before him, someone who still possessed an echo of that pre-war golden glory.

"Winnings," she got out. The bowl was empty. She had no idea if she had drunk it or spilled it.

"I have them, Weaponsmaster. We must go. I have had word. There were men asking for you."

"Let them ask it to my face."

There was a rod of iron in this one that somehow the Wasps had not broken. "They are hunting you, Weaponsmaster."

She just blinked at him blearily. Slowly, muscle by muscle, her perfect form collapsed until she was sitting on the floor again, her stained robes spread out about her.

"Fine. Go tell them where I am. There might be a reward."

But that was too cruel and his face showed it. She hated Eshe, sometimes. She had never asked to be responsible for him. She had tried to drive him off. He had not gone. She had refused to feed him. He had proved more than able to scrounge food for both of them. And these days, he kept hold of the money.

"Bad men," he insisted. "Killers. They will not care who dies, what burns, to get at you." He was shuffling from one foot to the other. "Please."

Why should I care? But the badge cared. The sword and the oh-so-honourable circle of the doomed order of Weaponsmasters, they cared, and they hauled her to her feet. *Will I seek them out?* she wondered. Apparently, she would not. Instead, she left town hurriedly – this place in the heart of the occupied Commonweal whose name she couldn't even recall. She made sure people saw which way she had gone.

Once she had staggered a sufficient distance, with the alcohol evaporating off her like mist, she covered her trail and doubled back. She wanted to look at her pursuers. Perhaps one of them would be good enough to kill her. There was always hope.

Sober, she could be stealthy as a shadow. An old, old shadow, it was true, but then all shadows were old. They were the only things in the world that even the rising sun could not renew but must either destroy or leave in hiding. Creeping like a creak-jointed thief back into that village, hiding and lurking, she felt in bitter need of destruction.

Eshe, she had told to stay away, out in the fields. No doubt he would ignore her, as he always did, but he was at least half shadow himself, and who would notice one more starving Dragonfly child in a land that the Wasp armies had chewed their way through?

She remembered the war: the one that had so recently ended. Back then she had been a prince's champion and her badge a source of pride. Sword to sword, she'd had no equal, and this in the Commonweal, where the art of the duel had been perfected centuries before. When the Wasp Empire brought their challenge she had laughed, they all had. Oh, certainly the Wasps had always been a hostile presence on the Commonweal's eastern border, but they were savages, soon riled and soon slapped down.

Those few merchants and vagrants who warned that the Empire had changed in the last generation were ignored. The Monarch of the Commonweal commanded a nobility unparalleled with sword and lance and bow, and a levy of peasants vast enough to swallow the Empire a hundred times over. The outcome of the war was never in doubt.

Of all their predictions, only that last had been true.

A fugitive in her own country, she crouched and spied on these men who had come to take her. There was no mistaking them: not soldiers but some band of trackers sniffing after the bounty the Empire would pay for her head. There were more than a score of them, men who had been peasants, and then soldiers, and were now just survivors. She saw Dragonfly and Grasshopper-kinden amongst them, and a handful of Wasps who were probably deserters. It was their leader who caught Ineskae's attention, though.

It wasn't that you didn't see Wasp-kinden women. They came with the army, but as slaves and kept women and whores. The Wasps had a firm idea of where women belonged in their Empire. And yet here was one of their delicate maidens out on her own, and in command of a pack of killers. This one had seen better times, it was true. She was lean and angular, and wore a knee-length brigandine that had been ill-used and stitched back together. Her fair hair was hacked short, and she carried herself with every bit as much belligerence as a man of her people. Across her back was the same style of Commonwealer sword that Ineskae herself carried.

What, then...? the old Mantis asked herself. *What does this one want? And what do I do about it?* The answer to that one came readily enough. *I suppose I kill her. That's how this usually goes.*

Yet there was something disturbing about her, impossible to define, impossible to ignore. Ineskae reached out for her sword – not an act of the body, but of the mind – and yet her hand remained empty. Something was wrong.

She was too old and too sick of her own existence to know fear. More, there was nothing about this tatty-looking mercenary to strike awe into her. This was just some runaway with a Dragonfly blade, some hunter for hire. There was *nothing*.

But still her sword avoided her grasp and she slunk away. There would be a clean death in some other place. Better to die crossing swords with some ignorant brigand or fighting beasts in a Wasp pit. So many better ways to die.

Two nights later, and Ineskae could not even find herself a fight.

This was some wretched little village, barely a half-dozen wooden huts and some animal pens. She was not welcome. The locals feared her. She had been rattling at their doors demanding drink this last hour, but each family had closed and shuttered their homes, just as they would if the fierce winter wind were crying outside. Eshe had stood in the centre of the village, the still point she was orbiting around, watching her sadly.

She had no wish to be sober. Sobriety brought memory in its wake like a leprous beggar. Outside, under the keen and starless sky, Ineskae took her sword in both hands, but this was an enemy she could not fight.

Past midnight, feverish and trembling, the last veil of her drunkenness was stripped away and she could not stop herself remembering Aleth Rael.

Weaponsmasters were supposed to pass on their skills, but in all her long life she had trained only the one student: Aleth Rael, the swift, the laughing. She had loved him. She had ached to see him fight, or dance, or paint. When he had won his own badge, in the secret trials of their order, she had felt her heart swell until she thought it would break. He had been all the children, all the family she felt she would ever need.

And he had gone out into the world, and she had known that he was destined for great things. He was going to be a general, a diplomat, a man who could have forged a future.

And the Empire had come, and he had come home and gone to war, as all of them had gone to war. When she was drunk she could forget that he was dead.

That was what Eshe did not understand. He was so well meaning. He tried to keep the drink from her hands because he thought that would make things better. But when she had to remember that her student, her surrogate son, Aleth Rael was dead, it tore at her like no sword or claw ever had.

By morning the two of them were gone, she staggering off into the wilderness, Eshe silently dogging her steps, following the faded track to the next town. The cold would not take her, the wild beasts and the bandits avoided her. And so she ended up as she always ended up, seeking the oblivion of drink, because it was the only oblivion she could find.

Three days later she dragged her feet into some other no-name place with the rising sun, weary as death but still not dead. This time she did not even have the energy to beat on doors and make demands. She sat down in the cleared space that formed the centre of the village, kicking aside a detritus of spent candles and the charred ends of incense sticks. During the war, places like this had looked to their traditions when the Wasps came. They had placed their faith in all the comforting lies and rituals inherited from generations past. It hadn't worked. Around her was the debris of a battleground where the present had slain the past.

How long she sat there in the morning chill, she could not say. Then she heard Eshe whispering her name, and a shadow fell across her. She reached for her sword, wherever she had left it, but her hands remained empty.

A boot nudged her knee none too gently. There was a stocky Dragonfly man standing before her, a cudgel in his hand. He was greying and leathery, and she guessed he must be the local Headman.

"What do you want?" she asked him.

"We want you to leave."

"Give me a drink first."

His face darkened. He could read the history of her descent in the stains of her robe. "Leave."

"Fight me." Abruptly she was on her feet, but the sword still refused to come. She had dropped it somewhere on the trail, but it would be in her hands the moment it knew she needed it. Apparently this was not one of those times.

"You want a fight?" the Headman spat, utterly disgusted. "Go to the garrison. They fight there. They fight and drink and turn our daughters into their whores. Go to the Wasps, woman. You'll fit right in."

"Sounds like paradise," she croaked sourly. "Just point the way."

"No, Weaponsmaster," Eshe whispered with a tug at her sleeve. "Not the Wasps."

"Well there'll be hunters through here within the day, asking after me," Ineskae snapped, slapping at the boy. "I wanted to fight them but you… wouldn't let me." It had been her sword and her badge, not the child, she recalled. Did the sword and badge object to her going to seek a blood match at the Wasp garrison? Apparently not. Fickle bastards, the pair of them.

The Headman was plainly glad to send her to the Empire, possibly because it would involve people he despised getting hurt either way. He said something to Eshe, too, and Ineskae thought it must have been an offer to find the boy a place.

Yes, say yes, she mouthed, but Eshe was proud. Eshe wanted to stay with her. She had no idea why. She should send him away.

With that thought, she felt a sudden cold emptiness within her, at not having the irritating child underfoot. He was no Aleth Rael, her golden protégé, but he was something. Why did she need something, in this ruin that history had made of her life? She could not say, and yet the need was there, insistent as her sword.

Where there were Imperial soldiers, there was fighting. Where there were soldiers there was drink. *I should have thought of this a long time ago.*

The garrison itself had been some noble's castle, built in the ancient days as four high walls surrounding a central courtyard. The ancient ways had not weathered well, which was why the structure was now just three walls and a low bank of rubble that the Imperial war machines had pressed down.

She took in the scene at a glance, guessing that the off-duty soldiers gathered in that space at nights, with with a half-dozen big fires bleeding their warmth out at the heedless sky. There was a raised stage made of piled stone carrion from that fallen wall. There were traders and vintners who were established enough to each have a patch of wall they made their own. When Ineskae appeared, she was immediately surrounded by a sour-looking mob in black and gold who thought she looked like a beggar. When she told them with exaggerated dignity that she was a Mantis come to fight, they let her through, no questions asked.

They had several matches lined up that night. It gave her plenty of time to get in the right state of mind. When Eshe would not fetch her a drink, she was not too proud to get it herself, and when she had found a Beetle-kinden selling the harsh, cheap spirits she was fond of, she saw no reason not to sit with him and give him money. In that way, the fights preceding hers passed in a blur: men against men, a man against a big tarantula, a gang of chained criminals against a Wasp soldier.

At her side Eshe huddled miserably, jostled by every passing Wasp. "We should go," was all he would say.

"Why?" she demanded. "Look how we're all getting on! You'd think there'd never been a war."

"Weaponsmaster, if there are hunters, there's a price. The Wasps love gold as much as any," he insisted.

"Let them come," she declared loudly, turning a lot of heads. The Beetle tapster was looking alarmed, holding off on giving her another filled bowl. She fixed him with a steel stare. "Try it, fat man. Just try and come between me and my love." When the words were out, she did not know where they had come from. They seemed abruptly pathetic.

Then someone was tugging at her sleeve again and she rounded on Eshe to snap, "I'm not leaving!" only to find it was a Wasp out of uniform. "What?"

"You said you were here to fight," he boomed over the crowd. "Your moment's here."

"About damn time." She got up, lurched, ended up clinging to him, then stumbled off into the crowd at a tangent, trying to set a course for the stone mound of the stage. When she got there, she rebounded from it painfully, and then someone unwisely tried to help her up, so she punched him to the floor.

The soldiers around her, with the exception of her bewildered victim, found this hilarious, whooping and cheering for her as she clambered up, her robe rucking about her knees. When she stood there, swaying, someone yelled out, "Did you forget something, grandma?" and another, "Where's your sword gone?"

"She drank it!" called some wit, and she only wished it were true.

She thrust a hand into the air as though calling for silence, and for once the sword knew its cue and was there. She heard the expanding ripple of surprise, a crowd of Apt soldiers – for whom a Weaponmaster's magic was just a story – hurriedly trying to rationalize what they had seen.

"Give me my fight!" she roared at them, as though expecting them to storm the stage and drag her down. "Come on, you sons of whores!"

But then someone was being shoved up to face her. Not a Wasp: somehow she had thought it would be one of their own.

It was a Dragonfly man in ragged clothes that had once been fine. She knew it was not Aleth, of course. Aleth was dead. This was some captured warrior or noble, hauled out to give the lads a bit of sport. When he stood before her, though, she could only see Aleth Rael in him. Her tear-blurred eyes would not focus on the reality. The drink betrayed her and let the memories pour in like the sea.

When he took up a stance against her, sword held high just as Aleth always preferred, she howled out her denials, staggering away but being jovially pushed back onto the stage every time.

"Come on!" her opponent yelled at her, and she knew that voice: it was the voice of desperation, of someone who wanted to die. She had heard it from her own throat often enough to recognize it now.

So she went. The sword wanted to fight. It wanted to put someone out of their misery and probably didn't care which of them. So she went with a will, with a vengeance.

Eshe hunched himself down until he had his back to the Beetle-kinden's barrels. Ineskae and her Dragonfly opponent had clashed three times, separating after each, long swords gleaming and leaping in the firelight. As always when fighting, the old woman was steady as steel: she was drunk but her sword was sober.

People thought she had taken him in for charity. They did not realise it was the other way around. He had grown up on stories of the Weaponsmasters. After the war, without family or home, those stories were all he had left of the world he had once known. Everything had been stripped from him but the dreams.

He had been begging when he saw her – that badge, unmistakeable. He had latched onto her not because she would save him, but because he might save her. He knew, miserably, that he was failing.

And then someone had sat down next to him and said, "Hello there," as naturally as anything, and he looked, and it was the Wasp woman, the one hunting Ineskae. She was here, bold as day, surrounded by men of her own kind who would rape her and put her on crossed pikes if they realized what she was.

He tried to bolt, but she had his arm in a pincer grip.

"I'm Terasta," she said conversationally. "What's your name?" Despite the roar of the crowd he heard her words clearly.

He would not say, but then her grip redoubled and he gasped out, "Eshe!"

She nodded, her eyes on the fight. "Hello, Eshe. You know we've a mutual interest? I'd say 'acquaintance,' but we've yet to be introduced. We will be, though, and very soon."

He wanted to cry out, to warn Ineskae, but there was no chance his voice would be heard and he was afraid Terasta would hurt him more.

"Look at her fight," the woman breathed, eyes gleaming as she stared at the stage. "Magnificent, isn't she?"

The duel had intensified, both of the combatants striking faster, blades scraping and rebounding from each other. Ineskae's face was set into an expressionless mask, every part of her bitter, sodden personality purged in the moments of the fight. Eshe was unhappily aware that this was what she sought, to be taken from herself. Simply being Ineskae was her own private hell.

"It looks as though things are about to become busy here," Terasta observed. She pointed out a band of Wasps who were forcing their way laboriously through the crowd. Unlike most of the off-duty audience they were in full armour, and it was obvious they were making for the stage.

"Why?" Eshe whispered, and somehow she heard him.

"The reward that has motivated my band of cutthroats is a powerful incentive to the army's more venal elements. Now…" And she was standing, dragging Eshe to his feet. "Time to get her attention."

For a blessed second her hand was gone and Eshe bunched to run, but then she had stooped and picked him up effortlessly. Almost like a proud mother, she hoisted him up into the air, holding his struggling form over the heads of the crowd.

Eshe did not think Ineskae would see. He did not think she would care. A moment later, though, she had swayed aside from a strike, failing to counterattack, and her eyes met his.

He would not cry for help. A Weaponsmaster would not. He kicked and scratched, and got nowhere, the Wasp just shifting her grip easily, anticipating every move. Then she was taking him away, and the uniformed Wasps were reaching the stage, and he did not see what happened next.

Ineskae was fighting Aleth Rael. The memory was stronger than her actual duel with the ragged Dragonfly nobleman. She had sparred with her beloved student so often, in those golden days before the fall. To relive those lost fights was far more satisfactory than to admit the truth.

Beyond the decaying vistas of her imagination, the Wasp crowd hooted and cheered as they danced, blade to blade. Who could have expected such a good show from a pair of old relics like this?

She could not know what her opponent was thinking, but when she crossed sword with him, when they tried ardently to kill each other with the razor edges of their shared steel, he played her game. It was as if she had asked him to wear her student's face, just as a favour for the woman she had once been.

And she knew it was all in her mind. She knew that she was fooling only herself. Tears drew their lines down her withered cheeks even as she fought. But while the fight went on she could pretend, and remember being happy.

And then there was a wrong note, and she fell from her killing reverie and opened her eyes.

The child: the annoying, unwanted, useless child who dogged her every footstep for no reason she could divine; the child was in trouble.

There was that Wasp woman, the hunter. She had Eshe struggling in her grip. She was taking the child. *Why was she –?*

The crowd had not noticed her distraction. Her sword had not stopped its dancing. Abruptly, though, she had somewhere else to be.

She changed her pattern and, to her joy, her opponent followed, his own sword leading him to her plan, enemy become accomplice. She went into the crowd, and he went with her.

She saw black and gold armour and heard a Wasp voice shout her name. They were arresting her. What did that mean? *Arrest means to stop*, she considered very calmly, as her sword lanced forwards. *I can't be doing with that.*

The lead Wasp, the officer, took her blade through his open mouth. By then there were already half a dozen brawls as other Wasps objected to the interruption.

Ineskae plunged into the crowd, running on heads and shoulders, hacking at arms, weaving from stingshot. Behind her, her opponent stopped and fought, buying her time though he owed her nothing.

Ahead, the Wasp woman was already out of sight, and Eshe with her.

The Wasp woman had near two-score villains assembled here, in tents and around fires. This land, a good mile from the garrison where Ineskae had been fighting, was broken and rocky. The hunter-brigands were strewn about wherever offered shelter from the cold wind. A handful were notionally on watch, and a Dragonfly man went from one to the other, kicking them if he found them asleep.

"You think they'll beat Ineskae," Eshe divined.

Terasta snorted. "They'd barely slow her down."

"Nobody can beat her. She'll kill all of you."

He expected her to slap him, or at least to sneer. Instead, her expression was thoughtful. "Could she?"

"You know the badge she wears!" Eshe snapped fiercely.

Terasta nodded. "Better than you'd believe. And I know that she has fought the desperate and the doomed in every pit across the Commonweal. And she was cut, back in Te Sora, and again in Mian Lae. Can you imagine? One of the Weaponsmasters, the ancient order, losing blood to some thug swordsman in the back of an army drinking den." She did not sound mocking, anything but.

"I hope the reward makes all your deaths worthwhile," Eshe hissed.

"Oh, my men want the reward, and we have fought off three other packs of hunters who sought it. Why else would I need scum like this? But that's not it. Not for me …"

Then there was a yell from one of the lookouts, and a moment later the gang of villains was scrabbling for weapons, leaping up as the spitting light of a chemical lantern heralded the Imperial army.

"Time for the scum to earn their keep one last time," Terasta murmured.

The soldiers who marched up were perhaps half the strength of her hunters but their faces showed only contempt for their lessers. "Who commands here?" their officer said. Eshe guessed they were the same mob who had crashed the fight back at the garrison.

"How can I help you, Sergeant?" Terasta's hand was

abruptly off Eshe's shoulder, abandoning him in the midst of her camp.

The lead Wasp raised an eyebrow at finding a woman in charge. "We want the Weaponsmaster."

Terasta nodded. "You want her; we want her."

The sergeant squared his shoulders. "We know she came this way. Don't play games."

"I never do," the woman replied, unintimidated. "I have papers authorising me to hunt fugitives from Imperial justice."

Eshe looked about him, finding that nobody seemed to be paying him all that much attention. He began a slow shuffle away from the camp's centre, edging towards the dark beyond the fires.

"I piss on your papers, woman," the Wasp sergeant snapped.

"Interesting," Terasta remarked thoughtfully. The transition from her standing there and her sword clearing its scabbard to cleave between neck and shoulder, was swifter than Eshe could follow, and yet so natural that it seemed rehearsed. The Wasp let out a gurgling yelp and went down, and then the fighting started in earnest, and Eshe ran.

He got quite far, hopping and stumbling over the broken countryside, his Dragonfly eyes wringing as much light from the waning moon as he could manage. He thought he was clear of them, the sounds of battle receding until they became someone else's problem.

Then he skidded down a scree slope, fetching up against a jutting rock hard enough to beat the breath from him, and Terasta stepped around it and took his arm again, as though she and he had been following the steps of the same dance.

Eshe struck at her with his free hand, but she twisted his arm above his head, driving him to his knees.

"I approve of your instincts, boy," she said softly. "Any other time they'd have been right on the money. But this is where I wanted you. Right here." She cocked her head, listening as the sounds of the fight were carried on the breeze.

"Your people are losing," Eshe spat at her. It was anyone's

guess whether it was true.

"Probably. But they're a pack of killers, thieves and deserters fighting a squad of equally greedy soldiers. Why should we spare any tears?" She shrugged. "My scum have served their purpose, in getting me this far and fending off the others who wanted Insekae's head."

A new voice growled out, low and dangerous, "And you think you'll collect it, do you?"

Ineskae had intended to avoid the bloody skirmish between the Empire and her hunters, but somehow she had ended up going through the middle of it, her sword and the dregs of her drunkenness just drawing the shortest possible line between her and Eshe and then cutting along it. There was blood weighing down her robes, mostly other people's. Her souvenirs were a thin line of red above one eyebrow and a ragged gash across the back of her left hand.

The Wasp woman regarded her coolly. "I'm not here for any reward," she said. "I'm here for you."

"Personal, is it?" Ineskae squinted. "I don't know you." She was tensed, ready to strike, sword and mind finding her a dozen solutions to the problem: kill the woman, not the boy. Eshe's eyes were burning on her.

"I know you, Weaponsmaster," the Wasp woman told her. "I have heard more stories of you than you probably know exist. I know everything of you, your history, your victories, your provenance."

"And how?" Ineskae demanded scornfully.

"Aleth Rael." The Wasp smiled tiredly, letting go of Eshe, abruptly nothing more than a shabby mercenary in ill-fitting armour. "Aleth Rael, old woman."

Ineskae was very still. "How dare you speak his name?" she whispered.

"Because he was my teacher."

"You? A Wasp?" Her fury was automatic, and also hollow.

215

There was something new come into Terasta's voice, an earnestness beyond her studied poise. Ineskae was practically spitting with insults, desperate to keep this confrontation as something simple: just another throat to cut. And yet no words came out. Her sword trembled in the air between them, fighting her, and her hand was stayed.

"I am Terasta of the Empire, and I was his student while he lived."

"Impossible," Ineskae got out. "Where's your badge?"

"I never had the chance to earn it," the Wasp said bitterly. "The war came. He went home to fight for his people, and against mine. And then he died."

"Yes." Something vital went out of Ineskae. Abruptly neither she nor her sword had the heart to continue their struggle.

"And I knew I should have been with him," Terasta added, "even if it meant killing my own kinden. I failed him."

"Yes," Abruptly Ineskae tottered over to a flat stone and sat down. "Yes," she said again. "But here you are."

"He left me with one thing only," the Wasp said. "He left me with his memories of you, the woman who gave him everything. He loved you."

The old Mantis looked at her bleakly. "So why are you here? To give me his fondest best wishes?" Eshe had retreated to her, half hiding behind her, and she reached up to him. His hand in hers was like a lifeline in a world that was draining away.

"I have tracked you. I have followed your path from fight to pointless fight," Terasta told her. "You are looking for death. A proper death. A Weaponmaster's death, worthy of the sword and circle badge. And you can't find it. Not here. Not any more."

"Seems that way," Ineskae grunted. "You're going to give it to me, are you?"

"If I can. Because I understand the sword and circle, even if I never earned it for myself."

The old Mantis stared at her. Wasp-kinden weren't noted for

any kind of honour that the fallen Commonweal might have recognized, but she saw it in Terasta: the stillness, the calmness; a woman whose life had been given over to the sword for its own sake, and not merely for what that sharp edge might win. Something rose in her at the thought: a proper fight, a final fight, a dignified exit from a world that no longer wanted her.

Her sword and her badge desired that. She had used them badly, since the war's end. They wanted rid of her.

But she was damned if she was their plaything.

"No," she said softly.

The Wasp started in surprise. "But... all this time, what have you sought, except this?"

"I know." Ineskae closed her eyes, feeling out this new thing she had discovered within herself as though it was an arrowhead too barbed to draw out. *So I have to push it on through.* "I thought so too, until now."

"Then what changed?" Terasta demanded, bizarrely infuriated that all her good work and planning had apparently been in vain.

"You took him." Ineskae squeezed Eshe's hand gently. "And I wanted him back. It was the first time I wanted anything that wasn't a drink or a death since the war. It was meaning." She managed a brittle smile. "And you did the right thing, by Aleth Rael, by me. You were right on all counts. And if you want to draw your sword and try your luck, I don't reckon I can stop you. Only now I'm not ready to go. Now I've got other business to deal with." It was absurd, she knew. She was too old, too worn down, and yet somehow she felt younger than she had in a long time. Somewhere in that flood of feeling was the ghost of the woman she had been back before Rael died, back when she had something to care about.

Terasta was looking completely lost. She had come a long way, engineered so much, and played by all the right rules, and now what did she have? "I don't understand," she complained. "What is the boy to you, really?"

"Who knows?" Ineskae stood, feeling her joints creak. "Maybe it's time I took another student. Can't let the old ways die out just yet, can we?" She weighed the thought in her mind, feeling a tentative and probationary approval from her sword, from her badge. "I could take two, maybe." Her gaze was still red-rimmed and wild, but it was steadier than it had been in a long time.

For a long moment, Terasta stood frozen, hand partway to her sword hilt, world yanked out from under her. And Ineskae saw that the woman's hunt – her relentless pursuit of her teacher's teacher – was indistinguishable from Ineskae's own quest for self-destruction: differing strategies to deal with an identical void.

"I will fight you, old woman," the Wasp said flatly, and Ineskae sighed, waiting for the strike, but then Terasta's shoulders twitched, the smallest shrug. "But not until you are ready," she added. "Until then, it would be an honour and a privilege to learn."

Then there were voices calling amongst the rocks, the survivors of the Imperial soldiers spreading out to search for their elusive quarry. Ineskae consulted her sword and her badge, but they felt no need to go and shed more Wasp blood today. There was no hurry to go picking fights, now that she had so much else to do.

FAIRYLAND

Jan Siegel

First of all, there wasn't a door. Just a thicket of shrubs in a woodland hollow, a sudden space where the branches drew back, arching over and binding together in a net of twisted stems. Birds did not come there, though they might have nested in secret beneath the leaves; insects skittered away from the gap; the small creeping things down in the leaf mould would flinch if they approached too near, and scuttle back the way they had come. Once in a while some creature in flight from a predator would cross the unseen boundary, and the pursuer would halt on the brink, and sniff the air, and gaze in bafflement after his vanished quarry. People did not know the place, not then, for people were few and far between. But when the village came, pushing back the trees, and the children invaded the borders of the wood, they would pause on the hollow's edge, feeling the hairs rise on their skin, and dare one another to go further.

One day there was a child who did not return. Then the wood had an ill name, and the children were kept out, and the people left gifts of flowers and food to placate the fairy folk who might steal their infants away. Scavengers ate the food, the flowers rotted, and only the village idiot went under the shadow of the trees.

O'Driscoll the blacksmith did not believe in fairies, or so he said, but he had a young wife, Bridie, who was pretty in the fairy-fashion, light-limbed and long-necked, with woodland eyes and hair as fine as mist. The birds came to her hand to be fed, and the hare did not run when she drew near, and the village idiot would sit with her beneath the trees and talk to her in a language only they could understand. In the tavern of an evening the tosspots and troublemakers would whisper about her, saying she and the fool did more than talk, and O'Driscoll heard the whispers, while he drank and brooded on his wife and her strange ways. Then he tossed the tosspots over his shoulder, and threw the troublemakers into the street, all without even shortening his breath, for he was a strong man. But afterwards he went home and brooded more darkly than before.

Bridie tried to please him in little ways, not comprehending what disturbed him, for she didn't listen to the talk of troublemakers and scandalmongers, and the whispers had passed her by. She loved her husband despite his moods, and was kind to all creatures; she was one of those who saw no wrong. So she cooked his favourite foods for him, and sang softly about the house to ease his heart, and she did not see the demon inside him, murmuring that thus the guilty behave to hide their guilt.

There came a day when O'Driscoll looked for his wife and she was gone. He did not know that the fool was ill in the priest's house, and Bridie there to nurse him; he was too proud to ask her whereabouts from anyone. He ran to the wood, and under the arms of the trees, blundering among the shadows, calling her name. Presently he came to the hollow, and he saw the branches curving around the doorless space, and only more hollow beyond: a place where the sun never reached, and the fallen leaves had gathered and rotted for year upon year, and the little darknesses had settled among the leaves, and the loose ends of a spider's web blew untenanted though there was no breeze, and the toadstool caps thrust upwards like the hats of tiny imps spying on the intruder. Evening was drawing in, and the wood grew dim; a bird screeched in warning, but O'Driscoll paid no attention. The darkness oozed from under the leaves like a miasma, and the many-legged crawlers on the woodland floor were still, fixed in their place, and out of the rustling silence came the pipes, faint as the wind's whisper, wilder than birdsong.

Within the pipesound there were words, spellwords calling, calling, and O'Driscoll followed them like a man summoned, down into the hollow, and under the arching stems, which grew to swallow his height, and then the wood was gone, and his feet trod a stony pathway into a waking dream.

The path descended into a valley of rock, a valley so deep it might have been at the bottom of the world. On either side there were red cliffs too high to guess, and the sky was narrowed to a vein of blue, and the path wound down and down into the red dimness. Then at last the valley began to widen, and the sun found its way in, a low, slanting sun carving the rock with shadows, etching strange shapes sculpted by the wind, which might have been forms, or faces, or nothing at all. There were pools on either side of the path, many-coloured against the rufous tint of the rock: scarlet and citron yellow and turquoise and acid green. He drew close to one and peered down; it seemed to be very deep, and steams rose from the surface, stinging his eyes, so he retreated, following the path downward, always downward. A bird like none he had ever seen before flew up from somewhere nearby, circling in the steams. Its beak was curved like a sickle and its feathers were many-coloured like the pools and sparks trailed in its wake. It seemed to have no song, only a thin weeping cry. And always there was the pipe-music, drawing him on.

Presently he saw the piper, not far ahead, a shape emerging from the rock-shapes, shadow-moulded and patched with shadows, appearing and disappearing among the whorls and ridges of stone. A shape that leaped and danced and spun, cheeks swollen with the puff of its breath, fingers flying along the multiple pipe-stems – three, four, five, he could not count –limbs hairless or hairy, feet cloven. Stubby horns seemed to thrust up from its skull, and its eyes were dark in the sunlight, and red as blood in the shade. And the pipe-music made words in O'Driscoll's head, calling and calling him on.

Come to the valley of Azmodel,
to the country beyond the door!
Follow the piper that pipes the spell –
the call of the sea in the whorl of a shell –
the high road to Heaven, the low road to Hell –
loreley, lullaby, philomel –
dance in the footsteps of Samael
to the kingdom of Nevermore!

Come to the country of Stolen Dreams –
to the garden where roses blow –
to the rainbow lakes where the moonshine gleams –
the phoenix soars in the rising steams –
the starfire melts in the sun's first beams –
the lily weeps and the mandrake screams
on the road to the World Below.

As it is in certain dreams, which appear so real that they thrust all other realities aside, so it was for O'Driscoll in the valley of stone. He forgot the woodland and the hollow, the village with its tosspots and troublemakers; this was the only world he knew. The cliffs on either side receded, and suddenly – he wasn't quite sure how – he was in a garden. It reminded him a little of the garden at the manse, with its rose-grown arches, twisty paths and tangled flower-beds and the topiary rambling out of shape. But of course he had no clear memory of the manse: all that remained was an echo of something lost and familiar, an eerie distortion of a place long gone. Strange plants had been clipped and coaxed and coerced into unnatural forms, cloisters and colonnades of greenery, sprouting cupolas, writhing columns of intertwining stems. Flowers poked out, some like little mouths, pink and pouting, others with protruding stamens and petals spotted as if with blood. Bush and box-hedge had been trimmed into the form of animals and demons. Insects, or things which might have been insects, buzzed and zoomed to and fro, moving too quickly for him to see them plainly, but he thought he glimpsed a dragonfly with a reptilian head, a moth with the body of a sylphid, a hornet with the face of a malevolent imp. And still the piper danced in front of him, and leaves flew off branch and twig to whirl around the leaping figure, and insects with iridescent wings spiralled above its head.

The sun was sinking into the valley's throat, a blood-orange ball swallowed up in the crack between leaning walls of rock. The lastlight melted into long shadows which came racing towards him, engulfing the garden in a wave of dusk; many-coloured fireflies emerged to swirl about the piper, and all around O'Driscoll there were rustlings and murmurings and the tapping of fairy feet. He thought he saw wisps of darkness detach themselves from root and tree-bole, rising upward into willowy forms which gathered about him and wove themselves into a pattern of airy dance-steps and floating limbs. Other shadows slid from under shrubs, from empty archway and spiny thicket, thronging round him in a crowd he could hardly see. He felt himself pushed and pulled into the dance, though no hands touched him. Capering, reeling, stumbling, he was drawn onward, following the phantom procession as it wound through the garden, chasing the last green traces of sunset before they were consumed in the cleft ahead.

The ground sloped slightly upwards and his feet trod on broad steps of polished stone. Then there was a circle of pillars, perhaps twenty yards in diameter, perhaps thirty; in the afterglow of twilight and his bewilderment of mind he could not tell. The ghost-dancers wound between the pillars, fading like smoke into the dimness, but the piper passed within, and O'Driscoll followed, finding himself beneath a huge dome set with star-gems which twinkled and faded like the unseen stars in the sky above. There was an altar on the far side with a stone idol squatting over it which looked ancient and misshapen, gnarled lips twisted into the parody of a smile, eyes narrowed under a knobbled brow. Twin basins of eternal oil burned on either hand.

The piper bowed before the idol, then blew a riff of notes unlike any he had yet played, piercing and unearthly as the call of a night bird in a birdless desert. And the idol moved. The heavy head lifted; balefire glared from the narrow eyes. The gnarly smile widened into a rictus, crumpling the stone cheeks, and something like a bellow issued from between malformed lips. The twin flames flared upwards. As if conjured, the phantom throng returned, pouring between the pillars into the circle of the temple. In the sudden light they seemed to grow more solid, becoming sprites with narrow faces all hunger, sloe-eyed, sly-eyed fauns, bogles and boggarts, goblins and grinnocks, and other beings even stranger: grotesques with random limbs, a mouth like an anus, an anus like a mouth – morlochs, pugwidgies, jikininkis, moguai. Outside the temple it was now altogether dark. The pipe-music grew shriller as the motley troupe cavorted around O'Driscoll, making obeisance to the altar even as they danced. The call of the spell was no longer the wind's whisper but a chorus, wild and triumphant.

> *Follow, oh follow, to Azmodel,*
> *to the garden where roses bleed!*
> *Hark to pipes of the last appel –*
> *melody, threnody, break the spell –*
> *vanquish the flame of the stars that fell –*
> *call up the Night where the shadows dwell –*
> *philomel, Caspiel, toll the knell –*
> *too late to look back, too vain to foretell –*
> *drink of the brine in the wishing-well –*
> *dance in the footsteps of Jezebel*
> *to the place where the demons feed!*

And there she was, as he had known she would be – Bridie, his Bridie, dancing through the horde on feet that seemed hardly to touch the ground, her hair floating like vapour, her eyes alight with reflected fire. She was naked, and her white body was the only pure thing in the valley; it seemed to him she shone like a fallen star. And dancing with her was the village idiot, but he looked no longer foolish: horns branched from his hair and his face was a-gleam with wickedness. There was a wreath on her brow of flowers whose names O'Driscoll had once known: helleborine, witchfingers, old man's deadnettle, forget-me-never. The rose-touched blossoms of maiden's folly nestled in the hair between her thighs. He tried to reach her but the crowd came between them, surrounding him, sweeping him away – he saw the fool laughing, lifting her above him, above the whirl of the dance – saw her gazing down at her partner with an expression on her face he had never seen, never should see, not on *her* face, not his Bridie. Then she was falling, falling into his arms, and O'Driscoll was borne away on a spinning tide, carried like flotsam through the darkness, until at last the tumult abandoned him and he was cast like a drowned man upon another shore.

He awoke later, much later. The morning leaked faintly between the trees. He was lying on leaf mulch down in the hollow, beside the thicket with its empty arch. He rose slowly, like one who has had a fever, still sweating and dreaming in the aftermath, and wandered through the wood towards his home. Bridie was sleeping in the parlour where she had sat to wait up for him when she saw he was gone. There were tear-tracks on her cheek, for the fool had died in the night, and fading flowers in her hair, gathered for her by some village child. O'Driscoll stroked her face, very tenderly, not wishing to wake her. Then he wound her hair around her throat, and strangled her.

When he did not arrive at the forge the villagers came for him. They found him sitting there with Bridie in his arms. He would not speak for a long time. They hanged him, for what else could they do? But there was no satisfaction in it. On the last night he told the priest his story, and when he was dead, swinging from the oak-tree bough which creaked with the weight of him, the priest sent for the best carpenter in the county. Deep in the wood they set an arching lintel, a wooden door – a door without

225

a wall, a portal going nowhere – and locked it with a key which the priest kept safe, binding it not with a spell but with a prayer, though in truth the priest did not know if prayer would be efficacious in such a case.

The years passed as years do, the decades became centuries, the woodland shrank to a coppice and the coppice was cut for firewood and houses grew where once there had been trees. The door was always locked, deep in a cellar now, and guardians kept the key, and other doors closed around it, and stairways and passages sprouted over it, and the djinn of Time yawned as the ages passed slowly by. The little lives of humans came and went, and with them were the stories, rumours, whispers of magic lands beyond the doors, glimpses of the past, visions of kingdoms that had never been. With rumour came fear, murmurs of things hiding in the dark, and enchantment that turned always to evil, so the house was untenanted, and the appointed guardian kept all intruders at bay, and in the end even curiosity was almost gone. The lost valley of Azmodel was forgotten, a thousand years forgotten, a tale penned only in the unread manuscript of a priest from long ago.

The world changed. Science and technology drove out superstition and magic. Folktale and fairytale were replaced by flickering screens and special effects and the cut-and-paste fantasies of a mechanical age. And one day a man came to the house, a man of the modern world with all its wisdom and knowledge, but the dreams of other days were in his eyes. The guardian welcomed him and gave him tea, as was the custom. Later, he gave him whisky. The modern world has many customs.

"The time has come," the visitor said, "to talk of many things. Of shoes, and ships, and sealing wax, the fall of ancient kings. Of doors that are forever locked, and times when pigs had wings."

And so they talked, and the man stayed in the ancient library a day, a week, a month, and read the fading manuscript which none had ever seen. Then he went to the guardian, and asked for the keys – the keys to the lands beyond the doors, and the one key, the oldest key, the key to the door which had stood unopened in an unused cellar for centuries beyond count.

"There are strange things in this house," said the guardian. "I was appointed to keep watch so that nobody could enter, nobody could leave, nobody could be harmed. But who knows? It may all be rumour and fantasy. Fairyland has been locked and forgotten for a millennium and more."

"Then there is nothing to fear," said the visitor.

"True," the guardian conceded. "Still… if the phantoms exist, behind the door, in some other place, some other reality the thickness of a molecule from our own, they may not be pleased to find their sanctuary invaded after so long. It is said none has ever entered here to leave unscathed."

"It is said by whom?" asked the visitor.

"Rumour," sighed the guardian. "Rumour has a lot to say for itself. Nothing substantiated, of course. Tell me, why would you risk this venture?"

"Because," said the visitor. And that was all.

They finished the whisky and the guardian gave him the keys, the keys to the house and the one key, the key to the door that was lost. The man took them, and weighed them in his hand, the hand of science, and contemporary wisdom, but the desire of things forgotten still flickered in his gaze.

"All I ask," said the guardian, "is that when you are done, whatever your condition – though you look in the eyes of dragon or demon, though you love a fairy woman and your heart is lost forever, though the phantom hordes of Azmodel dance with you till you drop – bring back the keys. I conjure you, as the saying goes, by all that is most dear and most dreadful, bring back the keys."

"I will not take them out of the house," said the visitor, and the guardian smiled a wry smile.

Then the man took the keys, and entered the house, and was gone.

A month went by, and another month, and still the guardian waited. He wondered if he would wait a century and more – for such guardians are long-lived – if the man would emerge at last white-haired, aged with horrors, or mysteriously young, spell-preserved, while all the world had gone on without him. But on Midsummer's Eve the man returned, a man of the modern world, and gave the guardian back his keys. The man's hair was not white, nor his face aged, and there was neither enchanted youth nor madness in his steady look. But the dreams of other days sat behind his eyes.

"So what did you see?" asked the guardian.

"This and that," said the visitor, and he drank the tea he was offered. The customary tea. A bird that sang in the garden was only a bird, and a bee that buzzed on a flower had no human visage.

"Who are you," the guardian said, "to enter the house, and leave, with no tale to tell, no shadow in your face, no gibbering saga of nightmare and delirium? Does the house stand empty now – have the phantoms fled – is my guardianship defunct?"

"No," said the man. "Keep the keys. Let no one in. Your task is unchanged."

And he held his teacup with a hand that did not shake.

"What did you seek there?" the guardian persisted, intrigued beyond curiosity. "What kind of a man are you, to cross the forbidden boundary, risking murder or madness, and return without a whitened hair, without an added line to your face?"

The visitor smiled. "I am a writer," he said.

Come then, oh come to fair Azmodel –
to the garden where stories grow!
Hark to the call of the notes that swell
from pipesong and swansong and sleeping dell –
follow the dream to the doors of Hell,
rattle the knocker and shake the bell –
none to resist and none to compel –

rhapsody, tantivvy, crack the shell —
hatch the demon and catch the spell!
Dance in the footsteps of Tinkerbell
Down to the World Below!

Mountain Tea

Sandra Unerman

The three suitors met by chance at the inn and scowled at one another. One, Lord Pertinax, was middle-aged, strong and swarthy, the second, Sir Lambert was young, tall and fair-haired, and the third, Sir Rufus, was a red-head, ageless, smooth and thin. All were dressed in multi-coloured finery, with jewelled pins in their hats and ribbons on their sleeves. Their hair and beards were perfumed and their gloves were new. So they wasted no time trying to mislead one another about their purposes. They sat together over breakfast and Lord Pertinax said,

"Where are you off to?"

Sir Lambert smiled. "To the House with the Golden Pavement, to court the Lord Mayor's daughter. And you?"

Lord Pertinax nodded and said,

"She will live in a castle newly built, if she marries me, and be lady over the finest farms and orchards in the west country."

Sir Lambert said, "I have brought the trophies from seven tournaments to lay at her feet. If she marries me, we will ride from city to city and I will wear her colours whenever I set my spear in the rest."

Sir Rufus said, "I've heard some strange rumours about the lady. Do you know how many suitors she has refused so far?"

Lord Pertinax said, "A dozen or so. But they say her father is anxious for her to marry. He wants a capable son-in-law to help him in his ventures."

Sir Lambert said, "I heard thirty. But her father's fortune is the greatest in the city and she is his only heir."

"Then why doesn't her father pick a husband for her?" Sir Rufus asked.

Sir Lambert laughed. "They say he promised his wife on her deathbed that their daughter should be free to make her own choice. And there were witnesses, who told the whole city, so he cannot go back on his word without damage to his reputation."

Lord Pertinax tugged his beard. "But surely she will be guided by her father's advice?"

"Not so far," Sir Lambert said. "Or she would already be married. She has refused her father's friends as well as his enemies."

Sir Rufus asked, "And have you heard what happens to her suitors afterwards?"

The other two looked at one another and shook their heads.

"Neither have I. She will entertain no wooing from a man she has not met, they say."

"That's reasonable." Sir Lambert looked at his reflection in a polished pewter tankard and tilted his hat. Sir Rufus said,

"Maybe. But I can find nobody who has spoken to one of the men she has sent away."

Lord Pertinax shrugged. "I dare say they've slunk home in shame. Why should we care about them?"

"I hoped to learn from their mistakes."

Lord Pertinax grinned. "If you care to wait, I'll come back here and tell you what I can. Only if I'm disappointed, of course. I'm going there this morning."

"I'll come with you," said Sir Lambert.

Sir Rufus shrugged. "Let's go together."

They arrived at the house and were left to wait in the hall, where they saw plenty to admire. The walls were hung with hunting tapestries, the ceiling was painted with fiery clouds and the floor was marble, inlaid with a labyrinth of golden lines.

Presently a boy led them past the grand staircase and ushered them through a door. They looked round in some surprise, for this room did not match the splendours they had seen so far. It was unadorned and dim, panelled with grey wood and furnished with a bare table and rough-hewn stools. The light came from a meagre fire in a low hearth, beside which a woman stood, waiting to be noticed.

They bowed to her.

"Where is the lady?" Lord Pertinax asked.

"We have come to seek her hand in marriage," said Sir Lambert. Sir Rufus did not speak but he smiled at the woman. She was small and plain, her clothes drab and coarse, her hair scraped back into a bun.

"I will tell you about the lady," she said. "Sit down and drink some tea while you listen."

She poured for them and sat down herself. She looked from one face to another and round again while she talked.

"When I was a child, I was very timid. I used to be too frightened to move if a cat looked at me and I could not touch the melted stumps of old candles, for fear they would burst back into life and burn me."

Lord Pertinax said, "But about the lady?"

"Drink your tea and you will hear."

He grunted his impatience but did as he was told.

The woman said, "I was not afraid of the dark but of bright lights and sudden movement. And noise: crows squawking, dogs barking, men shouting." She looked now at the fire and went on. "As I grew up, I began to feel safer. I walked in the garden and the grass did not cut me. I was given a pony to ride and so long as I was gentle with him, he was patient with me. I worked hard to learn my lessons, in music, languages and accounts, and my teachers were pleased with me."

Sir Rufus shifted in his chair and drew in a breath. But the woman looked at him and he sipped at the tea. She said,

"It has a refreshing taste, doesn't it? Not sweet but cleansing."

All three men put their cups to their lips and she turned back to the fire.

"I began to trust nature and learning. But other children teased me or laughed at me behind my back. A boy danced with me all evening once. I thought he was kind but I found out afterwards he had lost a bet to make me speak more than three words at a time. So when I was old enough to dream of love, I grew more afraid than ever. I was bound to be courted for my fortune and my father's influence and I did not know how to tell a true lover from a false one."

The men looked at one another and frowned. The woman said,

"I never learned how to judge people but there are other ways of making the right choice. When my grandmother died, I inherited a necklace, a long chain of golden flowers set with pearls and amethysts. I took it to the witch who lives in the mountains and begged for her help."

The woman closed her eyes. "I lied to my father. I told him I was going to visit my aunt in the country and went myself to find the witch. My maid was horrified when I confided my plan to her but she was more afraid of staying behind to face my father than of coming with me. We took three of my father's men-at-arms as an escort and they found us a guide who knew the mountains.

"The journey was the hardest I have ever endured and I was not sure I would survive it. We travelled on foot and all the paths looked indistinguishable among the black rocks, while the scrawny trees seemed to hide fierce, hungry eyes that waited for us to falter."

Lord Pertinax said, thoughtfully, "This tea has a tang of the mountains."

The woman opened her eyes. "All the better to quench your thirst," she said and she refilled their cups. "One night, as we huddled together in the shelter of a hollow tree, a white wolf came and grinned at us. It sat down on the path and when it howled, its companions answered from above and below. The men argued about whether to go out to attack the wolves at once, before they could gather their full force, or to wait for daylight. They had swords but my maid and I carried only small knives. I did not want the men to leave us but we could not lie there all night with nothing to do but to listen to the howling of the wolves. So we sang the loudest songs we knew, battle songs and marching songs. And we flourished our weapons in the moonlight until the wolves went away."

Sir Rufus said, "You had need of this tea then, to keep you from despair."

"Not as much as I have needed it since," the woman said. "We went as quickly as we could but the weather turned even more quickly towards winter as we climbed higher up. One day we saw a mountain hare which had frozen to the ground where it couched, high above us on the mountainside. We would not have spotted it but for its golden eyes and its red ears, which flapped as it struggled to get free. We had not eaten fresh meat for many days. Before I could stop him, the youngest of my father's men called out,

"One for the pot," and scrambled up the slope to seize the hare. It mewed and then went stiff as he drew near. But when he pulled it free of the stones, it kicked out with its hind legs. The youngster lost his balance and fell to his death but the hare ran free."

Sir Lambert said, "It tastes of sorrow, this tea."

"And of many other things." The woman poured again. "See how many flavours you can find."

"The guide led us well and the rest of us reached the witch's cave in safety. She was rougher than I expected: a great, heavy woman wrapped in bundles of felt, with a face as pale and round as the full moon. She seemed more than half asleep and she did not want to let us in.

"'You are too late,' she said. 'I seldom grant wishes and never in the winter.'

"We pleaded with her but she did not care about the hardships we had suffered on our journey. Only when we spoke of our companion's death, she roused herself to ask what had happened to the hare. We told her how it had run away and she said,

"'If it suffered any hurt, whisker, paw or tail, bad luck will follow you. Wait here while I find out what happened.'

"She came out into the cold and wild creatures came to surround her, deer and ravens, goats and hares. She listened to their grunts and cries, she looked at us and she laughed. She said,

"'My sister's hare lived where she might have died in the cold, because of you. Though you meant her harm, or your man did, a good deed deserves some reward, even when it is done in error. For the sake of the hare, I will hear why you have come, though I doubt I will do more.'"

The woman smiled for the first time. "I did not think I had the eloquence to move her, so I told her my troubles as simply as I could and I showed her the gift I had brought her. And one or the other, or both together, changed her mind. She said,

"'You are not such a poor thing as you look. You chose your gift well: my love is for treasures with stores of craftsmanship and strength in them, not mere bullion or uncut gems. Not many understand that. And you are right. Too many women do not fathom the nature of their husbands until after they are married. I will teach you how to make a man show his true self the first time you meet him.'"

The woman looked again into the fire. She said, "The witch gave me a bag of dried leaves from a bush that grows only in her garden and told me how to brew it into a tea. When a man drinks this tea, if he is true in mind and heart, he will remain a man. If not, he will be transformed into the shape that suits him best."

The woman looked up but there were no men left in the room to meet her gaze. A badger, a deerhound and a fox turned their heads away in confusion and she laughed as she opened the door to shoo them out.

The League of Resolve

Stan Nicholls

The god killer yanked his blade from a dying man's chest and let him drop.

Another fighter rushed in, shrieking a battle cry. He swung to face him. Their swords met with a jarring impact, rocking them both. They swapped blows, ducking and swerving in turn, seeking a breach in each other's guard.

He saw the opening first. His blade flashed out, striking deep and true. Belching blood, the man went down.

There was no let up.

He cracked the skull of a charging attacker, near severed the arm of a second, plunged his blade into the belly of a third. Next was an officer, judging by the imperial insignia on his bloodstained jerkin. The man was agile, but a fraction too slow to escape the thrust that found his heart.

For a small, miraculous moment no opponent was in sword-range, and there was a kind of stillness in the mayhem. The god killer became aware of the throb from the wounds he had taken, and knew that the blood covering him hadn't all been shed by his foes. Breathing hard, pouring sweat, he took in the scene.

He had started out with sixty-four men. God killers. Now half of them were dead. Retreating to the brow of a hillock, the survivors were fighting desperately as countless enemy swarmed up on all sides.

The battle proper boiled in the valley to their rear, a seething, hellish scrum. When his platoon had been cut off from the main body he led them to what he deemed the comparative safety of the valley's mouth. That proved an illusion. The reality was a last stand.

His fleeting reverie passed. He was conscious of clashing steel and agonised screams from all around.

His men were coming together as they drew back from the onslaught.

Hoarsely, he yelled for them to hold their ground. Clustered, surrounded, they hoped for no more than taking as many of the enemy with them as they could.

The carnage continued, and grew more frantic. At its height several of his men called out his name and pointed skyward.

A shadow fell across them.

Then a flash, heat and flames. The ground itself was afire. Men were burning. The sickly aroma of charred flesh filled the air.

Pain shot through the god killer, borne by the scorching heat.

Darkness took him.

The makeshift encampment was large, and lit with a profusion of torches and lanterns. There were upward of a hundred canvas tents of various shapes and sizes, pitched as need required rather than in any kind of ordered fashion. At the perimeter, and throughout the camp, flags flew, bearing a triangle in a circle, green against a white background. They made clear the function of the place, and its neutrality.

Wagons queued to enter, laden with casualties, military and civilian. Walking wounded were shepherded in columns, hobbling on improvised crutches or stumbling with eyes bandaged, their hands on the shoulders of the man in front. The military wounded wore the uniforms of both sides in the conflict.

Grey-robed men and women received them, tending the injuries of the lesser hurt, dispatching the worst to particular tents for more rigorous care. The bustle was punctuated by moans, shouting and occasional screams.

One healer, grey-garbed like the rest, moved through the camp with quiet purpose. He had seen perhaps thirty summers, was lean and sported a mop of ink black hair. Against prevalent custom, he was clean-shaven.

He observed, advised and issued orders. Where necessary he lent a hand. He helped hold down a man while his leg was amputated, with only rough alcohol to assuage the agony. He stitched gashes and bound wounds. He tried to comfort the dying, closing their eyes when they succumbed.

"Master Deras! *Master Deras!*"

One of his aides ran towards him. He wasn't much more than half his master's age.

"What is it, Ismey?"

"Yoreth Dunisten!"

"What about him?"

"He's *here*. Himself! The General's here!"

"As if we didn't have enough to cope with. What does he want?"

"To see whoever's in charge."

"Why?"

"You wouldn't expect him to tell *me*, master."

Deras sighed. He was dog tired, and the way things were going he had no idea when he might find time for rest. "All right, lead on."

They weaved through the shambles and came to a tent close by the camp's entrance. A pair of guards stood outside, their uniforms identifying them as Lycerians. Dismissing Ismey, Deras entered.

Inside, the General waited alone. He was of advanced years, with whiskers turned white, but his bearing was ramrod straight and his gaze held steel.

"You're in charge here?" he barked.

"I'm one of the overseers, yes." He nodded at the tent's flap. "And I'm not keen on armed men in the camp."

"There are those who'd see my death as an accolade. You're treating a number of them right here."

"They have as much right to be here as your men. This is a neutral area, recognised by treaty. If you were afraid to come in maybe you should have stayed away."

Dunisten bristled. "Were you under my command I'd have you flogged for talking to me like that."

"It's a good thing I'm not then. What exactly do you want, General?"

The man visibly bit back his anger. "I want my men looked

after."

"The League of Resolve offers healing to all, whether you demand it or not. If you came here to remind us of our purpose you've wasted your time."

"You don't understand. Some of our wounded have… special injuries."

"You'll find we're well versed when it comes to the many ways people try to destroy each other."

"But in this case –"

"Do you have credentials as a healer, General? If not, I suggest you leave the doctoring to us."

"Are you *sure* you're in charge?"

"I could drag another of the overseers from their duties, which probably involves ministering to one of your men, but they'd say the same."

"I'm sure they would, given the League's known sympathies."

"To what? Peace? Mending the broken? Giving a dignified death to those we can't put right? Are those the sympathies you have in mind?"

The General took a breath. "Look, I appreciate that you're not overly fond of the military. But I've fought a battle today, and its outcome's still uncertain. I don't want to round off the evening with more enmity."

"Neither do I. And I've a lot to do clearing up the human mess you and the empire have made. So unless there's anything else, I need to get back to work."

Dunisten regarded the healer. "What's your name?"

"Deras Minshal."

The General looked startled. "Minshal?"

"What of it?"

"And you're a Lycerian?"

"As it happens, I am."

"I thought there was a likeness."

"To what? *Who?*"

"Fate has played a nice little trick on us this night, Deras Minshal."

"What are you talking about?"

One of the guards poked his head into the tent. "They're coming in now, sir."

General Dunisten swept past Deras and went outside. Deras followed.

A fresh set of wagons were arriving, carrying Lycerian wounded. The General signalled the convoy to halt. He and Deras approached the nearest wagon. It held half a dozen motionless figures, but there wasn't enough light to make out much more. The General snapped an order and someone brought a torch.

The men in the wagon were badly burnt, to the extent that their flesh had blackened. Most of their clothes had been incinerated and they lay in tatters.

A couple of them writhed. One was groaning.

"These men need immediate attention," Deras said.

The General nodded and waved on the wagons. "Well, what do you think, Minshal?"

"We've dealt with burns before."

"Like these? Of such intensity? And from an area where no fire was used as a weapon?"

"How injuries are caused isn't our concern. We're only interested in repairing the damage."

"Those men are from a crack squad, what's left of it. They're a valuable asset. But there's one in particular I want saved. The best of them; their captain."

"None get preferential treatment."

"You might think differently when you see who I've got in mind."

"Who? You've done nothing but talk in riddles. Make yourself plain."

That was ignored. "He was brought in earlier. The ones with burns, where would they be taken?"

"We have a special unit where —"

"Take me there."

"As I said, I'm busy. I'll get somebody to guide you."

"I want you. *Humour me*," he added coldly.

"I'll not let armed men wander through the camp." He gestured at the guards.

"They stay armed. But in deference to your rules we'll conceal our weapons."

"That doesn't make you any less armed, General."

"The sooner you stop arguing, the sooner you can return to your duties. So shall we get on with it?"

"This is an infringement of the treaty."

"Which at base is unenforceable and you know it."

"I'll be taking it up with the Council."

"Good luck with that."

Deras hesitated for a moment, then said, "Come on."

They began to walk, flanked by the General's watchful bodyguards.

There was a lot of activity in the large tent the burns victims occupied. The General looked around, obviously having difficult identifying discoloured, battered faces. At last he exclaimed and pointed.

The cot he indicated held someone who superficially looked like all the others. He was attended by a woman of an age with Deras. Typically for a Casimarian, her skin was pale and her hair straw blonde. Her eyes were summer sky blue.

"Velda", Deras greeted.

She glanced up, smiled thinly. "Deras."

"How is he?" the General asked.

"Not good." She gently touched her patient's cheek with a soft, balm-soaked cloth.

Deras was staring at the injured man. He was barely conscious, and he was delirious, his cracked lips working soundlessly.

The blackened, ill-used face mesmerised Deras.

"I was right, wasn't I?" the General said.

Deras nodded slowly.

The man was his brother.

In the days that followed there was no end to the torrent of casualties coming in. A week later the battle petered out. Both sides claimed victory and withdrew to lick their wounds and fight anew. The flow of casualties thinned to a trickle and dried up.

The war moved on, but many of the wounded were too stricken to leave. As ever, the League remained, releasing its charges when they healed, consigning them to the funeral pyres when they didn't.

Deras saw to it that he had as little to do with his brother Goran as possible. He discouraged questions as to why. But Velda kept him posted, and reported a strengthening recovery. In that respect Goran was luckier than a number of his comrades. There would soon come a point when he was fully cognisant and able to speak.

Deras' reluctance to engage with his brother puzzled many, and particularly his aide, young Ismey Cleam, whose curiosity needed constant feeding at the best of times.

Nearly a month after the battle ended the League's encampment was starting to empty. Only the more serious cases, like Goran Minshal, were still being treated. And Velda Piran was the healer who most consistently cared for him.

One night, as Velda came off a long, tiring watch, Ismey took a seat by her in the healers' refectory.

"How's your charge?" he asked.

She put down her cup. "Which one?"

"Master Deras' brother."

Velda smiled. "Goran's making a remarkable recovery."

"Funny how some pull through and others don't, even when they've got less grievous wounds."

"It's to do with the individual's will. Some have a real passion to live. Goran has that."

Ismey steeled himself to ask about what he really wanted to know. "Why is Master Deras avoiding him? He practically chewed my head off when I asked."

"It is a sore point with Deras."

"You'd think, with it being his own brother and all, he'd want to spend time with him, catch up, whatever."

"Ismey, you're young." She grinned. "Don't look offended; I don't mean anything by it. But I'm wondering what you know about Lyceria."

"I know what people say about the Lycerians. Not that I've seen anything wrong with the few I've met in the League. And I know they don't really have a homeland."

"There's a reason for that."

"It was all a long time ago, wasn't it?"

"You're a citizen of the empire. Didn't they teach you about what happened?"

"Not a lot about that period, just that we should hate them. Maybe it would have come up later, if I'd stuck around to finish my schooling. But I wanted to be a healer, and came to the League."

"What did your parents think about that?"

"I'm an orphan."

"Oh. Sorry, I didn't know."

"Believe me, even the League's seminary was better than an Eagamar orphanage. And the seminary was all about healing, not history."

"It was a bit different for us, probably because Casimar's a near neighbour of what was Lyceria. My people had a front row seat, you might say."

"So what happened?"

Velda took another sip of water. "Lyceria, under the old king, Eynoss Silverstone, got into a dispute with its neighbour Chessolm. I'm not sure anyone can remember why. Anyway, Chessolm was a city state, and Lyceria laid siege to it. That was a dangerous move, because the empire was obliged by treaty to protect Chessolm. The pact existed due to Ranald Amentinus being based there."

"I've heard of *him*."

"Yes, you must have. A holy man whom many, inside the empire and out, considered a messiah. Some thought him an actual deity."

"Was he?"

She shrugged. "Who knows? There were stories of miracles and so on. But, as you said, it was a long time ago. The point is a lot of people believed in him."

"And the empire honoured the treaty?"

"Yes, but Eagamar was slow in mustering its forces. Chessolm's wheat fields went unattended outside its walls, and after several weeks of the Lycerians' siege starvation was rife. At which point Amentinus died. Whether from hunger, disease or, as some said, a besieger's arrow, no one knew."

"I can imagine how the empire answered that."

"You can't, Ismey. It was more savage than any battle I hope we'll ever see. The empire's army drove off the Lycerians with great brutality, killing many in the process. When Amentinus' death came to light the Lycerians were branded as outlaws, with all other states forbidden to harbour them. Lyceria itself was forfeited to the empire and the citizens remaining within its borders, however old, young or infirm, were slaughtered. What was left of the nation was scattered. Lycerian became a byword for outcast and criminal.

"To this day they're commonly called god killers."

"And that's when the war started."

"Wars, more accurately. A never-ending, bloody tussle between Eagamar and Lyceria's descendants."

"What does this have to do with Deras and Goran?"

"The thousands of Lycerians who survived the cull parted not just physically but in terms of ideas. Some accepted their lot and settled in other lands. Some took to the sword in a crusade to win back their home. A few chose the path of harmony and tried to make a difference to the world."

"My master and his brother were on different sides."

"Exactly. The fighter and the peacemaker, at odds since they were youngsters. Then some quarrel split them, and they haven't seen each other in years."

"Did Deras tell you all this?"

"Er, no." She seemed a little uncomfortable. "Goran."

"He has his reason back, then?"

"Near completely. Certainly enough for him to talk to his brother."

"Does he want to? Or does he feel the same as Deras?"

"He's wary, I'd say. But not as hostile."

"Do you think they'll talk?"

"I don't know. I hope so. But if they do, there's something else Deras will have trouble accommodating."

"What's that?"

"What Goran believes nearly killed him."

A further week passed. Goran grew stronger, and Velda more persistent in trying to persuade Deras to see him.

Velda and Deras were checking supplies in one of the storehouses when things came to a head.

"I don't see what harm it could do," she said. "He's your own flesh and blood. You should –"

"Let it rest, Velda." He rammed a bundle of dressings into a shelf with unwarranted force. "I don't want to see him, and that's an end to it."

"At least tell me why."

"We fell out."

"So badly that you can't swallow your pride?"

"Can *he*? Goran was the one who made the break."

"He doesn't see it that way."

"You two seem to have become... close. Everybody's noticed."

"What if we have, and more than close? What business is it

of yours?"

"How could you, Velda? He stands for the opposite of everything we believe in."

"He's doing what he feels he needs to do."

"And the result's the broken bodies brought here for mending. My brother's a killer, Velda."

"Goran just wants to put right the injustice done to your people. Don't you?"

"Through compassion, yes. Not with the sword."

"So you differ on methods. Should that keep you apart?"

"His way is butchery. How can we reconcile?"

"He sees himself as fighting for a righteous cause."

"He obviously has quite a sway over you."

"I've a mind of my own, Deras."

"Yet it took him no time to get you to dump your principles."

"It's called being open-minded. And I *haven't* abandoned my values."

"Really? I know my brother and how persuasive he can be."

"All right, enough!" she flared. "You're using me to argue with Goran by proxy, Deras. If you've got a grievance with him the grown up thing to do is damn well tell him yourself. Or haven't you the guts?"

Deras had been fussing with the supplies throughout their conversation, as though the distraction might shield him from what she was saying. Now he slammed down the crate he was holding.

Without another word he turned and stamped towards the door. She hurried after him, hoping that the catalyst of anger was doing what reason couldn't.

The encampment was much less crowded than previously, and the tent housing Goran was almost empty save a small number of slumbering figures. Goran himself was sitting up.

As they approached, Deras saw his brother's face for the first time since he was brought in. The impression was that someone had daubed him with scarlet paint, then slapped on several bluish-black blotches, resembling large, ripe bruises. There wasn't much flesh of a natural colour in evidence. His exposed arms looked to be in a similar condition.

Deras was used to injuries and disfigurement, but the sight of his sibling in such a state affected him more than he expected, no matter their estrangement. Given pause, his anger faded.

"Hello, Deras," Goran said.

Deras gave a small nod. "Goran."

"I'll leave you to it," Velda announced. A private, tender look passed between her and Goran, and she left.

Almost casually, Goran indicated his face with a scarred hand. "Pretty, isn't it?"

Deras seated himself. "Some of it will heal, given time."

"Some, yes. But most I'll have to get used to."

"I'm sorry."

"Why have you been avoiding me?"

"We hardly parted on the friendliest of terms. I thought it best to stay away."

"Even after this happened to me?"

Deras paused before replying. "I'm not saying it was a noble decision."

"Don't misunderstand me; I don't blame you. I wasn't sure about seeing you either."

"The past has a hold on you, too."

"I thought you were wrong. I still do. I don't suppose you've changed your mind since, seeing as you're here?"

Deras shook his head.

"Same old Deras. Still trying to change the world."

"Isn't that what you"re doing?"

"You'd always rather talk than fight, and dream of a peaceful future."

"That future we can agree on. It's the getting there that divides us."

"We'll only have it when our people stand in the

smouldering ruins of Wyndell, and that bastard emperor, Phylimorn, cowers at our feet."

"For all your wars, Lycerians have hardly breached Eagamar's borders, let alone reached its capital. Freedom from strife is what's needed."

"We have a better chance of realising our goal with swords than your pious words."

"Same old Goran. Headstrong and too partial to the blade."

"Perhaps we're both fools then."

Silence descended.

Deras broke it. "We were never able to change each other's minds, Goran. Neither of us is likely to do it now. Can't we put this rift aside?"

"We can try."

"Then let me speak frankly. I'm concerned."

"About what?"

"Velda. You two seem to have formed a bond."

"You could say that."

"It's not unusual for a patient to develop certain feelings for their healer, and –"

"I thought we were ignoring the rift, not making a new one. Whatever I feel for Velda is more than gratitude. And it's nothing to do with you."

"She's in my charge, and a friend. I don't want to see her hurt."

"What're you going to do if she is? Challenge me to a duel?" He saw his brother's expression. "I'm *joking*, Deras. I've no intention of ever hurting her. That would be a poor reward for nursing me through this, apart from anything else."

"I'll hold you to that."

"You won't have to."

Deras thought it wise to alter course. "What did it? What was it that harmed you so?"

"What comes by air and spits fire?"

"Oh, Goran, *please*."

"That's another way we see things differently."

"If you mean I believe in reason and you put faith in tales for the gullible, yes we do."

"We were nowhere near fire. Something came from above and vomited flame on us. What else could it have been?"

"Even if there was such a thing, where did it come from, and why attack you and your men?"

"Eagamar controlled it. The empire has magic, the way we used to."

"Supposedly."

"So what's your explanation?"

"Sarangela fire. Delivered by trebuchet, most likely."

Goran laughed frigidly. "*That's* a myth if ever there was one."

"Why should it be? You use flame in battle, don't you?"

"Nothing like Sarangela fire, that they say burns ten times fiercer than oil and fastens itself hard on everything in sight, men included."

"I find it easier to believe that the empire's brains thought of a way to increase the oil's potency, and make the fire more tenacious, than that they use spells to command mythical creatures."

"I've never seen Sarangela fire used in all the battles I've fought. Have you ever healed anyone afflicted by it?"

"Not until you and your men."

"You've no proof. If this stuff was viscous why wasn't any found on us?"

"The heat burnt it off."

"You'll never see the truth, will you?"

"I was just thinking that."

They talked on, trying to avoid the reefs their new-found truce steered through, but agreeing on little. Eventually Deras decided his brother needed rest and took his leave. He came away with conflicting thoughts.

And wondered how Velda could pair with a man who

believed in dragons.

The brothers spoke on most days during the following week. Their meetings grew easier, if only because they learned to avoid each other's sore spots. As far as the important issues went, the distance between them remained unbridgeable. They settled into a kind of wary tolerance, with the occasional smattering of good humour.

That routine was broken before dawn on the eighth day.

Someone shook Deras, violently.

"*Master!* Master Deras! Wake *up!*"

Deras blinked into consciousness and quickly rose. Ismey was there. He had blood on his face. "What is it? What's happened?"

"Raiders, master. They've… they've killed some of our people."

"*What?* Where are they? Are we under attack?"

"They're gone. And… they took Velda with them!"

The blood splattering Ismey turned out to be from the three healers murdered by the intruders. He had been roughed up but escaped lightly, and could give no description of the raiders other than they numbered upward of a dozen and wore dark clothing.

A sweep of the encampment confirmed that they were gone, but Deras had all the tents and storerooms searched anyway.

While that was going on, Goran came to his brother.

"This was because of me," he said.

"I know." Deras handed him a scrap of parchment. "They left this."

Goran scanned the hastily-written scrawl. "So they'll exchange Velda for me at the abandoned redoubt at Wilburr Reach, noon tomorrow." He screwed up the note and tossed it aside. "Why didn't they just go for me last night?"

"I'm sure that was their intent, but they were disturbed before they could locate you. I suspect Velda was very much a secondary target, settled on once they were discovered. She was bedded down near the periphery and would have been easier to snatch.

What I don't understand is how they knew about her connection with you."

"No mystery there. Somebody on the empire side you treated here passed on the word. Like you said, everybody had noticed Velda and I were close. Don't look so pained, brother. Gratitude to the League is one thing, but loyalty to their cause overrides it."

"So you reckon it was the empire, not some band of marauders?"

"Had to be. I've done a lot of damage to them, and they'd like to see me pay for it. I expect they've got a nice little public execution in mind."

"You have to get General Dunisten to storm the place."

"They'd certainly kill her if we did. That's something I couldn't bear."

He spoke with such conviction that any doubts Deras had about Goran's feelings for Velda were dispelled. "What, then?"

"I'll go there, of course."

"To give yourself up? With no guarantee that they *would* let Velda go?"

"I wasn't thinking so much of giving myself up as getting her out of there."

"How?"

"I'll think of a way."

"I'm coming with you."

"You're joking."

"Do I look as though I am?"

"With respect, Deras, I don't need a peace-lover along on this."

"You care for Velda, and so do I. I'll do whatever I can to help her. Besides, you might be glad to have a healer with you."

"I've no time to argue. Come if you must, but *don't* get in the way. Now I've got to think, and I've some allies to summon.

Wilburr Reach isn't that far. We'll set out at first light tomorrow."

They were up and ready well before dawn broke.

Deras went to Goran's tent, where his brother had something to show him.

"Take a look at this," he said.

He held up a black leather face mask. There were holes for eyes, mouth and nose, and inset studs. Some kind of soft fabric lined the inside.

"I got one of the female healers to make it for me," Goran explained. "Turns out they're not only good at stitching wounds. Here, let me show you." He put the mask on and tightened the straps at its rear. "What do you think?"

"Well, it's certainly striking. Doesn't it pain you to wear it?"

"A little. I'll get used to it."

"So, have you a plan?"

"Yes, and it involves you. But it's dangerous. *Very* dangerous. Are you willing to take the risk?"

"I am."

"Good. Now let's get ourselves outside. I'm expecting some people. I'll explain while we wait."

Shortly, twenty or more riders arrived at the camp entrance. Most were men, but there were three or four women, too. All had bows slung on their backs.

The one leading them was a red-haired, flame-bearded giant of a man. He dismounted and was greeted by Goran with a warrior's grasp.

"Gods, Goran," the giant exclaimed, "if that mask isn't an improvement on your usual dismal mug."

Goran took that in good part. "I reckon you could do with one yourself, Gled."

The giant roared with laughter.

"This is my brother, Deras," Goran went on. "Deras, this is Gled Brackenstall."

Brackenstall pumped his hand. Deras thought his fingers

might break.

"And this," Goran said, waving an expansive hand at the rest of them, "is his band of archers."

"God killers all," Brackenstall added with dry irony.

"Gled's band comprises an autonomous unit in the Lycerian army," Goran explained. "Today they're undertaking a little freelance work with us. I take it you haven't bothered to tell the general about your absence, Gled. "

"We archers tend to be independent minded. I didn't see the need for bureaucratic complications."

"I'm grateful. And you're all in agreement about this?"

"We owe you, Goran. For much. We're all happy to repay some of that debt."

The mounted archers nodded and murmured agreement.

"Thank you. By the way, Deras is coming with us."

"We're taking a *healer*? No offence, Deras."

"None taken,"

"I have a plan, Gled, and my brother's part of it," Goran said. He looked at the rising sun. "But we should be leaving. I'll fill you in as we travel."

"The sooner we get to grips with those Eagamar bastards the better," Brackenstall replied. "Let's ride."

Wilburr Reach was situated not far from the border with the land of Megaka, which in the shifting landscape of alliances was currently an ally of the empire. The area was contested and consequently perilous, and it had to be assumed that the kidnappers had lookouts posted along the way.

The latter turned out to be true, and proved the value of archers.

When they were close to their destination, but not yet within sight of the redoubt, they came to a wood. The neglected road running through it was the only direct route. Judging this a good place for an ambush, or at least somewhere the alarm could be raised, Gled Brackenstall sent six of his archers ahead on foot.

They fanned out into the trees on either side while the main party kept to the trail.

The ploy paid off. Barely halfway through the wood there was a commotion in the green canopy far above. Two men plunged from trees, peppered with arrows. They wore empire uniforms.

As the wood's rim came into view it happened again. A single man fell this time, bolts protruding from his chest and back. They saw no more lookouts after that.

At last they were free of trees, and found themselves on a rise affording a view of the derelict fortress. At one time a formidable bastion, it had fallen long ago in a battle half forgotten. Now it was a jumble of ruins, its pockmarked walls covered in ivy and showing the blackened evidence of fire. Only one of its towers remained, and that stood at a precarious angle.

They kept out of sight, and saw a group of men, perhaps twenty in number, milling about in the open in front of what had once been the fortress' entrance.

Goran looked to the sky. As near as damn it was noon. "Position the band, Gled. Deras, are you ready?"

His brother nodded, finding that easier than trying to talk.

"Then it's time. Good luck to us all."

The group at the fortress began to hoot and jeer when they saw the lone, masked man approaching them on foot. Several ran forward, seized him and frogmarched him to the one in charge.

He held the rank of sergeant, and was muscular, stubble-chinned and broken-toothed.

"Well, well," he mocked, "Goran Minshal, at last. I'd have staked a month's pay you wouldn't have shown up here for the sake of a *woman*."

"I want to see her."

The men laughed at him.

"You're in no position to demand anything," the sergeant said. "But yes, you can see her, god killer." He signalled.

Velda appeared from behind a large chunk of fallen

masonry, shoved forward by a trooper. Her hands were tied and she looked frightened. There was a bruise on her forehead, but she seemed otherwise unharmed. She stared at her lover.

"Are you all right?" he asked.

That sparked another gust of spiteful laughter.

Velda had a curious expression on her face, and looked about to say something, but instead simply nodded.

"We have something special in store for you once we get you back to Wyndell, Minshal," the sergeant promised. "Meantime, you can watch this bitch die."

The man holding Velda drew a knife and held it to her throat. The others began braying.

The sergeant raised a hand. "Hold it, lads." He moved closer to their prisoner. His breath was fetid. "You're not going to get the best view through that thing, are you, Minshal? Besides, we'd all like to take a look at your messed up face." He smirked and reached for the buckles on the mask.

It came away.

"What the –"

Velda exclaimed, *"Deras!"*

An arrow winged into and through the sergeant's arm, its tip jutting out bloodily. He backed off, yelling in shock and pain.

The man holding the knife to Velda went down with an arrow in his eye. One of the troopers guarding Deras took a hit. The other abandoned him, ran for cover and collapsed headlong as a bolt found his back.

Arrows fell like rain, striking men all around. One plummeted screaming from halfway up the crooked tower.

Then the band of archers was charging in, their bows replaced with blades. Brackenstall led them, Goran at his side, his spoiled face plain for all to see.

A cacophony of steel meeting steel rang out as the two sides engaged.

"Kill the woman!" the sergeant shouted. *"Somebody kill the woman!"*

One of his men rushed at her, a blade in his hand. She had her back to the fortress wall, bound hands held up in a vain effort to protect herself, eyes wide. Goran saw, with horror, but couldn't disentangle himself from the opponents he faced. All the others seemed equally powerless.

Deras sprinted towards Velda, praying he could reach her before her would-be murderer. The man got there first, weapon raised. Deras saw a discarded sword in his path. He scooped it up and ran with it levelled. The man half turned as Deras neared and the sword slid between his ribs. Eyes rolling, incomprehension on his face, the man sank to the ground.

Deras looked at the bloody sword he was holding and couldn't have dropped it more swiftly had it just come out of a furnace. Velda dashed to him and clutched his arm. They started for the slab of fallen masonry, and shelter.

But the fight was all but over already. Bodies littered the ground, including a couple of the archers, though to Deras' relief they looked wounded rather than dead. Their comrades were aiding them.

Goran had the whimpering sergeant on his knees, his sword to the man's throat. "As for you, you piece of shit –"

"*No!*" Deras cried. "Leave him!"

"*What?*"

"Spare him."

"After what he's done? And what he was about to do to Velda?"

"For me," Deras pleaded. "In consideration of what I just did, if nothing else," he added desperately.

"He's right, Goran," Velda said. "I wouldn't want that man dead, in spite of everything. That isn't how the League does things."

"Release him," Deras urged. "He'll be a message to his kind. It'll let them know they can't overcome Goran Minshal. That Lycerians are a force to be reckoned with."

Goran hesitated. For a moment it looked like he could go

either way. Finally he withdrew his sword and gave the man a kick, sprawling him in the dirt. "What the hell. They'll probably execute the swine anyway for bungling his mission."

They tied the sergeant to a horse and sent him away.

Velda and Goran embraced. She shed a tear and he comforted her.

"You're shaking, brother," Goran observed.

"I've killed a man." Deras was dazed by the realisation of what he'd done.

"And I'm grateful to you."

"But I *killed* a man," Deras repeated.

"And I didn't. Two miracles in one day."

"How can I take a life and call myself a healer?"

"What would have been the alternative? Soothing words?"

"It always takes them peculiar the first time," Brackenstall commented.

"First and last," Deras told him.

Goran squeezed his brother's arm. "Look at it another way. See it as saving Velda. Not to mention getting me to spare somebody, and that's never happened before."

"I'm grateful, too," Velda said. "It's not what we would have chosen, but you did the right thing." She planted a kiss on his cheek.

Goran surveyed the carnage. "And you created enough of a diversion to make the rescue possible. What more do you want, Deras?"

"I've been thinking about that. Why did you need me at all?"

"You wanted to be part of this mission, didn't you? Anyway, if they'd decided to kill me right away, or who they thought was me, I'd still be around to reckon with them."

"You are joking, aren't you, Goran?"

His brother just smiled. "We have wounded. See to them, healer. Go *on*."

Deras snapped out of it and made for the fallen archers. Velda went to help him.

As they rode back through the wood, Velda said, "I knew it was you, Deras. In the mask. Or that it wasn't Goran, rather. Even before you spoke."

"We're roughly the same build. We look quite similar. How could you tell?"

She smiled. "A woman can tell. If you ever get one of your own, you'll find that out."

"Only a saint would suit my brother," Goran offered.

"And he deserves one."

"Whoa!" Brackenstall said, halting the column.

"What is it?" Goran asked, hand going to his sword.

The archer looked up.

A great shadow passed over above the trees, momentarily blotting out the sun. As swiftly as it came, it was gone.

Velda turned to Deras. "What might that have been?"

A shiver tickled his spine. "I think I'd rather not know."

About the Authors

Joe Abercrombie was born in Lancaster on the last day of 1974, spent much of his youth in imaginary worlds, and left school with a good idea of how to make stuff up. He moved to the big city, learned to brew tea, and ended up as a TV editor, working on documentaries, events and concerts. But in the darkness of the night he was still making stuff up, and his first book, *The Blade Itself*, was published in 2006. He now lives in Bath with his wife Lou and their three children: Grace, Eve and Teddy. He makes stuff up full time.

James Barclay is mainly an author and sometimes Scott Barclay, the actor. He's published twelve books; seven about *The Raven*, two about *The Ascendants of Estorea* and three about his very own brand of Elves. He's also written two novellas for PS Publishing – *Light Stealer* and *Vault of Deeds*. Beyond writing and acting, James lives noisily but happily with Clare; their sons, Oscar and Oliver; and Mollie the Hungarian Vizsla.

Storm Constantine has written twenty-eight published books, both fiction and non-fiction, and well over fifty short stories. Her writing spans literary fantasy, science fiction, and dark fantasy. She is best known for her *Wraeththu* trilogy. Storm is founder of the independent publishing house Immanion Press, created in order to get classic titles from established writers back in print and innovative new authors an audience. She lives in the Midlands with her husband, Jim, and five cats.

Jonathan Green is a writer of speculative fiction, with more than fifty books to his name. He has written everything from Fighting Fantasy gamebooks to Doctor Who novels, by way of numerous

Black Library publications and myriad short stories. He is also the creator of the *Pax Britannia* steampunk series for Abaddon Books. To find out more about his current projects visit: www.jonathangreenauthor.com.

Tanith Lee was born in 1947, didn't learn to read until she was nearly eight, and started to write aged nine. Since becoming a fulltime writer in 1974 she has written around 100 books, nearly 300 short stories, four radio plays, and two episodes of *Blake's 7*. Her latest collection, *Colder, Greyer Stones* (NewCon Press), was launched at the 2013 World Fantasycon in Brighton, where Tanith was honoured with a Lifetime Achievement Award. Tanith lives on the Sussex Weald with husband writer/artist John Kaiine, in a house full of books, stained glass, plants and cat fur.

Juliet E McKenna has always been fascinated by other worlds and other peoples, myth and history. Her debut fantasy novel *The Thief's Gamble* was published in 1999, first of the *Tales of Einarinn*. In 2012, her fifteenth, *Defiant Peaks*, concluded *The Hadrumal Crisis* trilogy. She writes diverse shorter fiction and reviews for web and print magazines. She lives in Oxfordshire, fitting all this around her husband, teenage sons and cat, and vice versa.

Anne Nicholls' published works, originally written under the name Anne Gay, include the acclaimed novels *Mindsail* and *The Brooch of Azure Midnight*. Her short story 'Roman Games" was reprinted in the *Year's Best Fantasy*. Anne is now principally a psychotherapist, best known for self-help writing and broadcasting, but her paintings are also beginning to gain a following.

Stan Nicholls is the author of more than thirty books and approximately fifty short stories, but he is probably best known for his *Orcs* series, which have amassed worldwide sales in excess of a million copies. For six years he was the sf and fantasy book reviewer for *Time Out*, and his journalism has appeared in some seventy national and specialist publications. He has been Chair of The David Gemmell Awards For Fantasy since their instigation in 2009.

Gaie Sebold's debut novel introduced brothel-owning ex-avatar of sex and war, *Babylon Steel* (Solaris, 2012); the sequel, *Dangerous Gifts*, came out in 2013. She has published short stories, had several jobs, and is a member of T Party Writers. She now writes full time, gardens obsessively, and sometimes runs around in woods hitting people with latex weapons. Find out more at http://gaiesebold.com/ and follow the latest scandal and tidbits from Scalentine at http://scalentine.gaiesebold.com/

Jan Siegel has written in several different genres under several different pseudonyms. She also works as a poet, journalist, freelance editor, and occasional teacher, her interests covering a wide range of subjects. While a writer may be defined as someone who knows a little about a lot, Siegel claims she knows very little about a hell of a lot. An idealist, she is continuously surprised to find fact stranger than fiction and real human beings even more bizarre than any character in a book.

Adrian Tchaikovsky was born in Lincolnshire, studied and trained in Reading, and now lives in Leeds. He is known for the *Shadows of the Apt* fantasy series starting with *Empire in Black and Gold* and currently up to volume 9, *War Master's Gate*. His hobbies include stage-fighting, and tabletop, live and online role-playing. More information is available at www.shadowsoftheapt.com

Sandra Unerman lives in London and is a retired Government lawyer. She has written fantasy for many years and has had stories published in *Scheherazade* and *All Hallows* magazines. She has attended the Milford writers' workshop and recently graduated from Middlesex University with an MA in Creative Writing

(Fantasy and Science Fiction). She is a member of the London Clockhouse group of writers.

Ian Whates currently has two published novel series: the *Noise* books (Solaris) and the *City of 100 Rows* trilogy (Angry Robot), as well as more than fifty published short stories. His work has received honourable mentions in *Years Best* anthologies and two of his stories have been shortlisted for BSFA Awards. *Growing Pains,* his second collection, appeared from PS Publishing in March 2013. In 2006 he founded NewCon Press, quite by accident. "Return to Arden Falls" is the fourth *Fallen Hero* tale to appear to date.

For more information on how *Legends* came about, visit the blog http://www.ianwhates.co.uk/uncategorized/david-gemmell-and-legends/

And the interview conducted on the editor at the Fantasy Book Critic site:
http://fantasybookcritic.blogspot.co.uk/2013/08/interview-with-ian-whates-interviewed.html

Fables from the Fountain

Edited by Ian Whates

Cover art by Dean Harkness

Produced as a fund raiser for the Arthur C Clarke Award and containing all original stories written as homage to Arthur C. Clarke's classic *Tales from the White Hart*, featuring many of today's top genre writers, including:
Neil Gaiman, Charles Stross, Stephen Baxter, James Lovegrove, Liz Williams, Adam Roberts, Eric Brown, Ian Watson, and **Peter Crowther**

The Fountain: a traditional London pub situated in Holborn, just off Chancery Lane, where Michael, the landlord, serves excellent real ales and dodgy ploughman's, ably assisted by barmaids Sally and Bogna.

The Fountain, in whose Paradise bar a group of friends – scientists, writers and genre fans – meet regularly on a Tuesday night to swap anecdotes, talk of wondrous events, tell tall tales, reveal classified secrets, and, maybe, just *maybe*, save the world…

"*Fables from The Fountain* is a humorous and entertaining homage… Warmly recommended." – *SFcrowsnest*

"*Fables* is probably the closest I've ever seen to a multi-author anthology reading like a single-author work. I'm guessing this is what Whates set out to do, and if so he's achieved it admirably. There's not a poor tale in here."
– *The Future Fire*

"There are no weak stories here… Highly recommended for anyone interested in a good tall tale told well." – *The Green Man Review*

Anniversaries

The Write Fantastic

Cover art by Jim Mortimore

To commemorate the fifth anniversary of The Write Fantastic – an initiative by professional authors to introduce fantasy fiction to readers who have yet to experience the genre and to ensure existing readers are aware of the breadth and depth of current fantasy writing – NewCon Press released an anthology of all new fiction from the members of TWF.

Contents:

1. Introduction – Stan Nicholls
2. Remembrance – Juliet E McKenna
3. I Shaved Half Emperor Cyrrhenius – Chaz Brenchley
4. Song for a Naming Day – Sarah Ash
5. Persephone's Chamber – Freda Warrington
6. Birthday of the Oligarch – Kari Sperring
7. The Anniversay – Jessica Rydill
8. Smöergaen's Bane – Ian Whates
9. The Strawberry Grotto – Liz Williams
10. Authors' Biographies and Selected Bibliography

Available now as a specially priced A5 paperback for just £6.99
www.newconpress.co.uk

Colder Greyer Stones
Tanith Lee

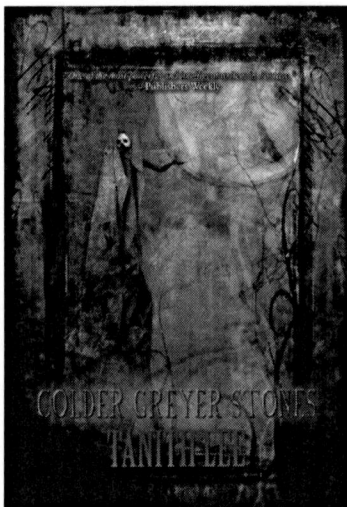

Cover art by John Kaiine

In 2012, NewCon Press launched their new *Imaginings* series with *Cold Grey Stones,* a volume of fiction from Tanith Lee: eleven wonderful and rich-textured stories, all previously uncollected, five of which appeared for the first time anywhere and all of which deserved to be treasured. The book was released as a signed limited edition hardback only and sold out in a matter of weeks.

Now, for the first time, we are delighted to release a paperback edition of the book, the contents expanded to include a brand new novelette *The Frost Giant,* 12,500 words of Tanith Lee at her best: a tale inspired by the book's cover art.

Come and experience the magic and wonder of Tanith Lee.

Colder Greyer Stones: available now as an A5 paperback £9.99.

Shake Me to Wake Me
The Best Short Fiction of
Stan Nicholls

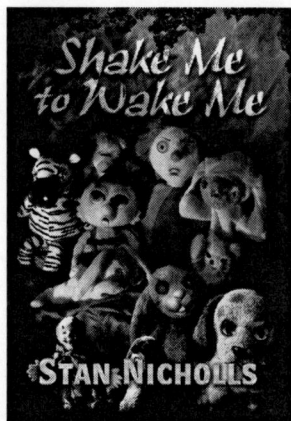

Cover art by Ben Baldwin

Shake Me to Wake Me features the very best of Stan Nicholls' short fiction, as selected by the author. Slipping effortlessly between fantasy, horror, and science fiction, the stories span twenty years of Stan's distinguished career, beginning with 1993's "SPOIL" and coming right up to date with "The Gripes of Wrath", a new story written especially for this collection. Prepare to be amused, prepare to be shocked, prepare to be entertained... Prepare to be *shaken.*

"Nicholls knows how to skilfully infuse abundant plot into easy prose and exceptionally smooth dialogue." – *SFX*

"Weirdly charming, fast-moving and freaky..." – *Tad Williams*

"Easily as much fun as you'd expect." – *Jon Courtenay Grimwood in the Guardian*

Launched in November 2013; available now from NewCon Press as a signed limited edition hardback, an A5 paperback, and an e-book.

NewCon Press is proud to work with

Celebrating Indepedent Publishing in Style
SPACEWITCH
www.spacewitch.com

books * art * audio
Proudly supporting the next generation.

Lightning Source UK Ltd.
Milton Keynes UK
UKOW03f1345181013

219296UK00001B/27/P